FALLING FOR HOME

JODY HOLFORD

COPYRIGHT

Original Copyright © 2016 by Jody Holford Reprint © 2018

This is a work of fiction. Names, characters, corporations, institutions, organizations, events, or locales in this novel are either the product of the author's imagination or, if real, used fictitiously. The resemblance of any character to actual persons (living or dead) is entirely coincidental.

All rights reserved. No part of this publication may be reproduced, stored in a retrieval system, or transmitted in any form or by any means (electronic, mechanical, photocopying, recording, or otherwise) without the prior written permission of the copyright holder.

Cover Designer: Christina Hovland

DEDICATION

To Matt & to Brenda
For everything
Always

CONTENTS

Chapter 1	1
Chapter 2	13
Chapter 3	37
Chapter 4	49
Chapter 5	63
Chapter 6	77
Chapter 7	83
Chapter 8	95
Chapter 9	109
Chapter 10	119
Chapter 11	129
Chapter 12	143
Chapter 13	163
Chapter 14	179
Chapter 15	191
Chapter 16	207
Chapter 17	223
Chapter 18	239
Chapter 19	253
Chapter 20	269
Chapter 21	279
Chapter 22	295
Chapter 23	305
Chapter 24	315
Chapter 25	327
Chapter 26	339
Chapter 27	347

Acknowledgments	353
About the Author	355
Also by Jody Holford	357

It takes courage to grow up and become who you really are.

e.e. cummings

CHAPTER ONE

*L*ucy slid one hand slowly along the firm edge, tracing every bump and dip. With her other, she reached into her pocket and pulled out her iPhone, hoping the light would give her a better look at the path her fingers followed.

"Son of a bitch! Where is it?" She stretched onto the balls of her feet, trying to inch her fingers along the grooves of the brick siding. For her whole life, her parents had kept a key tucked in a corner where the porch met the house, but now, when she wanted to get in without waking anyone, it was nowhere to be found. The weak sliver of moonlight wasn't helping any more than the narrow beam of light from her phone. She crept along the narrow garden path, careful not to step on the raised flowerbeds. Lucy kept her eyes wide, hoping to see the flash of silver that would let her into her childhood home and out of the night's crisp air.

The breeze blowing off the lake sent chills up her arms and she shivered. She decided to retrace her steps in case she'd passed it. Her boot caught on the branch of one of her father's beloved magnolia bushes. Stumbling, Lucy juggled her phone for a second before losing her grip entirely and dropping it into the dirt. As she crouched down in the shadows to find it, she realized she was going to have to do what a normal person would have already done and knock on the door. Cringing, she patted the damp soil, hoping the phone wasn't far. A sharp, low, masculine voice startled her from behind. "You're going to stand up real slow and turn around with your hands up."

Lucy closed her eyes and pulled herself out of her crouch, wondering if this night could get any worse. Her legs cramped as she straightened, reminding her that she was no longer the eighteen-year-old who had lived here ten years ago. She gave her eyes a second to adjust to the darkness. There'd never been much crime in Angel's Lake, but her heart still drummed fiercely as she turned, shaking her head at her bad luck.

"Nice and slow," the tall, broad-shouldered man repeated. Her pulse kicked into overdrive when she saw he was pointing a gun at her. Mind racing, her chest tightened.

"Hands up," he said. When her eyes left the gun for a split second, she noticed the Angel's Lake Police Department patch on the chest of his bulky jacket. Knowing he was an officer didn't help to settle her nerves, though, and another shiver raced through her body. She couldn't quite make out his features, but he had a good foot on her height wise, even though she was standing as tall as she could. Her back stiffened from trying to keep still, and she really wished he would speak. Or give her his jacket.

"It's okay. I live here," she said, her voice higher than usual. She would have been embarrassed by its squeaky sound, but the raised gun counteracted her pride.

He shined a flashlight into her eyes, blinding her. "Nice try, lady, but I live next door, so I know you don't." She squinted and held her hand in front of her eyes as she stepped forward.

"Freeze."

She froze. There wasn't a person alive brave enough to ignore that one-word growl. "You don't understand," she tried again, staying still. "This is my parent's house!"

"Sure it is. You thought you'd just creep around in their bushes before going inside?" he asked as he stepped toward her and lowered the flashlight. He gripped her upper arm and tugged her out of the flowerbed.

"Hey! Get your hands off of me," she demanded. "This really is my parent's house!"

"Prove it. What's your name?"

"Lucy! Lucy Aarons," she yelled, trying to wriggle free of his grasp.

He stopped abruptly and then used his grip on her arm to spin her around. The moonlight cast a thin glow over a face that was vaguely familiar. His square jaw had a hint of stubble and his dark eyes bore into hers. Where did she know him from? He arched an eyebrow at her obvious inspection. He lowered the gun but his steady gaze held her just as still. He emanated heat, and she had to stop herself from stepping closer to absorb it. She'd done enough to embarrass herself for one evening.

She really should have just knocked.

Alex fought a smile as she tried to work out his identity. She wouldn't. He would have recognized her voice if fear hadn't raised her pitch to ear-piercing levels. The moonlight slanting across the yard let him see those crystal blue eyes he'd know anywhere. Her pouty lips frowned while she studied him.

Disappointment tugged at his chest as she continued to stare.

"Alex. Alex Whitman," he finally supplied, letting her go and holstering his gun. It still took her a few seconds; he saw the moment it clicked and her lips turned upward into a kick-you-in-the-gut smile. She threw her arms around him with so much zest it knocked him back a step. Without hesitating, he wrapped his arms around her waist, immediately noticing the softness of her curves as she pressed against him. Bending his knees a little as she hung on, he breathed in the sweet combination of fruity shampoo and cold air.

"Wow. Alex. You're a cop!" she said with a laugh, her voice now closer to what he remembered from high school. She released him and stepped back, the smile brightening her face. His hands hung at his sides as he took her in. Her delicate cheekbones sat high, and though she'd filled out some, it was nothing more than how a woman should. She still looked like the girl he'd loved since sixth grade.

"Sheriff, actually. What are you doing here, Luce?"

"Sheriff? Seriously? Did you fire your dad?" Her eyes flashed with amusement even as she shivered. "No. He retired. I took over. It's been a long time."

"Yup. Seemed like a good time to visit," she remarked,

her eyes looking away as she rubbed her hands up and down her arms briskly. He'd interrogated enough suspects to recognize avoidance. He shrugged out of his department jacket and wrapped it around her shoulders, which drew her eyes back to his. The hint of sadness in them made him want to pull her closer. That and the fact that it was Lucy.

"How long are you home for?" he asked, continuing to hold the lapels of the jacket while she shoved her arms in with a smile.

"I don't know. We'll see what happens. I can't believe you're sheriff, that you still live here ... that you live next door to my parents."

"It's all true," he nodded as he chuckled. He wasn't surprised by her noncommittal timeframe. The only plans Lucy Aarons had ever made and kept were to get out of the small town that he'd grown to love.

The porch light came on, making them both squint in response.

"Evening, Mark," Alex called as Lucy's dad stepped out onto the wide porch. The sound of her dad's voice made Lucy's heart tumble in her chest. From the corner of her eye, she saw Alex watching her, but she couldn't stop looking at her dad. It wasn't like she hadn't seen him for four years, thanks to Facebook and Skype, but nothing beat seeing him face to face.

"Who do you have there, Sheriff?" Mark Aarons asked as he squinted into the darkness, his mellow voice causing the goose bumps to reappear on her arms.

Until she'd been standing in front of him, it hadn't occurred to her that she had missed him. She pulled away from Alex's gentle grip to move toward her dad's tall, lanky figure.

"It's me, dad," she muttered, shuffling into the light. He looked down from the top step, and she could see the gray peeking through his messy black hair. "Lucy!"

He stepped off the porch in a few long strides and then clamped his arms around her, squeezing her so tight she couldn't say a word. As she rested her head on his wide shoulder, she didn't know what she would have said, even if there weren't a golf ball-sized lump lodged in her throat.

"You're home," he whispered, as if he'd been waiting for her this whole time. His warmth seeped through her, settling her hammering heart. "For now," she replied more out of habit than belief.

"We'll take what we can get." He laughed and kissed the top of her head.

"Do I want to know why the sheriff brought you home, honey?" her dad asked, loosening his grip and pulling her into his side. Alex moved closer and she saw the yawn he tried to cover. He was not the meek shadow she'd met in sixth grade when he'd come to Angel's Lake to live with his dad. And he definitely wasn't the gangly teen she'd graduated with.

"Caught her lurking around the yard," Alex joked, smiling warmly at her father. They were clearly comfortable with each other, and she found herself wondering how long Alex had lived next door and why neither of her sisters had mentioned it. A hot next-door neighbor seemed like a sisterly thing to mention. She narrowed her eyes at him, but he just winked at her, making her stomach dip.

"Funny, Sheriff. Don't forget to mention the part where you manhandled me." He frowned at her and looked appropriately sheepish. She turned back to her dad. "Dad, where's the key? It's always on the edge of the brick behind the flower bushes," she complained. The wind was picking up, making the spicy scent of Alex's cologne drift up from his jacket. She pulled the collar tight, inhaled deeply, and had to stop herself from sighing with pleasure.

"It's not safe to leave a key out like that. Even in a small town," Alex answered first. Her dad laughed and the sound brought a flash of childhood memories to her mind. Lucy grinned.

"Yes. Sheriff Whitman admonished us straight away when he moved in six months ago. He spotted the key and gave us a stern warning."

Lucy caught a glimpse of Alex's slight blush at her dad's teasing. She watched him shuffle his feet and adjust his stance. *Hmm, maybe a little of the boy from high school is still in there.*

"You should get some motion sensor lights as well, sir." He looked at Lucy, studying her a moment, then said, "Now that I know you're not trying to break in, I should go." Alex nodded toward his own house.

"Long shift?" her dad asked. Lucy heard the concern in his voice and looked back and forth between the men.

"Usual. But there was trouble out at Old Man Cantry's farm," Alex said. He sighed and ran his hands through his hair, tousling it. She wondered if that was how he looked when he woke up in the morning. His gaze caught hers, and he arched his brow then continued. "Nothing major—

kids being kids. I'll be glad when Kate gets the youth center up and running so they have something to keep them busy. Somewhere else to hang out at night." He looked back at his house again and covered a yawn.

Lucy pulled away from her dad and shrugged out of his jacket. She wondered if Alex and her younger sister Kate were close. When she handed him the jacket, his fingers swept over hers to accept it. She felt a shiver of a different kind—the slow, teasing kind that started in her belly and traveled up her arms. Their eyes locked again.

"It won't be much longer now. She's been working day and night, pulling her plans together," Mark replied. Lucy's stomach dipped at Alex's intense look, but she stepped away from him and his delicious-smelling jacket. Her dad pulled her tightly against his side like he wasn't mad about how long she'd been gone.

"Yeah, I said I'd help with some painting tomorrow, which means I should get some sleep," Alex said. He turned to Lucy again, swinging his jacket over his shoulder. "Nice to have you home, Lucy. Maybe we can grab something to eat and catch up?" He gave her dad a quick glance after he said it, and she almost laughed. It had been a long time since she'd needed her dad's permission for anything.

"Sure. That'd be great." Her lips quirked when she added, "Thanks for not arresting me." He grinned widely, making her belly flip-flop. "My pleasure. Get a key." He winked at her before turning away.

Her dad hugged her tight as they watched him stride across the lawn back to his own two-story house with the same wide wraparound porch. As he got closer, motion lights flooded the yard. She chuckled and looked up to find her dad beaming. She noticed more lines creasing his eyes and mouth than she remembered from five years ago, but aging seemed to agree with him.

"You're home," he repeated, wearing a sappy grin. She laughed.

"I'm home." Lucy gave him another hard, quick squeeze before they moved toward the house. She kept the "for now" to herself this time. "Your mom is going to be thrilled." He opened the door and let her go through first.

"Well, let's surprise her in the morning because I really need some sleep."

He gave her a playful nudge on the shoulder, his eyes crinkling from his smile. "Just be grateful you're not sleeping in a cell."

When the porch light went out next door Alex let himself into his own home. Tossing his keys on the wide-planked entry table, he tossed his jacket on one of the hooks he had hung in the hall. He didn't let himself take a whiff to see if it smelled like her. Instead, he toed off his shoes. He yanked the hem of his shirt out of his pants, unbuttoning it as he walked over the oak hardwood floors he'd installed himself.

In his bedroom, he unloaded his gun, locked it up, and thought of the way Lucy had shivered in the cool night air. The way she'd laughed and given him a full-body hug. She looked good. Better than good. Long, rich-brown hair that tumbled down her back. Her face had matured with grace and filled out some. Her body ... well, it had matured just fine, too, from what he could see in the moonlight and feel in her embrace.

He tossed his shirt into the laundry basket at the end of his king-size bed, and ran his hand over Furball, who purred in response. As he headed for the shower, he couldn't get Lucy out of his head. He shrugged to himself as he blasted the water on hot and stepped under the spray. "Not the first time she's consumed your thoughts," he admitted. Tucking his chin, he let the water beat on his back and felt his muscles loosen.

The day had started out shitty. For the last month or so, the town's population of teens had banded together to cause as much grief as they could. Alex wasn't sure what had brought on the upsweep of petty vandalism, but the episodes were escalating. Today, he'd been called out to Mr. Cantry's farm because of a fire. Cantry was as old as the town itself and was probably its longest living resident. His ramshackle chicken coop had been burned to the ground. If the fire department hadn't responded so quickly, the damage could have spread beyond the small structure. There had been no good leads, which meant more paperwork for Alex. When he'd finally dragged his ass home, Lucy Aarons was the last person he'd expected to find. Now, rinsing away the worst of his day, the memory of Lucy's arms wrapped around him and the feel of her hair grazing his cheek came back. Her subtle, alluring scent had stayed on his jacket just as she'd always stayed in a tiny corner of his brain and maybe even his heart.

"Don't go there," he warned as he rinsed his hair. He'd had a soft spot for her since grade school. Realistically, Alex knew better than most that some women weren't the type to stick around. He was happy in Angel's Lake. It was more than a town; it was his home, and the people in it were his family. He needed stability the way an addict craved his next fix and had since his mom had ditched him fifteen years ago. He'd never lose that desire to settle and stay settled. Lucy didn't stay and she never settled. Still, when he crawled between his cool, navy sheets after pushing his disgruntled cat out of the middle of the bed, he fell asleep dreaming about her.

CHAPTER TWO

*L*ucy gasped and tried to sit up, but the hand on her face held her down. Eyes wide open, she saw Kate. Her younger sister's vibrant green eyes sparkled with mischief and absolute glee. Her fingers pinched Lucy's nostrils together.

"'Eriously?" Lucy gurgled. Kate nodded and removed her fingers.

"Fastest way to wake you up. You're home!" she squealed, sounding closer to ten than twenty-one.

"I'm home but I'm not awake. Get off my bed," Lucy pushed at her sister with her feet while trying to hide her head under the pillow, but she immediately regretted her actions when Kate applied pressure to the top of the pillow. She flailed her arms and Kate laughed and scooted off the bed before Lucy could smack her.

"You are such a brat."

"Get up!" Kate bounced from one foot to the other.

"I'm up." Lucy threw the pillow at her, but Kate tossed it back.

"Like out-of-the-bed up," Kate added, unzipping Lucy's suitcase and pawing through it. She tossed a bra at Lucy, followed by a pair of cotton underwear, a T-shirt, and black yoga pants.

"Hey!" Lucy protested when most of the clothing landed on her face. She threw the mountain of warm covers off her cozy body and sat up. Kate came back to her side and threw her arms around Lucy's neck.

"You're home," she repeated.

"Yes, I'm home," Lucy sighed. She gave Kate a tight squeeze.

"For now," they said in unison. Lucy tried to glare at her sister but couldn't pull it off. When had she gotten so beautiful? They shared the same cheekbones and hair, but Lucy could see features in Kate that she didn't have. Her father's elegant jaw and his long, straight nose instead of their mother's button one. When had she transitioned from teen to woman? *While you were wandering.*

"I missed you. Or I did, until you woke me up." She pushed at her sister's shoulders, but Kate bounced back, undeterred.

"Missed you, too. Come on. Get up!" She stood and yanked Lucy's arm while Lucy grabbed the pillow with her free hand and smacked her with it. Kate tried to keep a straight face as she told Lucy, "Mom's making whole wheat, honey, and oat pancakes. Apparently, they help with stomach problems."

Lucy scrunched her brows together. "I don't have stomach problems."

Kate nodded as she pulled Lucy's clothes out of her suitcase and began loading them into the same dresser she'd used as a teen. Lucy stretched and, left with no other options, stood to get dressed.

"None of us do." Kate laughed, tossing her long brown hair over her shoulder to look back at Lucy. Their mom was always on the lookout for the next non-existent problem to solve, often using her daughters as research for the self-help books she wrote.

Lucy pulled her top over her head and shook her hair out, figuring her slightly disheveled look was good enough for breakfast. She could use a shower, but that could wait.

"Are Charlotte and Luke coming over?"

Kate slipped two of her sister's handmade paper-bead bracelets around her wrists and stretched her arm out to admire them. "They'll be at the center later to help. I can't believe you haven't met baby Mia yet. These are gorgeous."

"I can't wait to meet her. Unlike you, I'll just call her Mia. I think it's fairly evident that she's a baby." Lucy tugged her covers up to the top of the bed and considered it made. She tried to ignore the pang of guilt that settled under her ribs when she thought of missing her niece's birth. Looking back at Kate, she gestured toward the bracelets. "Those were made by the women of one of the tribes I photographed. It's their primary source of income. Pretty amazing, actually."

"They're gorgeous. And look good on me," she said. Lucy shook her head. The bracelets shifted on Kate's wrist when she looped her arm through Lucy's and pulled her down the stairs.

Her parents were chatting about motion lights as Lucy and Kate entered the kitchen. Lucy's smile widened when her mom leaned in to kiss her dad on the cheek. Mark smiled up at his wife with the same fondness he always did, making Lucy grateful that some things really didn't change.

"I'll see how much—there she is!" Julie Aarons bubbled, catching sight of her middle daughter. She clapped her hands together and pressed them to her mouth. Her flowing mass of hair framed the soft angles of her ageless face. Lucy walked toward her, and Julie opened her arms, meeting her halfway. Her mom rocked side to side, holding tight as Lucy breathed in the fragrant combination of her mom's favored Oil of Olay body wash and the still-percolating coffee. Nothing else made her feel more at home than those two smells. Tears pricked Lucy's eyes as her mom continued the hug. She ran her hand up and down her mom's back.

"Hi mom," she croaked, surprised at how difficult it was to swallow the lump in her throat. Julie squeezed harder.

"About damn time you came home, missy," her mom lectured without heat. She pulled back and looked Lucy up and down. "I missed you." Lucy said. She hadn't even realized how much.

"I thought of you once or twice, too," Julie answered. When her eyes met Lucy's, they were damp. Lucy bit her lip and looked over at her dad. "Hey dad." Like her mom had, she gave him a kiss on the cheek. His hand came up to her hair and held her there for a moment.

"Hi, sweetheart. How'd you sleep?"

"Good. Really good."

Kate brought her over a cup of black coffee, adding one more reason she adored her younger sister.

"Great. There goes all my attention now that the prodigal daughter is home," Kate joked, stealing her dad's last rectangle of toast before sitting on the opposite side of the table.

"I'm pretty sure *you're* the reason I came home, brat," Lucy reminded, sitting down beside her sister while their mom just beamed.

"Sit down, Julie. It's not the first time we've all sat at the table. No reason to make a Hallmark moment of it," Mark laughed at the way his wife stood, hands clasped, staring at her family.

"Oh, be quiet. It can't be a Hallmark moment if Char isn't here. I need all three of my girls for that. You look tired, Lucy," she rambled, ignoring her daughter's frown at the assessment. She ran her palm along Lucy's cheek and added, "I can say that because I'm your mother. I have some tea that helps rebalance energies. I'll make you some after you eat."

Lucy shared a glance with her dad and Kate. Her mom had written several books on a multitude of topics that dealt with healing yourself, being yourself, and finding yourself. Lucy thought she needed to write one on how to lose yourself. She would make for great research for her mom—she'd spent several years trying to do just that.

They fell into an easy space of teasing and sharing, catching up and remembering, filling in the gaps for the time she'd been gone. Regardless of where Lucy was in the world, her family was her constant. Her north star. She didn't need to tend to them or check on them; she'd known that they'd be there when she needed direction. She tried not to think too hard about the fact that she needed them but they were all just fine without her. They thought she was home to help Kate, but truthfully, this trip was going to go a long ways toward helping herself. She hoped.

Alex pulled off his worn hoodie and tossed it onto the front seat of his truck. It was shaping up to be a warm day. He'd had to follow up on some phone calls in the morning, so he was later than he wanted to be, but he could see that Kate had no shortage of helpers for her community 'pitch-in' day.

Once upon a time, long before Alex had arrived in town, the paint-chipped, battered recreation building had been a centerpiece of Angel's Lake. After the new high school had been built, it was used less and less. Its parking lot saw more action than the actual building as a local teen hang out. The walls of the building had been tagged and uniquely decorated with both images and words that no one needed to see. Alex was glad the more colorful words were getting covered up today.

He wandered through the groups of people—some he'd known most of his life—waving and nodding. There were some people he recognized but didn't know, some newcomers, and some he wished he had never met. Being sheriff made him privy to secrets he would rather not know, pieces of their lives that weren't shared with the general population but ended up being, in part, his problem.

"Hey Sheriff!" The bank manager waved at Alex. As he waved back, he caught sight of Kate giving orders and directions, a clipboard in her hand. She pulled a pencil out of the knot of hair on her head and made notes as Lucy walked over to her with a bottle of water. All three of the Aaron sisters were beauties, but there was something about Lucy that made him feel like he'd swallowed his tongue.

"Well hey there, Sheriff," Lucy said. She smiled at him, her eyes playful, as she handed Kate the water. "Ladies."

"Hi Alex. Thanks for coming," Kate greeted.

She took a long swallow of her water and then passed it to Lucy, who did the same. Alex made himself look away so he wasn't focused on Lucy with her head tipped back, her hair flowing down her back, and her eyes half closed.

"Where do you want me?" he asked.

He arched his eyebrows as Lucy sputtered on her water. A little drop escaped down her chin when she lifted her head. She promptly wiped it away with the heel of her hand.

"You okay, Luce?" he asked, giving her a knowing wink. His chest filled with satisfaction. Maybe she wasn't as immune as she'd always seemed. "She's fine," Kate assured, pursing her lips and giving Lucy a look that he couldn't quite decipher.

"How about you go help Sam. He was getting all of the rolling pans ready. I want the first coat on today," Kate suggested, pointing in Sam's direction. Alex saw Sam, his closest friend, on the other side of the lot. When his gaze went back to Lucy, her cheeks were still flushed, and locked his eyes on hers. She broke eye contact first. "I'm going to grab my camera and set up for some shots," Lucy said.

"Perfect. But don't think that'll get you out of the heavy lifting later."

"Yeah, yeah. When did you get so bossy?" Lucy grumbled, scrunching her eyebrows and frowning at her sister.

Alex laughed at the look of indignation on Kate's face. From the outside, it was easy to find the back and forth sniping amusing. He had always wondered what it would be like to have siblings. With the mutual glaring contest happening between the two, he thought it best not to mention that he thought they were lucky to have each other.

"I'm off to find Sam. Play nice, ladies." He smiled, tipped an imaginary cap, and strolled away.

"He looks just as good walking away as he does walking toward you, huh?" Kate commented, her tone bland, her annoyingly ever-present clipboard at her side.

"Do you have a thing for him?" Lucy asked, pulling her gaze away from Alex's back. Which, indeed, looked pretty fine walking away.

"A thing? No. He's a sweetheart and I adore him, like most of the town, but no, I don't have a *thing* for him." Kate looked up from her list and pinned Lucy with a serious glare. "And you shouldn't, either."

They wound around two guys setting up a table saw, a couple of teens laying down painting tarps, and an older woman wearing an odd hat that resembled both a fedora and a sun visor setting up a food table for the volunteers.

Lucy's stomach rumbled even though she'd eaten her fair share of her mom's oatmeal pancakes.

"Why not? Is he taken?" She tried to keep her tone casual.

"No. But he's not for you," Kate evaded, her eyes on her list. Lucy reached out and grabbed the clipboard from her sister. "Hey!"

"Why did you say that?" Lucy demanded, her voice low. She held the clipboard out of Kate's reach while her sister chewed on her bottom lip then frowned. "He's long-term and you're not. He's forever, and you're ... for now," Kate answered. With a huff, she held out her hand for the clipboard.

"Well, don't hold back." Lucy gave Kate the board and turned away.

It was the truth, and Lucy knew it. She didn't understand why hearing it from her sister bothered her so much. She would grab her camera from Kate's car, and lose herself in taking pictures of the events around her without having to take part. Another thing she did well.

When Kate had asked her during a Skype session if there was any way she could come home and help with this project, it had been perfect timing. Vincent, the editor for the international magazine *Everywhere Around Us* had made it clear that the ladder to success would be a lot easier to climb if she were to sleep with him. When she had disagreed, vehemently, he had decided she didn't belong on that particular assignment or on any other with the magazine.

She snapped a picture of the woman with the fun hat as she shook thoughts of Vincent from her head.

She was a good photographer; better than good. She had freelanced countless jobs and had her work featured in a number of top magazines. She'd photographed models and movie sets, architectural wonders, and indescribable landscapes. Still, she'd only ever been a "contributor," and she now found herself wanting a more reliable income. Even when she was abroad, where costs were minimal, it was comforting to have a cushion, particularly since she never knew if the next job would be her last.

"Hey, Lucy! Nice to see you," a woman called out. Lucy turned. She recognized the woman but couldn't remember her name. She was almost positive she was a friend or fan of her mother's. Julie Aarons had many fans, especially locally. She used to come out and soak up the energy and feel good about seeing how her work affected people. It had surprised Lucy when her mom had insisted she needed to stay home today. Lucy gave a one-handed wave and snapped a photo in the woman's direction. Perhaps she'd put together an album for Kate. Ideas played in her mind as she continued to take candid shots. This community was so different from the one she had just come home from, yet the core elements were the same.

She had been on assignment in Kenya in a small village called Lwak. A clean drinking water project was making drastic differences in the lives of the people there, and Lucy had felt like she was a part of something special. It was certainly the longest-running feature she'd done. On other photo shoots, she was a background figure, like an extra in a cast of thousands. The size of Lwak, along with the nature of the job, forced an intimacy she hadn't immediately recognized as familial.

"Are you taking pictures of anything besides hot men?" a familiar voice asked sardonically. Lucy lowered her camera carefully, placing it back in the insulated bag hanging on her shoulder, a smile tugging hard as she bit her lip. She turned to look at her older sister, already leaning in for an embrace.

"Why? Is your husband offering to pose?" Lucy teased as she wrapped herself around Charlotte in a hug that settled the upset inside of her.

"He probably would if I let him, but he actually had to work today," Charlotte laughed, pulling Lucy impossibly closer. "You've been gone too long this time."

Lucy bit her lip to keep from crying, but the tears fell anyway. She held tighter and hoped the pressure would alleviate the ache in her chest. "I stay away to make sure you appreciate me when I come back."

Charlotte leaned back and eyed Lucy with her critical, steely blue gaze. This close, she could see the odd strand of grey in her sister's sharply bobbed, dark brown hair. Her narrow face and high cheek bones had always lent an elegance to her features that was matched by the way she presented herself. She could see the hint of late nights around Charlotte's eyes. To Lucy, and most others, she was perfect. Something that Lucy would never be.

"We appreciate you just fine. I'll appreciate you even more when you get your butt in gear and do your share of this project Kate has us all slaving over," she laughed, the seriousness in her eyes fading.

"Slaving. As if. You might chip a nail," Kate interrupted. In her arms, she held Charlotte's youngest daughter. Lucy didn't think she was the squealing type, but that was what she did as she reached for the bundle of pink. "Let me have her," she said when Kate took too long to pass Mia over.

"This is your auntie Lucy, Mia. She's a bit nutty and doesn't stay in one place long, but we love her. She takes good pictures and makes the best scrambled eggs ever," Kate cooed to the sleeping baby as she slowly shifted her from her own arms to Lucy's.

Lucy held Mia and stared down in awe at the wonderful mix of Charlotte and her husband, Luke. Some hidden pocket of longing slammed hard into her ribs, surprising her with its intensity. The Aarons nose and Donnelly lips stood proudly on smooth, porcelain skin. Her eyelids scrunched and fluttered, but didn't open. Lucy beamed silently at her sisters and caught sight of her dad walking toward them with Carmen, Mia's five-year-old sister, in tow.

"She's gorgeous, Char. She's just perfect." Lucy kissed Mia's tiny forehead.

"Obviously," Charlotte laughed as Carmen walked in between them. Lucy thought she'd stayed close to everyone —she Skyped and Facebooked whenever possible. She'd talked to Carmen and sent birthday gifts, but just like with her dad last night, seeing her in person hit Lucy like a punch to the stomach. Carmen was carrying a book, talking steadily to her grandfather, who nodded thoughtfully. Lucy gently bounced her arms when Mia peeped then looked down at Carmen.

"Hello there," she said to the animated five-year-old. Carmen didn't look away from her grandfather. "There are more than three hundred fifty types of sharks," Carmen stated. Lucy's dad nodded.

Char touched Carmen's shoulder to interrupt her, and when she looked up at her mom, Char said quietly to her daughter, "Your aunt said hello, Carmen. Can you say hello, please?"

Carmen's tiny face scrunched in uncertainty, or perhaps frustration from being interrupted. Looking back at her grandfather, she said, "Hello. Sharks hardly ever get tumors. That's very different from humans."

Charlotte glanced at Lucy, gave a tight smile, then kneeled down and touched Carmen's shoulder again.

"Your aunt Lucy has photographed several sharks," Charlotte shared. This caught the little girl's attention, and she turned toward Lucy now, face serious.

"Have you photographed a great white shark? Those are my favorite. They are known as the king of the sharks," Carmen said, her tone very matter-of-fact. With her shoulder-length hair and serious nature, she reminded Lucy very much of Charlotte.

Lucy kissed Mia's soft forehead once more, breathing in the delicious combination of baby shampoo and powder, and then handed her to Charlotte. Standing to take the baby from her, Char's lips turned down slightly. Lucy squatted down so she could meet Carmen's eyes, but her

25

niece looked beyond, her gaze darting everywhere but directly at Lucy.

"I haven't, no. But I did photograph a Porbeagle shark when I was in Chile," Lucy answered. Carmen's brown eyes widened even as her brows furrowed together. She opened her book, *The Anatomy of Sharks*, and looked through the index.

"I haven't read about that one. Do you have a picture?" Carmen asked, closing the book.

"I do on my laptop. I could show it to you sometime." Lucy weaved a little in her squatting position. She really had to work out more. Or do yoga. Or something.

"You photographed it?"

"I did. They're known as a playful shark." Lucy rested her hands on her thighs while Carmen looked her over.

"You look different. Mommy says we met before," Carmen announced. Lucy grinned at Charlotte's mini-me and the abrupt shift in topic.

"You look different, too. Bigger. But I was here when you were born, so we have met. You're cuter now than then, though," Lucy said. Carmen looked at Lucy for a moment, tilting her head to the side.

"You are, too," she replied solemnly, making her and her family laugh.

The sound of everyone's laughter reminded her that she was surrounded by almost all of the people she loved most in the world. The thought of what she'd missed out on twisted her stomach in opposing directions. She'd tried to cajole her mother into joining them this morning, but Julie had claimed she had a deadline that she couldn't put off any longer. Her father and Kate had exchanged a strange glance at this, and Lucy had wondered if her mom had been pitching in at the center. She stood and offered her hand to Carmen.

"Want to take some pictures with me, Shorty?"

"My name is Carmen. I'm five. Can I use your camera?" Lucy bit back a smile at the serious tone and expression. "Do you drop things often?" Lucy put a protective hand on her camera bag.

"I didn't drop Mia." She stared up at Lucy, one hand on her hip. "Good enough for me."

Carmen passed her book to her grandfather and took Lucy's hand. Lucy squeezed it gently and smiled at her sisters and her dad. With Carmen and her favorite camera in tow, she waved to their family as they went to see what different groups of townsfolk were up to. Carmen tugged her hand.

"What other sharks have you photographed?" she asked, making Lucy smile.

"Why don't you just toss the little jerkoffs into a cell?" Sam asked Alex as he held the board in place. They were putting together a portico that would apparently add character to the rundown building. Sam, an architect and carpenter, started to explain his vision, but Alex had insisted he just tell him where to stand and what to pass him when. He had done some repairs on his home, but he didn't have anything close to Sam's talent and capability. Which is why it came in handy that they were friends—Sam would be helping him make a few renovations over the summer.

"Not that easy. For one thing, I don't know how many I'm dealing with. I don't want to nail the lackeys if someone is behind them. It seems like more than just stupid kid pranks. Something isn't sitting right with any of this."

Sam took the triangular structure he had nailed together and put it to the side. Alex used the hem of his T-shirt to wipe the sweat dripping into his eyes. As he lowered his shirt, his gaze made contact with Lucy, who was strolling hand in hand with Carmen. She blushed when he caught her staring then went back to listening to whatever Carmen was saying. Charlotte and Luke's oldest was cute and had a free spirit. Kind of like her aunt. But she also had rigid

boundaries, and Alex suspected she might be on the autism spectrum. "You missed a spot of drool." Sam said, swallowing back some water. "Huh?" Alex looked down at his shirt and then at Sam.

Sam nodded toward the hem of Alex's shirt that he was still holding.

"You got the sweat, but now you're drooling. Though I don't really blame you. She's smokin' hot. Just like her sisters." He waggled his eyebrows comically. Alex frowned and grabbed a water of his own, opened it up, and then watched as Lucy showed Carmen how to point and shoot with her high-tech camera. He gave Sam a small shove. "Aren't you getting married? To an extremely hot woman of your own?"

Sam grinned, tossing his water bottle into a nearby bin already overflowing with empties. "That I am, my friend. That I am. But I'm not blind or dead, so it'd be hard not to notice the Aarons sisters," Sam returned easily, picking up his hammer.

"Fair enough. She's never around long enough to do more than take a glance anyway," Alex mumbled, grabbing the next piece of wood to attach to the triangular addition that he still couldn't fully visualize.

"You never know, man. Maybe she'll stick around."

"Sure. And maybe the pain-in-the-ass kids that are messing up the town will turn themselves in and ask to repair all the damage." Sam scoffed with a smile and the two of them returned to sweating and pounding nails in the Minnesota sun.

By late afternoon, Alex needed a shower desperately. There was a BBQ over at the Kellys' house, and Alex silently debated attending as he wandered around the side of the building. It backed up to a huge field that was surrounded by an array of forested hills. Alex heard the rushing of the nearby waterfall that had started to melt with the approach of summer. The entire center had received a fresh coat of paint today, which really made a difference. When he reached the back of the building, he smiled at the sight of the dumpster that still sat out back. He remembered, fondly, how at sixteen he'd tried to get Danielle Peterson to kiss him by the dumpster that still sat out back.

At the sound of clicking, he turned his head and found himself staring down the barrel of a camera so big it almost covered Lucy's face. "Hey, Sheriff. What's the smile for?" She snapped another picture.

"I was thinking about kissing Danielle Peterson right

here in this spot," he admitted, rocking back on his heels with his thumbs hooked in his pockets. He didn't flinch when she kept snapping but wished she'd put the camera away. He wasn't shy but he didn't crave the spotlight.

Lucy lowered it, frowned at him but before he could ask why, she gave him a smile that made his stomach tilt. She was more than just beautiful with the sun setting behind her, highlighting the red and gold strands peeking out of all that dark. He wanted his hands in that hair.

With her camera in front of her like a shield, she glanced at him through lowered lashes. "I hope that didn't make you feel special."

Alex grinned. Her lips pursed into a small pout that he found adorable. He probably wasn't the only guy with memories of Danielle behind the rec center, but he cared less about that and more about Lucy's slightly snide tone.

"At sixteen, I didn't care if I was special as long as I—"

Lucy cut him off by putting her hands up to her ears, letting the camera hang from her neck. Alex laughed and stepped closer to her but instead of pulling her hands down, he reached for the camera. Her hands came down immediately, stopping him from slipping it off of her neck. He arched an eyebrow and gave a small tug. With her lips pressed together, she continued to hesitate.

"You let Carmen have a turn." This close to her, it was hard to keep his focus on the camera and where it was resting against her chest. "She told me she held Mia without dropping her, so it seemed like she could handle *my* baby."

He slipped a strap over her head. "I held Mia without

dropping her, too, you know." He chuckled, putting his eye behind the viewfinder.

"Alright. Just be gentle." She put her hands on her hips and watched him.

He clicked the camera, surprised by the little thrill that the sound inspired. He turned the camera toward her and saw her frown in miniature. "Take pictures of the view."

"I am. It's an excellent view," he laughed. She rolled her eyes and walked toward the field.

Doors slammed from the parking lot as people loaded up supplies and families and took off for the evening. Alex was enjoying seeing the town come together for something that would benefit them all. Following behind Lucy, he found that it was a bit tricky to navigate the camera and move at the same time.

"I don't remember you dating Danielle," Lucy said, her tone stiff.

"Never said I dated her. She was just a girl," Alex said, wondering what all of the different buttons did. What was wrong with just 'point and shoot'?

Lucy and Danielle had never been chummy, but her tone suggested there was a reason for this. Confirming his suspicion, Lucy added, "Just a girl who kissed a lot of boys wherever she could."

Definitely a story there, but he didn't want to talk about the past. He was pretty damn happy with the present. "I know. But I didn't care at the time," he answered easily, zooming in on the trees in the distance. They were in full bloom, blending together and melding into one another as if they couldn't exist without touching. So much beauty. He loved this town and being in it.

Lucy stood beside him as he snapped a couple photos. His skin buzzed, like his body was completely aware of her next to him. He could feel her gaze. "And now?"

He lowered the camera, meeting that questioning gaze. Very clearly, he replied, "Now I still don't care who she kisses."

Her smile spread slowly before it reached her eyes and she nodded, accepting the camera as he passed it back to her. She carefully removed the extended lens and loaded it into the bag on her shoulder.

He was still staring at her with a smile of his own when she looked back up. A soft breeze had her brushing back a few strands of hair from her eyes. Then she turned and tipped her face to the sky.

Lucy sighed, as though she was tired or just happy to stand still. "I forgot how beautiful it can be here." Tendrils of hair stuck to her neck, reminding him he needed to get home and shower if he was going to make an appearance at the BBQ. Before he could stop himself, his thoughts wandered to her needing a shower as well.

"You heading to the Kellys'?" he asked, clearing his throat, hoping his train of thought didn't show on his face. She looked over at him with eyes that held a hint of sadness. Her smile matched.

"You okay, Luce?" he asked, giving into the urge and brushing the strand she'd missed behind her ear. Her eyes closed briefly and his breath stuck in his throat.

"I'm fine. I think I'll skip it. I'm tired and not really in the mood for another crowd. Especially since Kate has roped me into more work tomorrow."

He tucked his hand back into his pocket and told himself that the electricity between them was just a combination of lust and his own stupid memories. "Are you headed over?" She turned and began walking back toward the building, kicking blades of grass and stray rocks as she stared at her feet.

"I haven't decided. I don't know if I feel like another crowd either. How about some dinner? I'm starving." Their shoulders brushed as they walked side by side.

"Together?"

He laughed at the surprise on her face.

"It would be nicer than alone, I think. It would definitely be better than Bruce's burgers. I think it's some sort of sacrilege when a man can't BBQ." Lucy laughed and, finally, her smile reached her eyes.

"I don't know. Kate suggested that I leave you alone." She looked away, and he put a hand on her arm, pulling her around gently. "What? What does Kate have to do with this?"

He was sure he'd never sent mixed signals to Kate. He'd never thought of her that way. He'd only ever wanted Lucy. "She says you're long-term and should be off limits to a girl like me," she said, her tone flat.

He wasn't surprised by her candor—Lucy had always been direct. Though she made light of it, he could see she was bothered by what Kate had said. She stood in front of him, not quite meeting his eyes.

"Well," he mused, closing the small space between

them so their bodies were all but brushing against each other, "last time I checked, I didn't let anyone tell me who I should or should not get close to."

He could kiss her—press his mouth against hers as he'd been dreaming of for years. Her eyes were half closed and her breath was sawing in and out in short bursts. He could see the tiny spattering of barely there freckles on the bridge of her nose, and he had the ridiculous urge to run his finger from one to another. She wet her lips quickly, making his stomach—and lower—tighten. He took a deep breath and let it out slowly. He leaned in, moving his hand to

her arm, which was soft and sun warmed. He trailed his fingers up until he could cup her cheek. She watched him through lowered lashes and he wondered if he'd ever wanted to kiss anyone more than he wanted to kiss Lucy Aarons.

Regardless, he knew better than to let attraction rule over caution. "Besides," he murmured, his lips narrowly missing hers to travel up and graze her ear, "I only suggested dinner."

The sensual cloud scattered from her eyes and she rapped him on the chest. "Jerk, "she said, her lips curving up.

Shaking her head at him, she nudged him again and the tension, sexual and otherwise, between them eased. They walked back to the parking lot in time to see Kate loading up her trunk. He was surprised by how quickly the lot had cleared. Maybe others didn't know about Bruce's burgers.

Kate glanced over and gave Lucy another odd look as they walked toward her. He felt Lucy stiffen beside him.

"You know what? Dinner sounds great," she said, louder than necessary.

"You guys aren't going to head over to the BBQ?" Kate slammed her trunk closed.

"No. We're going to shower and grab a bite to eat," Lucy answered in what could only be described as a defiant tone. She seemed to realize belatedly what she had actually said.

"I mean," she stammered, her eyes darting back to him and then over to her sister, "we each have to shower. In our own showers. And then we'll eat. Together. After we each shower alone."

Kate chuckled and, just like that, the sisters were at ease with each other, despite Lucy's cheeks now looking sunburned. As Lucy stowed her camera gear in the backseat, Kate moved in and kissed Alex's cheek.

"Hang on to your heart. I love her, but she won't stay," she whispered so low he wasn't even sure he'd heard her right. "I'll drive with Kate and meet you at your house in an hour?"

"Sounds good," he agreed.

He watched as both women got into the car. The day had definitely not gone as he'd expected. There'd been no major issues in town, he'd actually enjoyed working with his hands, he'd almost kissed Lucy Aarons, and he would be having dinner with her, alone. He was more than a little curious to see what the night would bring. He caught himself whistling as he moved toward his truck.

CHAPTER THREE

*L*ucy ignored the not-so-subtle looks Kate was shooting from her position on the bed. Her sister had a far more expansive wardrobe than Lucy, who was currently rifling through to find something decent to wear.

"Stop it."

"I didn't say anything," Kate replied grumpily.

Lucy pulled on a black-and-white-striped V-neck tank top that was slightly longer in the back. It looked good with the dark cargo shorts she was wearing.

"You're shooting daggers, and it's starting to annoy me. You act like I'm some sort of femme fatale. I'm pretty sure Alex can take care of himself," Lucy huffed, turning around and waiting for Kate to comment on her outfit.

Kate glanced her way with little interest but gave a slight nod of approval.

"More like Julia Roberts in the Runaway Bride," she replied, closing her sociology text and pushing up off her perfectly made bed. Kate was in her final year of college and had taken the smart route, staying at home until she finished. She wouldn't be starting her career with a mountain of debt.

"Wow. That's low. And I've never left a guy at the altar," Lucy reminded her, doing her best not to stomp out of her little sister's room. She also resisted the urge to shove her down onto the bed as she walked past her and silently applauded her own maturity.

"How about the prom?"

Lucy stopped in the hallway and turned around slowly. People rarely brought up the prom. At least not people in her family. The story was legend in their small town. She'd refused to come down and meet her date, Lewis Mandrake, when he'd shown up with his limo and corsage, his tie the color of her lilac dress. She'd never shared the reason with anyone, so the story had snowballed and Lucy had never corrected any version she might have overheard with the truth.

"You know what, Kate? I think it's sweet that you're protective of Alex. If it's because you actually do have a thing for him—"

"I don't!"

"Then knock it off and mind your own business. I'm going for dinner with an old school friend. Our neighbor. The town sheriff. I'm not going to molest him or kidnap him or use his goddamn handcuffs on him, so let it go!"

Her hair whipped over her shoulder as she made an effort to turn dramatically and walked smack into her dad's chest. She closed her eyes and wished she had one of those trap doors in the floor like Ellen DeGeneres had for games on her talk show.

"Going out with the sheriff, honey?" Her dad's hands gripped her bare arms to steady her.

"Yes," she mumbled, keeping her eyes on the tiny check marks decorating his polo shirt.

"Well, I'm glad you ruled out handcuffs for the evening. I think Alex is kind of an old-fashioned sort," Mark said solemnly.

She looked up and tilted her head to the side. "When did you become funny?"

"Your mother wrote a self-help book on it. *How to Heal Others and Yourself with Laughter*," he grinned as Kate chuckled from behind her.

"You know, I'm not so sure I missed you guys after all."

Her dad let go of her arms and allowed her to move past him. She grabbed her purse from her own room before sprinting down the steps, ignoring both her dad and her sister, who were still chuckling like loons, their laughs so similar that it made her chest ache.

"Going out, Luce?" Julie asked as Lucy came into the kitchen. Julie was chopping carrots and Lucy snuck one quickly, popping it into her mouth. "Just out for a bite to eat with Alex," she replied lightly and moved to give her mom a quick squeeze.

"Alright, well, take a key this time," her mom suggested, moving to take her own off her key ring that still hung by the door on a homemade key holder. Lucy and Charlotte had made it for Mother's Day when they were ten and fourteen from a long stick and some hooks they'd found in the garage. Julie had treated it like prized silver, and looking at it made Lucy smile.

"You know I could probably buy you a new key holder now, right?"

"Don't you dare. There is no better gift than one that is made with love."

Julie pulled her in for an embrace, and Lucy realized that every time she left her mom's side, Julie hugged her as though she wouldn't see her again for a long time. Tears stung the corners of her eyes.

"Well, it was definitely made with more love than talent. Still, I need to do some shopping—I only have a few outfits. Want to come with me sometime this week? If I promise *not* to buy you a key hook?" she asked. Her mom pursed her lips and turned back to the cutting board, re-chopping the carrots that were already in small chunks. Her shoulders stiffened, and Lucy thought for one brief moment that she was mad.

"This week is quite busy for me, honey. If I don't stick to my schedule, I get behind in my writing. It really doesn't take much to throw me off track. I'm sure you had deadlines and cut-offs while you were taking pictures, right?" Julie answered, glancing up briefly before pulling all of the carrots toward her and scooping them up.

Lucy knew her mother meant well, but she hated that she referred to her work as taking pictures. There was something grade school and inadequate about the term. Still, no sense in picking on little things. She shrugged off the irritation and sense of unease.

"I'll see you when I get home, okay?"

"Of course."

"I love you, mom."

"I love you more."

"Just call me if anything about it seems overly suspicious," Alex told Mick, his aging deputy. Alex was pretty sure that Mick Harper was nearing seventy— though no one dared to ask—but he was one of the sharpest men that Alex knew. He'd rather have Mick at his back than any of the twenty-somethings coming straight out of training.

He heard the knock on his door and frowned as he checked his watch.

"I gotta go, Mick. I'm going to dinner but, seriously, call me if you need to...Yeah...Alright."

He moved toward the door as he turned the phone off and tossed it onto his couch. Water droplets dribbled underneath the collar of his still partially open shirt. Fastening the first few buttons, he opened the door to find Lucy kneeling down, playing with the strap on the sexy sandals that wrapped around her calf.

"Hey," he chuckled, smiling down as she glanced up. He finished doing his shirt.

"Hi. My strap isn't tight enough. Actually, Kate's strap because I stole everything I'm wearing from her. Well, not the underwear or the bra but—you know what? I'm going to shut up," she babbled and stood up.

"Don't stop on my account. I have no problem hearing about your bra or your underwear. And in the spirit of full disclosure, I'm also wearing my own underwear."

"I don't remember you being so funny. Must be something in the water around here," she smirked at him and moved into the house, her strappy sandals clicking on his hardwood floors.

"I don't remember you hanging out with me enough to know."

He walked toward the kitchen to find his wallet and heard the tapping of her step behind him. He wondered if the fact that he was thinking about whether her shoes would scratch his floors made him old.

"This is breathtaking, Alex."

He could hear the smile in her voice and turned to see her taking in the newly renovated kitchen. Sam had done a great job. The floor matched the rest of the house but seemed darker surrounded by the antique white wood of the cabinets. The granite countertop shot little specks of gold and bronze when the sunlight from the wide window over the sink hit it. The smile of genuine appreciation on her face warmed him, as it was his favorite room in the old house that he was working so hard to make his.

He liked the permanency of owning a house, having a mortgage. It still surprised him that he wanted that sense of roots here, in Angel's Lake. At twelve, he had hated the thought of his mom leaving him with his old man in this nothing town. Then he'd spent some time hating her and the town. Once he got the chip kicked off his shoulder, he'd come to love the town and tolerate his mother. His love for the town came far easier.

"I had some help from Sam with the design and

construction, obviously," he told her, watching as she ran her hand along the granite top of the island.

"It's so rich but still homey. This is the kind of kitchen that makes me wish I knew how to cook," she laughed. He liked her laugh. It had a musical quality to it that made you feel like humming along. He wanted to be the reason for that laughter.

"Would you prefer we stay in? I could make something," he suggested. She sat at one of the barstools. "I don't want you to have to cook for me," she blushed.

He wouldn't have admitted it to any person he knew, but as he looked at her across the counter, the pink spreading up her cheeks, his heart and stomach fell into one another, sending a tremor up his spine.

"I would love to cook for you. Unless you're picky."

"Not really, no. I prefer things without tentacles," she considered. He walked over to her side of the island. She turned in the swivel stool as he approached so that they were facing each other. Lucy smiled somewhat awkwardly, and he wondered if it made her nervous for him to stand so close.

"No tentacles. I can work with that."

"Do you cook for a lot of women in your kitchen?"

"Not all at once. That never works out well."

She rapped him on the chest and he captured her hand, holding it over his heart, which he was certain she could feel drumming out of his chest. It was a strange duality to be playful with her while being so incredibly aware of everything that made her Lucy. It was like feeling relaxed and hyper at the same time.

"I think I would have remembered if you were this funny in high school," she said, her voice low, her eyes on his hand covering hers. "You would have if you'd paid more attention," he replied. She'd been too busy working toward her ticket out of town.

"My mistake. I'm paying attention now," she answered, staring into his eyes without hesitancy.

He made a sound of agreement in his throat that he couldn't describe. He couldn't stop looking at her, right in front of him, touching him. The first time he'd met her, she'd had her hand in the exact same spot it was now, and he wondered if she remembered at all. If she remembered the moment that made him fall for her as a boy, respect her as a man, and ache with want for her now. He'd likely made too much of their first encounter, but it had changed something inside of him—given him strength. Still, a crucial moment in one person's memory could be irrelevant in the other person's life. Alex figured it might be best to leave the past where it was and see if they could start from right here.

Lucy had meant it when she'd said his humor surprised her. They hadn't really hung out in the same crowds. She remembered him being kind, serious, and dorky-cute. Now, he was intense, sexy, and confident. Having his solid frame stand over her magnified every sensation. She kept glancing at her hand, which was tucked inside of his, barely visible against his chest. She liked the sensation of being wrapped up in him. She could feel his heartbeat and would bet money that the pace of hers was faster. Almost uncomfortably fast. Perhaps she was still jetlagged. Though when her gaze met his, she knew she couldn't blame the energy pulsing between them on a long flight. She stood slowly, without meaning to—without thinking it through—and the movement brought the rest of her body up against Alex's. She heard his intake of breath and felt the warmth of it when he exhaled.

"I'd say we're both paying pretty close attention," he murmured roughly. "It makes me wonder what else I didn't notice."

"Well, obviously you didn't pick up on my charm."

When she breathed out, the movement seemed to bring her closer to him. She inhaled—held her breath as he watched her.

"Maybe you were too busy using it on Danielle Peterson," she tried to joke, but she could hear the squeak in her voice—a combination of nerves and holding her breath. He smiled and lowered his head slightly.

"Who?"

The air burst out of her lungs on a half laugh. "Good answer."

Unable to wonder any longer, she put her free hand on his waist, pushed up onto her tiptoes and pressed her mouth to his. She had barely a second to think of how soft his lips felt on hers, when he took control of the kiss, letting his tongue touch hers. The quick motion cracked the emptiness inside her and filled her with need. And for once, what she needed, what she wanted, was right there in front of her.

Pushing aside the self-doubt that had Kate's voice, she anchored herself to him and changed the tone of the kiss. His growl of approval as he moved his free hand to the small of her back, pulling her as close as he could, encouraged her. He released her hand and she used the opportunity to wrap both of her arms around his neck as she continued to consume him and be consumed in return. Without breaking the kiss, he pressed her back against the countertop. She hung on tighter. Lucy's lungs refused to work properly so she gulped in air when he shifted his focus to her neck, then the underside of her jaw, as he trailed kisses over her, leaving tiny, restless sparks of want along her skin. She found his lips again, framing his face with her hands. He gentled the kiss and ran his hand along her hair.

When they pulled back slightly, she could still feel their combined heartbeats pounding against each other as if they were doing some sort of repetitive fist bump. She watched his eyes open slowly; they were clouded with lust. Had it been just that, her heart wouldn't have twisted. Her stomach wouldn't have seized. As she looked at him, she saw more than desire. She recognized the look of hope in his gaze and understood what Kate had been trying to tell her. Alex believed in long-term, going steady, planning-a-future commitment. In fact, he craved it.

She might not have remembered much, but she remembered the boy with sad eyes and a chip on his shoulder, who had been dropped on the side of the road by his own mother. She'd left him in front of his father's house when he was twelve years old and went off to find something that would fulfill her, making it clear that the *something* wasn't her son or ex-husband.

"Alex," she whispered around the ball of regret forming in her throat.

"Let's go out to dinner instead," he said, easing back. His words surprised her, as did the realization that she missed the feel of his body against her own. "Uh ... okay."

She smoothed down her top and kept her eyes on the floor under the pretense of rechecking her straps. "Luce."

He waited until she looked up at him to step into her space again. He nudged her chin gently. "You look like I just asked you to have my baby," he smiled tightly.

"This is what Kate meant ... you're long-term, and I'm just—"

"You're just going to go for dinner with me, forget what Kate said, and remember that I'm more than capable of making my own choices. I don't need you—or Kate—to try to figure out what I want. I can do that for myself."

She bit her lip and resisted the urge to cry. Instead, she nodded her head, stiffened her shoulders, and took his hand. "Okay," she exhaled hard and asked, "so where are you taking me?"

CHAPTER FOUR

*S*he worried it would be tense as they drove to the edge of town, but instead, he pointed out what might have changed since her last visit Alex had not lived next door to her parents when she'd last been home, so she hadn't seen him, really, since high school. She twisted in her seatbelt so she could look at his profile while he drove. The sky was darkening and looked like someone had taken gel pens in red, orange, and yellow and streaked them across the clouds. His dark hair was spiked messily like Brad Pitt's before he'd gone grunge.

"What brought you home this time?" he asked, turning the music down a bit. The lyrics sat in her chest, heavy like lead: *"Going down, but no one knew, I was losing altitude."*

"Kate wanted help with the center, particularly with fund raising. Plus, she's graduating soon. Mia was just born, and I wanted to meet her, and both of those things aligned perfectly with me getting fired, so it seemed like fate."

"You got fired?"

He glanced her way before looking back at the road. He held his hands at ten and two the way she'd been taught in driving school and never done since. He was so by-the-book that she couldn't help but smile.

"I did."

"And?"

"And it sucks, but I'd rather lose my job than sleep my way to the top," she answered casually, switching the radio station.

He slammed on the breaks. "What?" His tone was vicious. She checked behind them, but there were no other cars on the road. She looked over at him, and though his face looked calm, his eyes were fierce.

"Your boss tried to make you sleep with him?"

"He suggested it, yes. Um ... we should keep driving. Unless you can't see through the haze of mad in your eyes." She laughed and went back to switching stations.

"I'm sorry, but how is this funny?"

"It's not funny, but it's cute, and a little bit sweet, that you look so mad about it. Welcome to the big, bad world, sheriff. Some people aren't nice."

He was quiet for the rest of the short drive to the diner she remembered well. It held both good and bad memories for her. She bit her lip as they parked, and she thought of how the bad memories seemed more trivial from her adult perspective while the good ones seemed shinier than they probably were. He turned in his seat after taking his keys from the ignition and leaned over to pop the latch on her seatbelt.

"I'm well aware of the realities of the world. What I

don't like, other than some jackass trying to get in your pants, is that you're so flippant about it. It's not okay. Does your family know?" He spoke carefully, slowly, with measured patience.

"You're right. It's not okay. But there's no use getting worked up about it. And no, I didn't tell anyone."

She covered his hand with hers and smiled at him. He was so easy to smile at and to be with. Like coming home to an old friend. A friend who was an exceptionally good kisser.

His hand tensed before he turned it so their palms were touching. "I hope you kicked him in the—"

"*No*. I did not. Because even though the world seems vast and huge, the photography world is small, and I like what I do. I'd like to continue doing it. And kicking anyone anywhere isn't the way to make a name for myself."

"You have a name," he said quietly, leaning forward and putting his forehead against hers. She held her breath, wondering if he'd kiss her again. He pulled back a split second later, got out of his truck, and came around the hood to open her door for her.

She looked up at him for a moment as she stood in the space between his arm and the open door.

"You're very sweet," she murmured before he lowered his arm and they made their way into the diner he'd eaten at more times than he could count. He wasn't sure if sweet was something he wanted to be in her eyes; it seemed a little too close to "such a good friend."

"I haven't been here since I was about twenty."

"Nothing has changed. Still the best burgers in the county."

They moved through Calvin's Diner, known to the locals as Cal's, waving hello to the few people that sat in the booths and at tables. The faded tabletops and vinyl seat covers gave it a retro feel. To Alex, it was another home. He'd hung out there with buddies after games and brought dates there. He had eaten many breakfasts, both before and after a long shift, at the rectangular, white Formica counter with the padded-top, swivel stools. He waved to Danielle, who had waitressed there for about five years now, and felt a moment of awkwardness when he saw Lucy's eyes widen. Perhaps he should have thought this through a little more.

"You bring all your dates here? So your ex-girlfriend can check them out and approve?" she asked curtly while sliding into the corner booth. Definitely should have rethought the game plan. Or at least had a game plan.

"No. And she was never my girlfriend. Just a girl I ... never mind. She wasn't my girlfriend."

He gave an awkward smile when Danielle came to the table, her Cal's uniform looking tighter than appropriate. The pocket of the pink apron over the yellow, collared dress was full of pencils and notepads. Her sandy brown hair was pulled up into a haphazard bun. She was still attractive but looked like the years hadn't been kind to her. Having been the responder to most of her domestic abuse calls, he knew first hand that they hadn't.

"How you doing, sheriff?" she drawled, her eyes on Lucy. "I'm good, Danielle. You remember Lucy?"

"Course I do. Hard to forget any of the Aarons sisters. How are you, Lucy?"

"I'm well. You?" Lucy fidgeted with the menu, not meeting Danielle's gaze.

"Not bad, I suppose. Can I get you some drinks?"

Danielle took their orders of cheeseburgers and fries with a couple of colas and left the table. Lucy was folding her napkin into tiny squares. He reached across the table and put his hand over hers. He didn't like how good it felt to touch her—it would be so easy to get used to touching her. She hadn't been home two full days yet and here he was, in over his head again. Drowning in Lucy. Good thing he knew how to swim.

"You okay? Did you and Danielle have some sort of rivalry that never made the rumor mill?" he teased. Her lips firmed and she kept her hand still under his.

"No. No rivalry. I'm fine. Their burgers better be as good as I remember, because I'm starving."

"I should have cooked for you. Next time?"

He waited until she realized he was asking for another chance before he smiled. Thankfully, the smile that warmed her face actually met her eyes. "As long as you cook better than I do."

"You'd have to cook for me first so I'd have a frame of reference."

He stretched his legs under the table, essentially caging her feet between his just as Danielle came back with their sodas. She set them down with a tight smile, turned away, took a couple of steps, and then stopped.

"Lucy," she said in a quiet voice when she turned around.

Lucy looked at her as something unspoken passed between the women, a look that made Alex's insides feel like they'd been doused in ice water. Neither said anything, but Danielle's face held a sadness he had not seen before—regret. Lucy bit her bottom lip. The bell over the door rang, and new customers laughed their way inside. Danielle nodded, even though nothing had been said, and went to say hello to the couple that had just entered.

"What was *that?*" Alex asked, sitting up and leaning forward on his crossed arms. Lucy's eyes looked close to watery, and she still held her bottom lip tightly in her teeth.

"Lucy."

"Nothing. Sometimes the past is better off left alone."

Since he'd had the same thought earlier that evening, he let it go. She switched the topic to her photography and started telling him about the village she'd been staying in. Her face became animated when she spoke of her work, and he lost the thread of what she was saying by getting caught up in her smile, her voice, the way her eyes widened when she talked about the changes she had witnessed. He cringed inwardly when he realized he was hanging on her every word. He was a grown man, yet one day with her home and he reverted to a lovesick kid. Alex had dated plenty of women so he knew he should have a little more… game. But none of those women had been Lucy.

Lucy waved her fingers in front of his face, laughing as she pulled him from his thoughts. "What's going on in that pretty little head of yours, sheriff?"

Danielle dropped their food off and asked if they needed anything else. She hesitated again and looked right at Lucy. "It would make me feel better if I apologized," Danielle said quietly, leaning over the table slightly.

"That's a lousy reason to apologize for anything, isn't it? To make yourself feel better," Lucy answered, reaching for the ketchup. "Maybe it is. But it doesn't make it any less true. I'm sorry, Lucy."

Lucy poured ketchup on her plate and then handed the bottle to Alex without meeting his eyes.

"Thank you. Apology accepted," Lucy finally replied, looking up at Danielle, her lips firmed and her eyes revealing nothing. Danielle nodded and left their bill on the table. Lucy bit into her burger and sighed in pleasure, distracting Alex for a moment while he watched her, trying to figure her out.

The burger was delicious, but it was hard to swallow past the lump in her throat. Humiliation had a flavor of its own, and the rancid taste of it was making her regret taking such a large bite. Her eyes stung as she grabbed her pop to wash down her food.

"Lucy," Alex said her name as though she was a child that had just told a completely obvious fib. "Good burger. Just like I remember."

He bit into his and eyed her from across the table. She didn't want to look down. She met his gaze and challenged him to push her further. She wondered if he thought she'd talk first. Like maybe he thought his gaze could break her like a perp.

"I'm tougher than you," she blurted. He laughed. Not

at her, but still. "Are you coming up with ways to prove that?"

"No." She sulked, feeling stupid. "I just know you're trying to get me to fess up, and it won't happen. Your cop glare won't work on me."

"My cop glare? Jesus, what kind of T.V. do you watch? If they say 'fess up' on the shows you're watching, maybe you should rethink them," he chortled, taking another bite of his burger.

She did the same and they passed the rest of the meal engaged in an amusing staring contest. When they finished, he dropped some bills onto the table and they walked out of the diner to what Lucy was sure was the sound of the gossip mill hard at work. He opened the door for her, and she hopped up into his truck. Slipping behind the wheel, he turned the key in the ignition, gave her a sweet smile, and started to drive without a word.

"Where are we going?" she asked when he turned right instead of left and they wound their way farther out of town. "Oh, you're talking to me again?" he laughed.

She frowned and went back to silence, using the opportunity to stare out the window. It didn't matter where she had been—the beauty of Angel's Lake always astounded her. There was a purity here that she hadn't found anywhere else. She looked over at Alex when he parked in a makeshift, gravel parking lot. Getting out of the car before he could reach her side, she arched her eyebrows at him. He chuckled and took her hand, leading her down a narrow walkway. Just past a small footbridge, they walked through a cluster of heavily leaved trees, and on the other side of them, she lost a small piece of her heart. Or perhaps, found it.

"Oh. Why didn't you tell me to bring my camera?" she gasped.

She felt like she was sitting in the middle of a colored Ansel Adams print. They were surrounded by trees as they stood at the base of the mountains, water rippling over rocks below them. She could hear the steady flow of it like background music. They stood on a worn foot deck that might have, at some point, been part of the bridge they had just stepped down from.

"Sometimes you don't need a camera for the picture to stay in your head," he commented quietly, standing so his side was brushing hers, their fingers touching. "I don't have any pictures of you, and I've never been able to get you out of my mind."

She turned to face him even though he stood staring at the water. She put her hand on his forearm. It was solid, like him, and warm. Also like him. "What are you talking about?"

He shoved his hands into his pockets and turned so they were face-to-face.

"Do you remember when we met? I was in the middle of a fist fight in sixth grade."

"I remember you being in a fight. I remember getting in the middle of it. I don't remember who or why."

"It was Davey Morgan. He was a punk-ass bully who had been spouting off since I moved in with my dad. One day he sucker punched me, and I let him have it."

"I hated that guy. Last I heard, he was living in a

rundown shack selling homemade whiskey. Or drinking it," she recollected with a frown.

"Probably both. I tossed him in jail a few times a couple years ago for drunk and disorderly. Haven't seen him for a long time, but I wouldn't doubt the stories. Anyway," he shrugged, pulled his hands out of his pockets and taking her hand before he continued. "You rushed over just as I was about to kick him in the ribs. I was so mad I couldn't see anything else. But I saw you. You came right up to me, grabbed my wrist, and turned me to face you. You put your hand on my chest."

He placed it there now and her heart ricocheted in response. She stepped closer to him.

"How do you remember this?"

"Some things stay with you. Define you. Change something inside you. You leaned in really close and told me he wasn't worth it. You kept your hand on my chest, just like this, looked me straight in the eye, and told me he wasn't worth it but I was. That I was better than that. Better than him."

"Looks like I was a pretty good judge of character even at twelve," she smiled, drawn in by the memory, by him.

"Maybe. But it was the first time somebody had made me feel worth anything in so long. That sounds dramatic, but it's true. You made me feel like I mattered."

"You did. You do."

"You told the principal that he'd called you a white-trash whore and I was defending your honor. I never even got suspended," he reminded her. She smiled, not sure if she remembered authentically or because he was filling in the gaps for her.

"Huh. Looks like I was a quick thinker, too," she laughed.

He put his hand on her arm and rubbed it up and down, sending shivers up her back despite the warmth of the evening. Linking his fingers with hers, he started walking back in the direction they had come.

"You were. But the point is, that moment made me step back and think about who I was and who I wanted to be."

"That's giving an awful lot of power to a twelve-year-old girl."

"Maybe. But from that moment on, I knew two things: one, I didn't want to be a dickhead like Davey."

"And two?"

He stopped at his truck. She could still hear the water and promised herself that she'd come back to take pictures.

"And two, if I ever got the chance, I'd tell you how much that moment mattered to me. So I'm telling you now. And saying thank you, I guess."

"You're welcome. Though I think your thank you is misplaced."

"See? No, it's not. That's part of why I'm telling you this."

He pulled her past the passenger side door and released her hand to open the tailgate. Before she could stop him, he picked her up under the arms and lifted her to sit on the truck so he could stand between her legs.

"You're worth it," he said seriously, his hands resting on her thighs. They were mostly covered by her cargo shorts, but the gentle grip of his fingers still caused a nervous distraction in the pit of her stomach.

"What?"

"When I needed to hear it, you told me and you made sure I listened. You told me I mattered, and now I'm returning the favor and telling you right back that *you* matter. Not your name, or your job, or anything else. *You.*"

She wasn't sure why she felt like crying. He was in her space, his eyes locked on hers. His words took away some of the ache that she hadn't realized was residing just under her ribcage.

"I think you're telling me wrong," she whispered, trying to ignore Kate's ever-present nagging voice that told her not to do this, not to go where she wanted to be. Not to mess something else up.

"What?"

She took his hand, brought it up to rest on her heart, and then covered his large hand with her small ones. His breathed hitched and his eyes widened. A tremor traveled up her spine and ended in her shoulders.

"Say it again."

"For the love of God, Lucy. Are you trying to kill me?" he shook his head with a wry smile on his lips. She tightened her legs on his hips and waited. He leaned in, close enough that she could feel his breath, warm like the air around them.

"You matter, Lucy Aarons. You're worth something. Worth so much."

She tried to bite the inside of her cheek to stymie the tears, but she knew it didn't quite work when she felt one slipping. His cupped her jaw with his free hand and began to close the small space between them.

"So are you," she whispered.

As he kissed her, as she let herself tumble into the seduction and sweetness of his mouth on hers and ignored the voice telling her she was right and he was wrong. That he deserved better. For just this moment, she wanted what he said to be true. She pulled him closer and let herself believe it, for now.

CHAPTER FIVE

*M*ost of the week was uneventful, which meant that by Friday, Alex was tired of flipping through the pile of paperwork that never seemed to get smaller on his desk. Though it was a fairly decent distraction from thinking about Lucy. Which he had done nonstop since she had returned home a week ago. He could hear Dolores's music playing from the front desk outside his office. If she played another Britney Spears song, he was pretty sure his mood was going to turn "Toxic."

Dolores Edgemont was fifty-something going on fifteen. She'd been divorced twice and liked airing her dirty laundry the way other people liked getting massages. Personally, he could do without either. He didn't want to hear about her last husband's lack of performance any more than he wanted a stranger's hands on him. He pushed back from his desk and went to the Keurig coffee maker that his dad had given him last Christmas.

"Don't be a cliché. Don't drink shit coffee because it's

available," his dad had grumbled around his smoker's cough. They'd sat on opposite couches after sharing way too much Chinese food, as was their Christmas tradition.

"And make sure to have it on hand when you drop by?" Alex had answered with an easy smile, earning a nod of agreement and a hearty laugh from Chuck Whitman.

Once he'd gotten through the anger of his mom leaving and over the angst that sucked the soul of every teenager, he and his dad had gotten along pretty well. His dad was straight-up strict with him, but he was also fair. Chuck dropped in at least once a week to make sure his son was actually 'pulling his weight,' and possibly to flirt with Dolores a little.

Alex pulled up the ancient blinds in his ten-by-twenty office, letting the sun shine on the dimly painted walls. Drumming on the windowsill while the aroma of chocolate-glazed-donut coffee infused the room—he didn't give a damn about clichés—he watched his sleepy town wake up. At twelve, he had thought Angel's Lake was the most boring place on earth; it didn't even have a 7-11 or an arcade back then. He liked the routine and predictability of it just fine now.

Across the street from the sheriff's office was the long, U-shaped property that housed most of the town's main businesses. Nick, of Adam's Apples, the town grocer, was just opening up his store. The bakery and post office wouldn't open until later in the morning. There was also a barber, a mini mart and two vacant stores. Compared to years ago, the town was booming

"You okay sheriff?" Dolores asked, surprising him out

of his thoughts. He looked over to see her helping herself to his coffee. Wearing a pair of skin-tight pants of unidentifiable material, she had her hair teased extra high today. She took a slow sip of his drink.

"Help yourself."

"I'll put another one in. You know I can't resist this one, so serves you right for making it. You look like you've been up all night but not for a good reason," she laughed, winking at him. With long blond hair and a syrupy sweet voice, she was attractive from a distance. If you didn't get too close, you couldn't see how leathery and worn her skin had become from spending too much time in a tanning bed. From where he was standing, it was harder to see the piles of makeup she put on to cover the fact that she was aging and didn't want to. Still, nothing in the world could hide her huge heart.

"I'm fine, Dee. Just waiting for everyone to open their doors and see that everything was status quo last night." The town's teens had been remarkably quiet all week. Maybe his old man was right and the small vandalism wave had been the kids reveling in the freedom of summer that was fast approaching.

She selected a new packet of coffee for the machine and slipped it in with a fresh cup underneath. "Rumor has it you were dining with Ms. Lucy Aarons the other night. Doesn't sound so status quo to me," she prodded, leaning a hip on his desk.

"I'm guessing rumor's name is Cal since it was his diner we went to. It was just dinner, and that's all I'll say about that. Don't you have something to do besides bug me and steal my coffee?" he asked, going to the machine to make sure he actually got this cup.

"Sure do, sugar. But nothing as fun as watching you blush when I bring up Lucy's name," she replied as the phone rang. "Oh, you're actually saved by the bell!"

He shook his head and hoped the day would stay slow, even if it meant putting up with Dolores's nosey ways and shitty taste in music.

If she hadn't left the house when she did, Lucy would have been subjected to one of her mother's surveys. She smiled remembering her timing of heading out the door as Kate had stumbled down the stairs, still in her Mickey Mouse pajamas.

"Well, I need one of you girls to answer the questions so I can see if it's a valid survey," Julie had complained as Lucy grabbed her camera and purse, claiming she had something important to do.

"Kate's here. I'm sure she would be a better test subject. Besides, I had a date this week, so it seems like she should do it," Lucy had said, with an evil grin aimed at her sister.

"Huh? What should I do?" Kate had yawned loudly on her way to the coffee.

"How do you please yourself? I'm writing a new book, *How to Make Yourself Happy: In Every Way*. It's about—"

"See you guys later! Love you," Lucy had called while Kate belatedly realized what was happening.

Now, walking down the road that led to the main street of town, she could feel the sun warming her back. It had been uncomfortably warm in Africa, and she welcomed the more tolerable weather.

"Well, hey there, Lucy," Mr. Kramer called from where he was putting out fresh produce in front of Adam's Apples. She wandered over, adjusting the thick strap on her camera bag.

"How are you, Mr. Kramer?"

"You're close to thirty now, Lucy. I think you can call me Nick," he laughed, polishing up a Granny Smith on his long apron and handing it to her.

"Ouch. Thanks for the reminder. How are you?" she asked again, taking the apple and a large bite. He'd always given her and her friends apples on their way home from school, looking just as he did now, as if he'd come into the world as a gray-haired, smiley-faced old man.

"I'm very good. My Fiona is getting tired of the grocery store. Keeps talking about visiting foreign places, but I don't want to go to Arizona and play golf," he complained, his soft cap of hair moving along with his exaggerated golfing gestures.

"I don't think Arizona counts as foreign. Don't you have a houseful of grandkids yet?" Lucy laughed, the perfect blend of sweet and sour on her tongue.

"Ginny's a few months along with her first. She'll be happy to see you, I reckon. You kids are taking longer and longer to settle down. I don't understand the hold up," he groused, pulling bags out from underneath the fruit stand. A couple of cars meandered past them as other shops switched their signs to open and merchants called out hellos.

"I'm not quite sure what to say about that, but I'd love to see Ginny. Tell her I'll come by. She's on the outskirts of town, right?" Lucy asked, stepping back a little. This conversation didn't seem any safer than the one in her parents' kitchen.

"Sure is. They bought a big old house on Westwood that they're restoring. It's going to be something, for sure."

"It definitely is," Alex's voice agreed from behind her. She felt heat creep up her cheeks and knew that when she turned, her face would be flushed. "Hey," she said as casually as possible given the not-so-casual somersaults taking place in her chest.

"Lucy," he nodded, a quiet smile making him look like he knew something she didn't.

"Morning, Sheriff. You want an apple?" Nick asked, wiping his hands on his almost white apron. The little apple decal over his chest was peeling off slightly. "No thanks, Nick. Where you headed, Luce?" he asked, that same smile in place.

"For a walk. I had an idea to raise some funds for Kate's project and wanted to get started. I should go. Thanks for the apple, Mr. Kramer. Tell Ginny I'll come by and say hi."

"I will. See you soon, dear. Good to have you home."

Alex nodded to Nick, who made his way inside, and then fell in step beside Lucy as she wandered past the now-open shops. They walked in easy silence, waving here and there to people she knew and didn't know. Everyone seemed to know Alex, which she supposed made sense. She busied herself by pulling her camera out of the case and attaching the lens. She could smell his cologne every now and again when a slight breeze shuffled past them. She inhaled through her nose louder than she'd intended.

"Smells good, doesn't it?" he asked, looking down at her as they moved to the edge of the town U. "Uh," she stammered, not sure how to answer.

"It's the bread. They make it fresh every morning. It's one of my favorite smells."

With his hands in the pockets of his jeans and his shoulders relaxed, he looked more like he was headed out for a hike than he did like he was surveying his town, keeping a watch over everything.

"The bread? Yup. Smells good. Delicious, actually," she smiled up at him from behind the viewfinder. "Don't start that again," he groaned, putting his hand up to block the lens.

"Aw, come on, Sheriff. You're very photogenic."

"As are you, but I seem to remember you don't like being on the other side of the lens, either."

They turned up Maple Street, which branched off in two directions: toward Angel's Lake Elementary and to the hills that held some of the best hiking trails in Minnesota. They veered toward the trails.

"I'm a much better photographer than I am a subject."

She turned the camera toward the easy foot trails that were lined with a rainbow of wildflowers.

"I'd say you could be either, given that you look like a model," he mumbled, picking up a handful of rocks from the path. "Don't you have a job to do?" she scoffed, adjusting the zoom lens.

"I'm doing it. I'm making sure you stay safe."

"I see. Well, as long as I'm not keeping you from anything important."

"I don't tend to wander where I don't want to be, Luce."

She snapped a close-up of a black-eyed Susan while he paused beside her, in her space. They moved along the trail, farther from the town center toward the quiet and the still.

"Do you like being the sheriff?"

She kept snapping, letting the routine of it and the continuous clicking sound soothe her, knowing she'd likely have to delete most of the pictures when she got home.

"I do. It's not a big town, but it's busy enough, and I feel like being sheriff lets me give back to a town that has given so much to me," he said thoughtfully. He seemed to say most things thoughtfully, which she figured made him good at his job.

She snapped his profile, the quiet serenity of him, and knew that she wouldn't be deleting that particular picture. "You act like this town saved you from something," she murmured, lowering the camera.

"It did. When my mom ditched me, I hated everything. I hated her, my dad, this town ... myself. But to be honest, I'd started hating most of those things before I got here," he looked at her like he wanted her approval to go on. She settled herself back onto a large boulder surrounded by thick trees and kept her camera on her lap. She could smell the perfume of the flowers dancing with his cologne.

"We lived in Chicago, me and my mom. My dad left and moved back here when they divorced," Alex continued, tossing the rocks he'd picked up into the stream down below them. "He had his parents here and a job if he ever wanted it. He phoned, kept in touch. But it didn't matter. I was ten and pissed off that he'd left. She went from one guy to another, looking for someone to take care of us. I gave up trying to prove to her that we didn't need anyone and started doing shit to make her mad. Getting in trouble at school, tagging buildings. Anything to keep her too busy to find another asshole that she thought would take care of her. Of us."

His shoulders didn't relax even after he'd thrown the last of the pebbles. She took a picture of the stream, wanting to hear the rest. He moved forward and she fell in step beside him.

"Did it work?"

He laughed without humor and looked over at her. His eyes were dim with what looked like regret. It surprised her how badly she wanted to make them bright again.

"A little too well. She packed us up and said she couldn't do it anymore. 'It' meaning taking care of me. She dropped me off at Chuck's without telling him and didn't look back for ten years. She needed some money about five years ago, so she got in touch. I accidently hung up on her," he chuckled. The sound made something tighten deep in her own belly.

"Think you'll ever forgive her?"

"I think I mostly have. I just don't want her in my life, you know? You're lucky, Luce. You have a family that loves you. Misses you when you're not here." She firmed her lips and tucked her camera back into the bag.

"I know," was all she said. But inside, she wondered how true it was—at a certain point, didn't you stop missing someone and just get used to them being absent? She looked up at the sky where the clouds made fluffy pictures and the sun hedged toward noon.

"How long do you think you'll be home?"

She turned, unsure of how far they had wandered, and started back down the trail. She had a feeling she knew the answer deep down in her soul but was afraid to think about it. Afraid to want it.

"Not long enough to go steady," she joked.

He stopped her with a hand on her arm, and she closed her eyes to absorb all the sensations. The sun beating down on them was not as warm as the spot where his hand gripped her gently.

If he were looking to have his heart stomped on, torn out, and lit on fire, pursuing Lucy was the way to go. A smart man would walk her home, go back to work, and see if he could connect with a woman at the bar outside of town later tonight.

Lucy had her eyes closed. Her hair was tucked into a braid with little pieces falling out, like she'd been in a hurry and wasn't really concerned with how she

looked. She was wearing a plain-Jane tank top and a pair of shorts. Simple, dainty sandals, not at all fit for the trail, were on her feet. Yet, there was nothing plain or simple about the way she clung to him when they'd kissed the other night. Nothing ordinary in the heat that was coursing up his arm just from touching her—like he couldn't touch enough of her at once. He pulled her closer. She let him.

"Who asked you to go steady? Maybe I just want to get

laid," he grinned, knowing that she deserved prettier words than that but knowing she'd run if he said any. She laughed loud and her shoulders released the tension she'd been carrying in them.

"Oh yeah. Because you're just the type to go for a one-night stand. I bet you have a three-date minimum rule," she smiled, her body brushing up against his.

"A minimum rule?"

"Yes, dating etiquette 101. Take girl on three dates before trying to get in her pants."

"Okay, clearly that rule gets taught after high school."

She laughed again, and he moved his body slightly so she could feel how well they fit together. "Are you leaving tomorrow?" he asked, his voice lower.

"No."

"Then it wouldn't be one night."

"Alex. You know what I mean. I don't know how long I'm staying. I can't promise you anything."

"I'm not sure where I got the reputation that I was holding out for an engagement ring, but I promise I can do casual just fine. You can't deny there's heat between us."

He willed his body to stay calm as she tilted her head, pushed her chin out, and considered him. He tried to focus on the scent of flowers instead of her hair, on the sound of birds instead of her breathing. Breathing was a necessity and should not be found sexy. Yet on Lucy, it was.

"I won't deny it. What do you mean by casual?" she asked, caution in those heart-stomping eyes. She moved her hands to his chest, which gave him permission to move his to her waist and pull her just a little tighter.

"I mean we enjoy each other while you're here, and when you need to go, you go."

"Just like that?"

"Just like that."

She frowned, narrowing her eyes—measuring him. He ran his hand up her back, catching it slightly on her camera strap. "We'll just enjoy each other with no strings?"

"Well, as long as no strings means that while we *enjoy* each other, no one else is enjoying you. Because then I'd have to shoot someone." She grinned, making his heart pound too hard and his face stretch with a stupid grin.

"Hmm. That would probably not bode well for your job," she considered, going up onto her tiptoes and nipping the underside of his chin. He should have shaved this morning. Would have if he'd thought Lucy would be this close to him. She didn't seem to mind.

"No. And I'll need it to keep me busy once you leave and break my heart," he whispered teasingly as he gripped the back of her tank top and closed his mouth roughly over hers before she could protest or say anything else.

She tasted like summer—like heat and fresh air all rolled into one. She stole his breath, and when her tongue met his, he wasn't sure he cared about anything other than this moment, right now. Her. He thought he heard a car alarm off in the distance, but it seemed so far from where he was, wrapped up in Lucy. Her hands found their way under his lightweight shirt that read ALPD on the right pocket. Her touch pulled him back and under at the same time, and he framed her face with his hands, trying to regain a little bit of the control he needed to survive her.

The alarm sounded louder, breaking through the buzzing that he thought was a direct result of his brain overloading with lust. When Lucy pulled leaned away and looked down at his waist, he briefly thought about seeing how secluded the woods really were.

"You're buzzing," she said huskily. He yanked her closer, kissed her hard, and felt the vibration of being this close to her run through him. "You have that effect on me."

"No," she said, laughing and pushing at his chest, "you're actually buzzing. Is it your phone?"

He looked down just as his phone sounded again on his hip. Lucy laughed harder, which did nothing to abate his desire, but it did make him grin. "Shit. Whitman," he snapped.

He held Lucy's waist as he listened to Dolores's panicked, screechy voice. At the same time, he heard sirens in the distance. Fire trucks from the closest town coming in to help.

"Son of a bitch! I'm on my way. Call everyone in and tell Mick to meet me on-site."

He pressed END and hooked the phone back on his belt loop, already moving forward. Lucy followed immediately, concern lacing her words. "What's wrong?"

"The rec center is on fire." His pace increased, and he tugged Lucy with him. She stopped, pulling her out of his grasp. "What?"

At her screech, he turned to see a look of panic in her eyes and her mouth hung open in shock.

With a gentler tone, he said, "I don't know anything. Our local fire department is there, but I need to get there as quick as I can." He held out his hand and she took it, letting him set the pace. But when she stumbled he stopped again. "Shit. Sorry. You alright?"

She nodded but her voice was strained. "Alex, go. I'll catch up. Just get there."

"I don't want to leave you here alone."

"Don't be silly. Go. I'll be right behind you, but I can't run with this equipment or in these shoes," she assured, pushing at him. He nodded grimly and took off, pissed at himself for not being where he was needed.

CHAPTER SIX

The last time Lucy had seen her sister cry had been five years ago when Kate, then sixteen, had realized that her boyfriend's claim that he "needed time" had actually meant that he "needed to make out, frequently, with other girls." Lucy had rubbed Kate's back while she hiccupped through her tears and said she'd never date anyone else again. Lucy had smiled when Kate had calmed down enough to admit she might date but would never fall in love again. And Lucy had hugged her tight when Kate had asked her how something that was once so special could hurt so much. With her twenty-three-year-old wisdom, she knew that her sister would bounce back, date again, and most certainly love again.

Standing beside Kate now, her arm wrapped around her sister's waist, she didn't know what to do. She felt like she'd had more wisdom at twenty-three than now and had no words to offer for her sister's sadness. She didn't know if a smile or a tighter hug would dry the silent tears spilling down Kate's cheeks. Lucy stood as Kate did, motionless, soundless, watching heavily geared firefighters put out the blaze that was destroying the freshly painted, worn down building. Lucy could feel the heat from where they stood behind the tape Alex's deputies had put up. Charlotte had shown up not long after Lucy and stood on Kate's other side, her arm overlapping Lucy's. The angry, orange haze fought back hard as the firemen beat it down with water from varying angles. The smell of wood and smoke thickened the air, making it impossible to breathe in deeply. Alongside the two fire trucks, one from the neighboring county of Cook, were three Angel's Lake cruisers. Lucy recognized Mick, who had been part of the police department since the dawn of time, talking to Alex.

"We're doing it for them," Kate uttered. "What do you mean, sweetie?" Char asked.

Lucy looked over at her sisters. They had several of their mother's features in common, but Lucy saw the differences between herself and the other two. More than she saw the similarities. Char had their dad's strength and would say all of the right things. Lucy remained quiet.

Kate crumpled the Kleenex she was holding. "Why would the teens do this when the whole thing is being done for them?"

"We don't know *who* did this, honey," Char said.

"It's got to be whoever has been putting graffiti all over the buildings and causing trouble around town. It doesn't make sense for this not to be the same person or people, does it?"

Even Char had no answer for that. The flames were growing weary, giving up against the steady fight of the men in yellow. The voices in the crowd were almost as loud as the roar of the fire. .

"Kate, why don't we go home? There's nothing we can do here. Not right now," Lucy suggested, her arm tightening as people inched closer to see the fading flames uselessly try to regain strength. Alex trudged toward them, a heavy jacket covering him despite the heat. His face was dirty—blackened like he'd played in the ashes, saddened like he had lost something as well. Lucy imagined they all looked similar as ash still floated around them silently.

Alex stopped directly in front of Kate and bent his knees so he could be eye to eye with her.

"Look at me," he commanded, putting his hands on her shoulders. Lucy and Char continued to hang onto their sister.

"I *will* find who did this, Kate. I promise you," he assured with such conviction that Lucy's heart felt lighter. When he said it, she believed it. She looked at Kate to see if she also felt the truth in Alex's words. More silent tears streamed, and Kate bit her lip, nodding in agreement. Alex leaned forward and kissed Kate's cheek with genuine affection. Lucy's heart squeezed with an uncomfortable tightness.

"Go home. I'll come by later with an update. You don't need to be here for any more of this," he suggested, turning his gaze on Lucy. His eyes changed slightly, his gaze softening in a way she hoped only she would notice. "Take her home. Get cleaned up and have something to eat. I'll come by, okay?"

The three sisters nodded and navigated their way through the curious onlookers. No one spoke directly to Kate, but Lucy heard the murmurs of "so sorry," "such a shame," and "poor girl."

"What a fucking mess," Sam assessed, hands on his jean-clad hips. The trucks and the crowd had gone. The sun was almost done for the day, and so was Alex. His head hurt, his body hurt, and his heart hurt. The rec center lay in blackened bits and pieces, ruined by someone with nothing better to do than tear apart his town.

"That's an understatement. Fire chief said it was deliberate. Figures they used gasoline-soaked cloths to start it up. Doesn't take long for something like this to rage out of control," Alex sighed, running his hand through his smoke-matted hair.

"So they're not only assholes but they're idiots, too?"

"Pretty much. I need to know you can fix this. I told Kate that I'd come by with an update. I want to be able to tell her that you can put it back together."

"Shit, Alex. There's no *fixing* this. It's a do-over."

"But you can do it?"

"Sure, you know, with all my spare time these days, I'll just draft up some plans and get started tomorrow," Sam snapped without feeling. He glared at Alex and walked forward to where the building looked like it had crumbled.

"Don't be a dick," Alex returned.

Sam scoffed and shook his head while Alex followed him around the decimated lot.

"You want to say that everything will be okay. You can sugar coat it for Kate, but this is going to take work. And money."

"The city must have insurance. Once the fire inspector signs off on it as arson, they should be able to move forward with a claim," Alex mulled. The sky was a fuzzy, unwelcome grey even though the fire had been put out for a while now.

"Who the hell would do this?"

"I don't know. Not for sure anyway. But I will find out. And whoever it is will wish they'd chosen a different town to screw with." Sam grinned at his friend and gave him a hard clap on the back.

"Looks like you have your work cut out for you. No more lounging in your office with a box of donuts."

Alex shook his head and treated his friend to a one finger salute, but he also smiled for the first time all afternoon.

CHAPTER SEVEN

"What are you working on, honey?" Julie asked as she padded into the kitchen, coming to stand behind Lucy where she sat at the long and wide, wood planked dining table. As a girl, she had done her homework at this table.

Looking over her shoulder, Lucy saw her mom's eyes were wrought with concern. Little creases marred the corners, and Lucy could see her biting at the inside of her cheek—something Lucy did, too, when her thoughts weren't settled. Julie's hair framed her face in loose curls that made her look younger. She smelled like mint and Lucy breathed her in as she rested her head against her for a brief moment. Her mom stroked her hair gently and something twisted inside of her stomach.

"I'm doing up some brochures. I thought that I could offer photography as a trade for townspeople pitching in with the center," Lucy said. She straightened and scrolled through the screen, showing Julie the brightly colored document she had been working on. "How's Kate?"

"She's alright. She's tough like all my girls. She's lying down. I was going to make some soup. You know that there's actually a link between soup and feeling better, don't you?" Julie asked as she peeked a little closer at the brochure.

"Uh—sure."

"So you'll take photos in exchange for what? Money?"

Julie moved to the cupboard, her flowing sweater waving behind her, and rooted around for some soul-healing soup. Lucy stretched her arms above her head, yawning.

"Money, labor, supplies. Whatever they have to give. Anything."

Lucy felt cooped up even though she had spent a good portion of the day outside. Even after showering, she could still smell the fire and taste the ashes on her lips. She pushed back from the table to grab a drink. As her mom opened a couple cans of soup, she eyed Lucy with a bit of doubt.

"Why would someone give supplies and labor for a few photos?"

Lucy's jaw tightened and she fought back the irritation. Her family didn't truly understand the depth of her talent. She didn't need them to build up her ego, but it would be nice if they recognized that not every photographer's work was featured in *National Geographic*, *Cosmo*, and *Rolling Stone*—all of which were on her résumé.

When Char had become a dentist, they'd rented a hall and held a celebration. They were planning something similar for Kate when she graduated with her degree in social work. When Lucy had graduated, they wondered why she would go to school to study something that was clearly a hobby. She had taken off on her first trek to Europe before any celebrations could be mentioned or overlooked. They had never purposely made her feel *less*, but standing beside them did that all on its own. They were proud of her; she knew that, most of the time. Still, it would be nice if they understood the measure of her success. Before she'd gotten fired, of course.

"People love to be photographed, mom. High-quality photography isn't cheap. People are doing photo shoots of everything these days—not just weddings. And I'm not just an average photographer. I'm offering something they'll want in return for something that the rec center needs. You'll see," Lucy said. Her tone was clipped, but she didn't try to soften it. Her mom mumbled a "Hmm," as she continued to stir.

Lucy busied herself by grabbing drinks and bowls, setting them down roughly on the counter. From the window over the sink, she saw Alex trudging up his porch steps, his grimy jacket slung over his shoulder. Her heart ached for him. It wasn't hard to see how much pride he took in taking care of this town and the people in it

"I think it's nice you want to do something to help Kate, honey. I think it matters to her that you're home. Probably a lot now. You want some of this soup?" Julie asked, dishing up the miniature, oddly formed vegetables in red broth. Lucy shook her head, still staring at Alex's house, even though he'd gone inside.

"Nah. I'm going to go check on Alex."

"He's such a good man. I have no doubt he'll find who did this," Julie replied, kissing Lucy's cheek before picking up a bowl of soup to take to Kate. She didn't doubt it either, but until he did, he would blame himself for this and whatever else might happen.

The shower had washed away the grime, but not the heaviness that sat in the pit of his stomach. He pulled on a pair of athletic shorts and towel dried his hair a bit more before tossing the towel into the laundry. Wandering into the kitchen with the intention of getting a beer, he almost tripped over Furball. Swallowing a curse, he leaned down to pet the cat, which had stopped him in his path for that very reason.

"I know, bud. You're being neglected."

Furball meowed in agreement and followed Alex to the kitchen. Alex dumped some food in a bowl and after setting the dish down, he ran his hand along the cat's back. He grabbed a beer for himself; he'd think about food later. Turning on the T.V., he leaned back on his couch right when the doorbell rang.

Closing his eyes, he silently cursed and stood to see who wanted what now. When he opened the door, he was pleasantly surprised to see the only person he would be willing to invite in at this particular moment.

"Hey there, Sheriff," Lucy smiled up at him, a pizza in one hand and a laptop case in the other. He smiled back when she eyed his bare chest a moment too long before bringing her gaze back up to his.

"Hey yourself. If you're sharing that pizza, come on in."

He moved aside and shut the door after her. She toed off her baby blue Converse shoes and walked through the house into the living room as though she came over all the time. Putting the laptop bag down, she looked over at him.

"You want plates for this?"

"Nah. I'll grab some napkins, though. You want a beer?"

"Sure."

He grabbed the napkins and a beer for her. Then, because it seemed polite, yanked on a T-shirt before joining her. She'd already started on her first slice, making him chuckle.

"Hungry?"

She looked away from the T.V. and nodded unapologetically.

"Yup. They were having soup at my house. Apparently, it heals. I saw you come home and figured you'd probably be hungry, too." He sat down beside her and grabbed a slice. She put hers down to open her beer.

"You figured right. Did you go get it or did they deliver?"

"Delivered. Had to wait on the porch so my dad didn't try to steal any. He's not a big fan of vegetable soup," she laughed in her musical way and the sound drained some of the tension he'd been carrying. Beer, pizza, and Lucy. Not a bad end to a shitty day. Also not something he should get used to.

"I don't mind soup. On cold nights. When pizza isn't an option."

She tucked her legs beneath herself and took a long swallow of her beer. He liked the slender column of her neck and enjoyed the swell of her breasts when she arched back—but he should probably try to keep his thoughts, and eyes, from straying there.

"Pizza is always an option. Unless you're in the backwoods of some tiny town in the middle of nowhere," she amended, setting her beer down. She turned so her body was facing his, making their knees touch.

"I don't need to be anywhere pizza isn't an option," he replied.

She looked sweet and soft in a pale pink hoodie and black stretch pants. Her socks were polka dotted and cheerful. "How are you?"

"I'm okay. Pissed. Tired. Pissed. Not quite as hungry as I was five minutes ago. Come to think of it, not quite as pissed or tired as I was five minutes ago, either, so thank you."

She pursed her lips, and he had the urge to kiss her. He thought better of it since he was still finishing up his pizza.

"You're welcome. I didn't know if you'd want company," she said, almost shyly, which was something he'd never thought of her as being. He grabbed a napkin, wiped his mouth, and took a drink of his beer before answering.

"What if I hadn't?"

"Oh, I would have said I was just bringing you pizza and dropped it off."

"Then you would have gone home and had soup?"

"Yup. And I would have been mad thinking about you over here eating my pizza," she said with a smile. She crumpled up her napkin and tossed it onto the coffee table.

"I like this better," he said, reaching out and twisting a soft strand of her hair around his finger. "How's Kate?"

He noticed that she shifted a bit closer before she answered, which was more than fine with him. He put his arm on the back of the couch behind her head.

"She's sad. I hate seeing her cry. She hardly ever cries. But, she's resilient. She's got some ideas for how to rebuild. She's going to talk to city hall tomorrow to see who needs to fill out the paperwork for the insurance."

He couldn't help touching her and played with her hair while she spoke.

"Well that crosses one thing off of my to-do list, so tell her to let me know what she finds out. I talked to Sam. We went to school with him. You remember?"

"I don't really remember him from going to school, no. I mean, I knew who he was, but it's not like we were friends," she recalled.

He poked her teasingly in the shoulder. "He wasn't cool enough for you?"

She pursed her lips in an adorable way before frowning at him. "What's that supposed to mean? As if."

Lucy had always been in her own little world, but maybe she truly didn't realized how appealing she was, back then or now. This only made him want her more. He let it go, without answering her and tugged a strand of her hair playfully. She spent her life capturing beauty and yet she didn't seem to see it inside of herself.

"Anyway, Sam's an architect and does construction. He says it's going to be expensive to rebuild, so I sure as hell hope the insurance gets it started. What Kate is trying to pull off is going to matter to the community."

Because he didn't think he could resist kissing her—which would make him want to touch her, which would make him want to do more than touch her—he stood and picked up the pizza box. She rose with him, grabbing their beer bottles and following him to the kitchen.

"You know your voice goes all soft and sweet when you talk about my sister?"

She rinsed the empties before lining them up on the counter. Alex blinked, unsure he'd heard her correctly. Scrunching his face, he chose his words carefully. "I like Kate. She's sweet."

She turned her head, glancing at him for a second. "And gorgeous."

Alex frowned, running a hand through his hair. Kate was a kid. "And, what? Twenty?"

Lucy turned to face him just as he closed the refrigerator door. Alex moved closer, putting his hands on the countertop, gripping it on either side to stop himself from touching her. His eyes were drawn to the pale freckles on the bridge of her nose. He wanted to kiss each one.

She stared at his chest. "You're my age. Not that much older than Kate."

Shaking his head, his heart thudded heavy and slow in his chest. "You know I'm not into your sister, right?" he asked. He smiled, warmed by what sounded to him an awful lot like jealousy. He leaned in and kissed the side of her neck softly, then placed another kiss below her ear. She kept her hands at her sides.

She had to clench her fists to keep from touching him. He might be older than Kate, but he was probably a lot better suited to her. Driven, settled, solid ... very solid. She felt her nails dig into her palms.

"I was just mentioning how you sound when you talk about her," she replied in what she hoped was a flippant voice. His nose nuzzled against her as he replied, "Hmm."

The sound he made vibrated against her neck at the same time he pressed his lips there, causing a shiver to skirt up her spine and settle deep in her belly. The smell of his soap was ruining her ability to think clearly. "Wanna know how I feel around you?" His voice was low and gruff.

She would have answered him, but her tongue stopped working the moment his gently touched her ear. She put one hand on his chest and another on his waist. Just for balance.

Alex pressed against her with his hips. "Not soft. And not sweet."

"I know what the opposite of soft is, but isn't the opposite of sweet sour?"

He laughed and pulled back to look at her. He shook his head, but his eyes were bright with amusement and unrestrained affection. "You're damn hard to seduce," he chuckled. "Maybe you should stop talking."

She laughed and let herself run her hand over his chest, which was, indeed, very solid. She knew that he likely deserved someone better than her, but he was a grown man, pressed up against her, capable of making his own choices. From the hungry look in his eyes, she didn't think she was forcing him to be with her, and he was well aware that she didn't stick around.

"I'm trying to give you an out. A chance to come to your senses," she said, her voice breathy, her eyes not lifting to his.

"Lucy," he said in a low, firm voice that made her stomach feel like it was being tickled from the inside. He put his fingers to her chin and lifted her gaze as his thumb stroked her cheek.

He really had nice eyes. Direct. Warm. Sexy.

"I was twelve years old the first time I thought of kissing you. Do you really think, now that you've given me permission, I want an out?"

He answered his own question by leaning down, inundating every one of her senses, and pressed his mouth to hers. He kissed her like he'd been waiting just as long as he claimed. His hands moved immediately to her back, and she gave up trying to do the right thing. She might not stay, but she was here

now. There was nowhere else she would rather be.

He was twenty-eight years old and had been with enough women to know what he was doing. He knew how to seduce, romance, tease, and flirt. But any finesse he might have prided himself on seemed to have vanished when Lucy's tongue touched his, when her hands gripped the fabric of his T-shirt, making him wish he hadn't put it on. He went from pulling her near to boosting her onto his counter so he could step between her legs and wedge himself against her. She didn't seem to mind and looped her arms around his neck, devouring him with just as much energy as he felt. He was almost dizzy with need, but when she started to yank at the hem of his shirt, he was able to pull back enough to realize that if he only got one chance with Lucy Aarons, he was going to make it count.

"Slow down, Luce."

"Why?"

"So I don't miss anything," he smiled, pulling her closer and lifting her up. She wrapped her legs around his waist, and he walked to his bedroom. She teased his neck with her lips and her tongue, making his fingers flex into the soft fabric of her pants and the gentle curve of her ass.

"Alex," she whispered, her eyes clouded by desire and doubt. It was clear she wanted this, but she was holding back, worrying about hurting him, as far as he could tell. Truthfully, she could –probably would. But it would be worth it.

"I promise I won't ask you to put a ring on my finger after," he teased. She gave him a glare that only made him laugh. "It's not funny. You're the last person I would hurt on purpose," she said seriously.

"My eyes are wide open, Lucy. I'm a big boy. I can make my own decisions."

He pushed his bedroom door open with his foot and brought her to his bed. He didn't want to put her down, so he continued to hold her until the doubt in her eyes cleared and all he could see was the desire.

"Well, then what are you waiting for?" she asked, leaning back and pulling him off balance so they fell together onto his bed. His heart tumbled along with their bodies as he covered her, but he'd keep that to himself.

CHAPTER EIGHT

She couldn't stop grinning, which was ridiculous. It was like she had never been to bed with a man before. Granted, she hadn't been to bed with many, but enough to know feeling giddy afterward wasn't the usual. Or maybe she had just never been with a man who had made her *want* to smile so much after.

During. Before.

"Talk about the cat that caught the canary. What are you smirking about?" he asked on a laugh, running his hand up and down her side, sending ripples of renewed longing through her.

"Funny, sexy, and exceptional in bed. Why didn't I notice you sooner?" *Probably because in high school her focus had been on travelling and stretching her wings.*

His fingers continued to trail up and down. "To be fair, you've been gone, and I'm pretty positive I've improved in most areas since we went to school together."

"Well, then I guess it was worth the wait," she said

more seriously, leaning into a slow, sweet kiss. His hand gripped her hip possessively and before she could stop herself, she snuggled into him, letting herself relax against him. He ran his hand up her side before moving it to her hair and stroking it gently. The combination of sensation, happiness, and his utter sweetness made her feel like the scattered pieces inside of herself had shifted, aligned. The realization stole her breath, literally.

"You okay?" he asked, his eyes darker from this distance, more compelling. "Yeah. Of course. I, uh ... I wanted to show you something."

"Sweetheart, you're going to have to give me a bit more time before you show me anything else."

She rolled her eyes but laughed, even as her stomach fluttered from his term of endearment. Lucy scooted out of the bed as gracefully as she could, which was not really graceful at all. He went up onto one elbow and watched as she looked for his shirt, which she had pulled off of him and tossed ... somewhere. She found it at the end of the bed and hastily popped it over her head.

"What are you doing?" he asked, a lazy smile on his face as he lay back down onto the pillow, hands tucked behind his head. Unable to resist, she pressed a quick kiss to his lips. "I'll be right back."

"You sure? You have a tendency to run," he teased.

Lucy gave a half-hearted laugh but what he said stuck in her head when she headed out to the living room to grab her laptop. *It's not a tendency, it's a choice. A choice that has sound, professional reasons.* She was always getting teased about having one foot out the door, so why did Alex saying it bother her more than it did when others said the same? She brought her case back to the bedroom, sat beside him, and then pulled the laptop out while he sat up against the tall headboard. She kept her eyes on the screen while she waited for it to boot up.

His voice was soft. "Lucy."

She turned to look at him and saw that his eyes were sad. He reached out his hand and covered hers before saying, "I'm sorry. I was teasing but it was in poor taste."

She couldn't hide her surprise. She arched her brows and continued to look at him. "What? I didn't say—"

"Lucy. Do you think I can't read your face? That I didn't notice the way your smile fell and the quickest flash of hurt came into your eyes?"

"Actually, I didn't think you'd notice. I thought I hid it better. Maybe you just look too closely," she mulled on that thought as she turned back to the screen. He distracted her again by pulling her against his side. The laptop slid from her legs to the bed.

"Why would you hide it at all?"

"Because it's silly. It's not like it isn't true. I *do* have a tendency to run—or, at the very least, to not stick around."

"It's not silly if it bothers you to have people say things, even if it's teasing."

"It's not a big deal. Look, I want to show you this." She didn't like the flutter erupting in her chest at the serious expression on his face. "Lucy."

"*What?*"

Instead of being put off, he smiled at her show of impatience and kissed her quickly, lightly. "I plan to keep looking closely, so don't hide from me, okay?"

Lucy shrugged. "Sure."

"I mean it. No hiding. Not from each other."

She rolled her eyes at him but saw that he wasn't going to put it aside, so she reluctantly agreed. "Fine. Want me to cross my heart?"

"How about another kiss?" he asked softly, capturing her lips and distracting her, making her fall into it, into him. When he pulled away, she kept her eyes closed for an extra moment.

Opening them, she pulled the laptop onto her knees again and smacked his blanket-covered leg. "Pay attention."

She pulled up the mock advertisement that she planned to have printed on large paper. She had photos of the rec center in its glory days along with photos of the town working on it last week. She had taken a couple of shots during the fire: kids, parents, community members watching the devastation. In the middle, she had put a photo of the rec center as it had been next to a photo of the wreckage. Under these two photos, the large bold font read: *The future relies on us rebuilding the past.* Under that, in smaller font, it read: *What can you do to help?* She had started an Angel's Lake Rec Center Fundraising Facebook page and put the link on the poster. She planned to post current news and hopefully have people sign up to help. She was about to flip to her next file to show him the flyers for her photo exchange idea when he spoke.

"You made this?"

"Yeah. It's just a bit of graphic design. I dropped it off at a printer today so we can hand them out. I'll do basic photos—kids, families, couples, that sort of thing, in exchange for a monetary donation and volunteer time for the center. They'll have the option to add on to their package for a fee, which covers my costs."

"You're going to take photos in exchange for their help?" he asked, making her stomach twist. *Not him, too.* He looked at her and his smile was so wide she wondered if it hurt his cheeks.

"You take photos for *National Geographic* and *In Style*. You're going to spend your time and use your incredible talent to take kid pictures and family shots?"

Her pulse beat double time. He knew where her photos were featured. "That was my plan. It's not—"

"It's generous and thoughtful and pretty damn clever. You're hardly the photo booth at the mall. People are going to be lining up to get photos done by you." It settled her erratic pulse when she realized he liked the plan. And he'd seen her pictures; admired them. She had a flash of him as a boy, riding up on his bike to buy lemonade from Kate. Alex had overpaid on purpose and made Kate's day. Lucy might not have seen it then, but if she thought about it, he'd always kind of been there; a silent supporter.

Warmth pooled in her belly at the memory and from the way his hands never stopped touching her. But she didn't want to get distracted; yet. "I'm glad you said that. I'd like to take some of you. And some other men ."

His easy smile turned to a grimace and his eyes narrowed. "Didn't we have this conversation?"

"What conversation?"

"That I wasn't too worried about the timeline on whatever this is between us, but for however long it's going on, it's exclusive." Because she liked the thought of him only wanting her a little too much, she tried to make light of it. "Aww. Are you jealous?" She laughed when his frown deepened but stopped when he pushed back the covers, grabbed his boxers, and yanked them up. "Alex. It's for charity. I have no intention of seeing anyone else while I'm with you."

He gave her a smug, self-satisfied grin that she shook her head. "Happy now?" He leaned over her, his nose touching hers. "I am."

"And a tad insecure," she said quietly. She wished she didn't feel the same, but it was good to know she wasn't alone. It was likely every eligible woman in town was interested in their handsome sheriff.

He ran a finger along her cheek, like she was special. "I just don't like surprises. Or sharing."

"Me neither." Though she'd never thought much about it before him, the thought of another woman cozying up to him turned her stomach. Pushing that thought away, Lucy leaned forward and kissed his lips, quick and light. She did it again when it deepened his smile.

"Sit back down so you can see this. Tell me what you think and then you can show me how much you only want me. Again." She winked at him. A laugh rumbled out of his chest. "Damn right."

He sat beside her again, a smile on his face and his arm draped around her as he looked at the screen.

"So, I'm thinking a fundraising charity event. A dinner, an auction, selling some calendars of the town's best-looking men—created from favors I'm hoping to cash in—and maybe some really awesome door prizes," she explained in one long breath.

"A calendar? Of who?"

"You. Sam. Maybe Bruce. My brother in law, Luke. My dad said he'd do it. Nothing provocative, so you won't have to hide it from your dad," she said, poking him in the ribs when he looked too serious.

"Why would anyone buy a calendar with us in it? I mean, yes, I'm good looking," he said and laughed at her eye roll before continuing, "but honestly, why would they pay for it?"

"They'll pay for it because every calendar they buy gets their name entered in a drawing to win one of the bigger prizes. I told you I have some connections that I'm working on, trying to see if they can donate some big ticket items. A trip to Mexico, for one. A stay in the Four Seasons in New York for another."

"You know someone who could offer a trip to Mexico?"

"Sure. A friend of mine is a travel agent. He books all of my trips. He said he'd arrange it."

"A *friend*?" he waggled his eyebrows comically.

"For goodness sakes, Alex. Stay focused. Yes, a friend. I have a few of them."

"Lucy, these ideas are incredible. I worried about the insurance money being enough, but this is going to make it work either way. I'm not crazy about being in a calendar, but I'll do it, and most of the guys I know will, too. Tim, he's the fire chief, will be all over it. I can't believe you've put all of this together already."

She could feel herself beaming at him. She didn't need his praise, or anyone else's, but it washed over her nicely. His words warmed the cold spot that took up residence in her stomach when she was around her family. The spot that reminded her she didn't quite fit in; that she wasn't *actually* one of them.

"What are you doing?" she asked when he lifted the laptop, rose from the bed, and put it on the low, walnut-stained dresser. He looked over his shoulder at her and flashed the grin that warmed a lot more than her stomach.

"Showing you how much I like your ideas. And you," he laughed, throwing himself back onto the bed and then on top of her. She wasn't sure how he could make her laugh and need at the same time, but as his mouth closed over hers, she felt a nagging worry that she could get used to it.

Alex stood near the stage of the community hall and watched as the Aarons sisters charmed and worked the room. Together, they were a triple threat of looks, character, and ambition. Though, he didn't think any of them would own up to it, which made them that much more special.

The town hall was full. Lucy had set up a small podium and mic on the stage, which was really just an elevated platform, one step up from the actual floor. Like the rec center had been, the hall was rundown and worn. It had seen countless weddings, sweet sixteen parties, stags and stagettes. The scuffed floor had been danced on, puked on, and cried on. It held as many memories as the high school gym for most of the people raised in Angel's Lake.

"Quite the turnout," Mark said as he strolled over to stand beside Alex. Lucy had been in his bed every night that week, but she went home to her own bed before midnight, like she had a curfew. He wasn't sure what she'd told her parents, but there was something about standing next to the father of the woman he was sleeping with that made his stomach cramp. *There's no sign on my head that says, 'I slept with Lucy'.*

"Did you?"

Alex did a double take, his mouth open. "What?" he finally stammered. "Did you help her with this? You alright, son?"

"Yes sir. I—uh," he garbled. "No. This is all Lucy. And Kate, too, I think. Maybe Char?"

"My three girls. They can do anything. Have to say, I'm surprised to see Lucy step up like this, though. She's not one for grand gestures that draw in crowds. Bit of a loner. Always has been," Mark considered. His tone was affectionate, as though he didn't begrudge his middle daughter but simply accepted what he saw as her.

"Maybe you underestimate her."

Mark turned, hands in his pockets, and kept his gaze level with Alex's. The stomach cramp crept back in, pushing at his ribs.

"Maybe I do. Doesn't seem like she's surprised you. Mind you, I've looked at a woman the way you're looking at my Lucy. You're seeing all the good. Which there's plenty of. But there's flaws, like with all of us, so you keep looking at her like that, you're liable to get hurt or be in it for the long haul."

"Mark—"

"No, let me say my piece. Don't often get to. Lucy's always halfway across the globe, Kate's too busy to date, and Char ... Well, I liked Luke right from day

one. Just like I like you. And I'll keep on liking you as long as you don't hurt my girl. We tease her about being fickle and on the run, but she's got a heart in her that I sometimes suspect is bigger than any of ours. So just be careful with it. Even if you figure out it might not be for the long haul."

Lucy's voice came through the tinny PA system, drawing Mark's attention. Alex stood looking at him for a moment longer. It was the most Lucy's father had said to him in one conversation. Had he just warned Alex to be gentle with her while telling him she didn't stay put?

"Thank you for coming, everyone." Lucy spoke clearly. She didn't seem daunted by the audience, the rapt attention, or being up on the stage. Char and Kate flanked her. Lucy was slightly taller than both of them even though she wore flats instead of heels like the other two. Easels were set up behind the three of them, and a projector was shining on the long, white screen at the back of the stage. Her voice took away some of the discomfort her father had caused, and he watched as she shared her ideas for rebuilding the rec center.

Lucy looked out at the sea of faces and couldn't really tell who she was reaching with her words.

"When you leave here tonight, you'll receive a card

with the link to the project's Facebook page. This will be our way of communicating, but you can also contact Kate or myself if you have any questions. The first fifty people who sign up to offer labor, supplies, money, or time will be entered to win a sixty-inch flat screen TV," she shared, looking back at the screen to make sure the image of the LG LCD came up properly. She heard a few intakes of breath and some murmuring in the crowd. If her words didn't pull them in, the TV was a good start.

"Can you win that if you offer to model for the calendar?" Nick Kramer called out from the back, earning several laughs from the crowd and a swat on the arm from his wife.

Lucy chuckled and scanned the room. Her eyes locked on Alex's, and she felt the jolt in her stomach and her chest when he smiled and winked at her. He stood next to her father, which she wondered if she should worry about, but they were both smiling, glasses of punch in their hands.

"Absolutely, Mr. Kramer," Lucy laughed. "Kate's going to tell you how you'll be giving back to the community by helping." She moved aside, squeezed her sister's trembling hand, and stepped beside Char.

"Look at you. You've got quite a way with people," Char whispered. "Ha. Maybe. Or maybe it's just an easy room."

Kate began to tell the crowd how many different programs would be offered, not only for teens, but also for children, families, and seniors. "Hey," Lucy whispered, leaning toward Char as Kate continued, "What's with mom? I couldn't get her to come tonight."

She felt Char stiffen beside her before she looked over. "Mom doesn't leave the house much. She doesn't like to go out." "What's not much?" Lucy asked, noticing that a few hands went up to ask questions about who would run the programs offered.

"We hope that different members of the community will participate in teaching and taking the classes, but I've also established a rapport with the YMCA in Little Falls. Many of their staff are working toward degrees in education and need volunteer hours," Kate explained. Char listened to their youngest sister with so much pride, Lucy's heart missed a step. Char looked back at Lucy, her expression shifting, darkening.

"I don't know. Not much. She's fine. She just...started leaving the house less and less. Leave it alone. You won't be here long enough for it to bug you," Char finally whispered. Lucy stepped back as though Char had slapped her, and tears immediately stung her eyes. Char's face softened and she started to grab Lucy's arm.

"I'm sorry. Lucy," she whispered, but Lucy shook her head and walked off the side of the stage to make sure that the flyers and information cards she had printed were by the door where people could easily grab them as they left. She passed the table where Bean's Bakery had graciously laid out donated snacks for the evening and made a mental note to enter them in the draw for the television. Alex came up behind her as she straightened the perfect stack of flyers.

"You okay?" he said quietly, his body crowding in behind her, his breath brushing over her, smoothing out her hurt even though he hadn't caused it. She blinked quickly several times then turned to him with a smile in place.

"Of course. It's a good turnout. I think people will enjoy pitching in once we get started," she answered, keeping her voice low while Kate finished answering questions.

"Hmm," Alex murmured, pushing a strand of Lucy's hair behind her ear. His eyes watched her. She had spent every evening this week with him and was surprised by how much she enjoyed and looked forward to being with him.

"I should —"

He frowned. "Not try to hide things when you're upset. Not from me. What did Char say?"

Lucy winced. Of course he had noticed. The man saw everything—if she tried to sneak out of his bed, avoid a conversation, pretend something didn't bother her when it did ... It was like he had a radar.

"She just said my mom doesn't leave the house much, and I wondered why. Not a big deal. It's nothing."

He leaned in and kissed her, soft and gentle, like he didn't mind anyone looking. Still, she didn't want the attention on them and whatever they were. The town was here tonight to support Kate. She pulled back and smiled at him.

"I have to go check in with my deputies, finish up some paperwork," he said, moving with her even as she stepped back. "Okay. Thanks for coming. The town loves you so much that if you support the rec center, they will."

"The town is here because they care about your family, Luce. About you."

She started to make a caustic remark but noticed that people were starting to mingle and Kate was finished on stage. "Do you want me to come by later?" she asked.

His smile was wide and warm. And a little bit cocky. All of which, apparently, appealed to her. "Yes. I really and truly do."

She laughed and gave him a quick kiss. "Then I'll see you later."

CHAPTER NINE

Lucy hadn't seen her brother-in-law since she had returned home almost two weeks ago. Between organizing the plans for redoing the rec center and jumping into what was suspiciously resembling a relationship, time had suddenly flown by. And she'd really been enjoying every moment. She'd only seen Mia and Carmen a few times at her parents'. It wasn't enough, but for the first time in forever, she didn't feel like she had to cram everything in because she was on her way to somewhere else.

She knocked on the white lacquered door. They had moved since Carmen was born, and she felt a small trickle of shame that she hadn't even been inside of this home. It was gorgeous—a white, two-story cross between country and colonial with a wide front porch and baby blue shutters. The cement walkway that led to the four-step porch was lined with pretty flowers. Bright blues and yellows mixed perfectly, reminding her that, of the three of them,

Char had gotten the green thumb. Lucy considered pulling her camera out, snapping a couple shots of those vibrant petals, just as the door finally opened. Luke Hanson stood there in his jeans and T-shirt, his feet bare, with a slight snarl on his handsome face.

"Jesus. I thought you were a salesman," he said, breaking into a happy smile.

"I'm not Jesus, either, so I hope you're not disappointed," Lucy returned, stepping into him. He wrapped his arms around her and squeezed her tight, lifted her off of her feet, and spun her in a half circle. She laughed in delight as he set her down and shut the door.

"You show up about as often," he teased, kissed her cheek, and grabbed her camera bag from her.

Slipping off her shoes by the door, she followed him down a short hallway that led to a kitchen and sitting area. Char was standing at the counter, gripping it with both hands, as Carmen rocked back and forth on her heels, muttering under her breath.

"Hey," she said curtly, then turned to look at Luke, "you didn't pick up peanut butter."

He frowned, glanced at Carmen and back at Lucy, his cheeks turning a pale shade of pink. Looking closer, Lucy noted that his dark hair was peppered with some grey around the ears and needed a trim. Char looked half dressed—unless she actually planned on pairing her pretty button-up shirt with the pajama pants she was sporting.

"I only like peanut butter sandwiches," Carmen muttered a little louder.

"Aunt Lucy is here, Carmen. Aren't you glad to see

her?" Luke asked, going over to Carmen and putting his hand on her arm. "I want a peanut butter sandwich," Carmen replied, not looking at her dad.

Lucy put her bag on the counter, noting that Mia was sleeping in a bassinet in the sitting area. Curbing the impulse to pick her up, bury her nose in the crook of her tiny little neck, and inhale her, she walked to Carmen. Luke's lips firmed. He stood and walked to Char.

"Sorry, babe. I'll go get some," he said in a low voice. Lucy tried to focus on the tenderness she heard in his tone and not the stifling amount of tension that had permeated the room.

"I brought you something," Lucy told Carmen in a quiet voice. She stopped rocking and looked at Lucy. "Peanut butter?"

"No. But it sounds like daddy's got that covered."

Carmen stood staring, but not really *looking* at her, while Luke kissed Char's cheek and said he'd be back in a few minutes.

"Do you mind if I go finish getting dressed, Luce?" Char asked. Lucy couldn't ignore the sound of fatigue lacing her sister's normally upbeat, solid voice. "Of course not. Go."

She waited until Char left then went back to her camera bag and picked it up, moved to the sitting area, took another peek at Mia, and sat in the large recliner closest to the bassinet. She opened her bag and pulled out the photos she had brought for Carmen. Mia made cooi ng noises in her sleep and Lucy's fingers itched to pick her up. Carmen came to stand beside the chair.

"What did you bring?" she asked, looking at Lucy with curiosity.

"I brought you some of the shark pictures I took when I was in Australia."

"People think Australia and New Zealand are the same, but they're not."

"No. They're not."

"Did you go to New Zealand?"

"No. I was sent to take pictures of the Grey Nurse Shark. When I get sent on an assignment, I usually go where they send me," Lucy explained, scooting over when Carmen leaned against the chair, looking at the photo album.

"Sharks are endangered," Carmen said, running a small finger across one of the photos.

"Many of them, yes. Why do you like sharks so much?" Lucy asked, handing the book to Carmen. She smiled when Carmen wedged herself into a sitting position beside her on the chair. Mia stirred, made a few snuggling noises, and stretched her wee fists.

"They're strong. And powerful. No one wants to be near them because they're scary, but they're also beautiful if you just look," Carmen said after a moment of thought and turned another page. Mia began to whimper in her cradle, and Lucy looked down at Carmen and then ran a hand gently along her springy, dark curls that smelled like baby shampoo. Carmen pulled back, away from Lucy's touch.

"You need to pick her up. Make sure you hold her head," Carmen instructed, without looking up. Lucy smiled and bit back a laugh at the serious instruction. Standing, she leaned over the cradle and picked up Mia, snuggling into her neck and breathing her in, just as she'd been dying to do. Mia's little fists pushed against her, and she moved her head around like a little chicken pecking at Lucy's neck. Lucy laughed, making Carmen look up.

"She's hungry. You can't feed her," Carmen said, turning another page.

"You look good with a baby snuggled into you like that," Char said, walking in, her hair damp and her clothing fresh. "Did you shower?"

"I most certainly did, and it was amazing. Seven and a half uninterrupted minutes of heaven," Char answered, moving to the fridge. She pulled out some juice, held it up for Lucy in offering, and then poured them both a glass.

"I think that's half a minute longer in heaven than you're allowed," Lucy joked, happy to see Char smile. Lucy wandered over with her pecking niece. The kitchen was separated from the sitting area by an L-shaped counter. A small, round table sat in the center. Sitting, Char motioned for her to do the same.

"I think Carmen's right. She's hungry," Lucy said, smiling down at Mia as she sat.

"She's good for another couple of minutes. I'm going to switch to formula," Char told her. Lucy wasn't sure if she was supposed to have an opinion about that, so she just nodded her head.

"Everything okay with you and Luke?" Lucy asked tentatively. She had always been able to talk to Charlotte about everything. But right now, she felt like her sister had an invisible, and somewhat impenetrable, shield cloaking her.

"Things are fine. We're good. Tired. New parents with a five-year-old tired, but we're good. Speaking of good—how's our town protector? Dad says you've

been spending copious amounts of time with him."

Lucy bounced Mia in her arms while Char held her gaze. She wondered, for a moment, why her dad had been talking to Char about her at all. *Stop over- analyzing*. Still, she felt a twinge of resentment and misplaced jealousy. Why hadn't her dad talked to *her* about Alex?

"You going to answer me?" Char asked, amusement lacing her tone. She twisted her wedding ring as she spoke, and Lucy's eye was drawn to the delicate platinum bands, one with a diamond in the center.

"Things are fine," Lucy replied, throwing her sister's words back at her with a cheeky grin. "We're just hanging out."

"Alex isn't really the hang-out type. In fact, I can't think of him hanging out with any one woman on a regular basis."

That information sent a thrill through her but she tried to keep her voice playful. "Well, I am more alluring than most women." She wasn't sure what to do with the pleasure it gave her to know Alex might be falling as hard as she was. Or the sickness in her stomach when she thought about leaving before she had time to find out.

Mia gave a short cry then returned to rooting around Lucy's neck, which tickled. The moment was enough to remind her she didn't have to worry about something that wasn't happening. Right now, she was here with no plans of going anywhere and Alex wanted only her. She'd focus on that.

"Of course. The one that can't be tamed is always alluring," Char said. Her tone was teasing, but the words still cut Lucy's heart. There was no humor in her voice when she asked. "Tamed? Cause I'm a wild horse? Seriously?"

Char held up a hand. "Hey. I was just joking. And yeah, you kind of are the wild card of the family. And that's not a bad thing," Charlotte said. Lucy bit her lip. If she and Kate only *knew* how much of a wild card she really was. Still, the hurt in her chest was soothed by Char's genuine tone. She felt the barrier shift, like there was a chance for them to really connect. *Finally.* Lucy heard the door and smiled when Luke walked back in with a large jar of peanut butter.

"This should last us for a while. What do you think, Carmen?" he asked, tossing his keys onto the counter. Carmen looked up and smiled brightly at her dad, making Lucy wish she had her camera out and ready.

"Can we have peanut butter sandwiches now?"

"Sure. Come help me make one," Luke answered.

Lucy smiled at the way Carmen clutched the photo album to her chest as she walked into the kitchen with them. Luke was a good dad. Alex would be a good dad like Luke. Before she completed the thought in her own head, her pulse tripled. She'd been home two weeks and Alex was one of the longest relationships of her adult life. What the hell was she doing thinking of him as a dad? Or herself as a mom. But something in the way Luke was with

Carmen pulled at Lucy's heartstrings and made her wonder. Wondering was as dangerous as wandering. Both led to uncertain paths.

"Aunt Lucy took all of these photos," Carmen told her mom without releasing the album.

"She's a very good photographer," Char responded. Lucy glanced at her with an appreciative smile, warmth multiplying inside of her chest.

"Speaking of which, I was hoping to do some family shots of you four, now that there's a new addition. I also want to talk to you, Luke, about posing for the calendar idea I had," Lucy told them. Standing, she moved toward Char and then put Mia in her arms. Char stood and moved into the living room, making way for Carmen to sit down while Luke continued making her a sandwich at the counter.

"Is your calendar featuring geeky accountants?" he joked, a wide grin in place. In jeans and a T-shirt, he didn't look like any other accountants she knew.

She gestured to him. "Right, because you fall into the geeky category. Hey, how come you're not at work?" she asked, taking a sip of juice and watching Carmen look through all of the photos again.

"You didn't tell her, Char?" He glanced at his wife, who was snuggled into the corner of the couch, discreetly nursing Mia. Looking over at Lucy, he placed a sandwich in front of Carmen. "What do you say, Carmen?"

Carmen continued to turn the pages. Luke placed his large hand over hers, but she pulled away and tried to turn the pages again. "Carmen." His voice was sharp but low. Carmen looked up at him. Her brows pinched together, and her small mouth puckered in a frown. "This is mine."

"And you can look at it when you finish your sandwich. What do you say?"

"Thank you."

"You're welcome."

Luke's face became less strained when Carmen uttered the words grumpily and began to eat her sandwich. Lucy didn't know what to make of the exchange or the family dynamics. She was hardly an expert—on anything, really—but she had spent the last ten years of her life surrounded by people of all walks of life, all ages and abilities. No one spoke of Carmen's behavior as anything out of the ordinary, and her sister and Luke—and the rest of her family—were wonderful with her, but Lucy couldn't help wondering what good it would do any of them to pretend everything was status quo.

"Tell me what?" she asked, redirecting her thoughts.

Luke poured Carmen a glass of milk while Char made herself more comfortable, tucked her feet under her on the couch, and stroked the bits of light brown hair on Mia's head.

"I'm going back to work. Luke is going to work from home. We're feeling the strain with me being off. And we're looking into getting some help." Char's eyes moved to Carmen when she said help, lightening Lucy's heart with the realization that they were confronting their daughter's challenges. The bang on the table when Luke placed the glass of milk down startled Mia and Carmen. Luke's face colored slightly. He grabbed a cloth to wipe up the spilt milk.

"It just makes more sense for me to stay home since Char can't exactly fix teeth here."

"I think it's great. All of it. As long as you guys are happy and doing what you need to do for your family, that's all that matters. Maybe I can help out a bit? Give you a break one day a week or something?" Lucy suggested to Luke, bringing her glass to the sink and rinsing it.

"For what? A few weeks while you're home?" Char asked. A sharp, quick pain stabbed Lucy in the chest. So much for connecting. But she smiled around it and pushed back the hurt at the sarcasm in her sister's voice.

"*Char*. That's a really nice offer, Luce. We'll take you up on it anytime," Luke replied, smoothing things over with a less-than-subtle glare at his wife.

"Sure," Lucy said too brightly, avoiding eye contact with either of them. She picked up her camera case, unhooking the latches as Char finished up with Mia.

"Well, if you guys are okay with a few candid shots, I'll do some of those now. I'll let you know when I need you for the calendar, Luke."

CHAPTER TEN

*A*lex put his hand on his gun, not something he had to do often in Angel's Lake. He and Cam, one of his younger deputies, walked to the door of the pub on the outskirts of town. The Catfish was basically the only place within fifty miles that people could go to dance, and it was usually crowded with twenty- somethings. Alex shook his head when he realized that he still fell into that category. *Sure doesn't feel like it most days.*

"Keep your hand on your weapon, but keep it holstered, alright, Cam?" he said, pulling the heavy, scarred door open. Cam was only a month on the job and showed a lot of drive and enthusiasm. But he also looked downright scared about going into the Catfish to deal with the drunk and disorderly call they had received about ten minutes ago. Cam nodded his head, his eyes wide; his military haircut made his forehead seem too big.

The sound of country music rang out into the starless night. The waft of colognes and perfumes, sweat, and beer raged out at them as if opening the doors had been the escape hatch for the combined scents. A couple—probably a little too young to be there—clung to each other, kissing, the girl giggling as they moved past Alex and Cam. Alex could hear shouting over the din, laughter that was too loud and too phony.

Walking in, he noticed it was not as crowded as it had sounded. The stained, carpeted floor was some sort of geometric pattern meant to hide the nasty things that happened to spill nightly. A long, scuffed, and well-used bar took up almost the whole back wall. Two steps led up to a few pool tables that always had a line of quarters waiting. Through the dim lighting and the cloud of needy desperation that filled the room, Alex saw Davey Morgan towering over a woman, his arm raised to strike. Alex lengthened his stride and nodded to Fast Eddie, the bartender and owner who was anything but fast. Grabbing Davey's wound up arm, Alex swung him around, placing his foot behind Davey's heel. The other man turned sharply, and he tripped and fell back onto his ass. Letting out a stream of curses, some of which Alex was sure Davey had invented, he looked up and glared at Alex.

"What the fucking hell?" Davey sputtered, a slur elongating his enunciation. Eddie meandered over, his large stomach peeking between his T-shirt and jeans, crossed his arms over his wide chest, and frowned.

"He's been cussing and screaming like that at all my customers. Won't go home. Won't settle down," Eddie drawled out. The music switched to a slow number, and the pool table balls smashed together as if to emphasize the shift in tone. Davey started swearing again, and Alex kicked him with his boot.

"Shut up," Alex instructed over the noise. He looked toward Cam and nodded, which brought Cam shuffling closer to pull Davey up by the arms. "Get your hands off me, boy! You know who I am?"

"This here is Davey Morgan, Cam. He's our town drunk and all-around loser. Davey, this is Cam. He's our newest deputy and the one who's going to escort you to our fine establishment back at the sheriff's office," Alex introduced, hiding his grin. Hell, maybe he wasn't being professional, but there were some perks to this part of the job.

"You okay, ma'am?" Alex asked the wide-eyed blonde watching them, still looking a little frazzled.

"I told him we should go. I told you we should go, Davey," she replied, her voice low and breathy. Alex wondered if she was scared of Davey or of ending her night in a cell.

"Did you come here with Davey?" Alex asked. She nodded. Alex looked back at Davey, who had stopped talking altogether. His ragged, whiskered face made Alex wonder if he looked anywhere near that old. Time had not been a friend to Davey. *Correction. Davey has not been a friend to Davey.* The man's plaid shirt was untucked, and his jeans rode low on his thin hips. He was truly the definition of disheveled. His hair looked like it hadn't been combed in a week and was sticking up at odd angles. Stepping a bit closer, Alex squinted to see what was making Davey's hair stand up.

"What the hell is in your hair?" he asked, reaching out. Davey tried to swat Alex's hand away, but Cam held both his arms strong and steady. "You gonna take him out of here?" Eddie interrupted after being called by one of the waitresses.

"Yeah. Thanks for phoning, Eddie ."

"No problem, Sheriff. Davey, you know you're welcome in here when you can behave yourself."

With that, Eddie shuffled his large girth back behind the bar, tucking his shoulder-length, curly locks behind his ears before grabbing a glass to pour some beer.

"What's in your hair?" Alex asked again.

"Nothin' man. How do I know? Shit, can this punk-ass kid let me go now? My arms are fallin' asleep," Davey whined.

Alex looked down at Davey's date. She was probably a couple of years younger than them, and even in the deceitful glow of the bar lights, Alex could see she was relatively attractive.

"You can do better. Do you have a ride home?"

"Yes. I have a friend here. She's dancing. I'll see you later, Davey."

Muttering under his breath, Davey didn't say bye as the girl made her way to the other side of the bar where people were crowding the dance floor. "Let's take him in," Alex said.

Looks like Cam was going to get taught quite a few things tonight, He took a breath of the fresh, crisp air and felt thankful that he didn't see the need to spend his nights off in places like The Catfish.

Alex rubbed his eyes with the heels of his hands after he dropped his keys onto the hallway entry table. Shrugging off his jacket, then tossing it on a chair, he toed his shoes off and left them in the middle of the hall. He was tired. Not sleep tired—though he was that, too—but he hated not being able to put all of the pieces together. He grabbed a bottle of water from the fridge and shuffled toward his bedroom. His breath caught as he stepped through the doorway, and every other thing slipped away.

Lucy lay curled on her side, her hair falling into her face like it was a blanket for her cheek. Her hands were up near her chin, and Furball was nestled against her, curled into Lucy's stomach, purring loudly. His ears pricked up when Alex gulped in a breath of air. He moved to the other side of the bed and put his water down on the nightstand. Chucking his shirt off, Alex tossed it into the corner, somewhere near his laundry hamper. His pants were thrown in the same direction, leaving his boxers on, and he lay down on the bed. He curled into her, his hand on her hip, and breathed her all the way in until he felt like she was nestled inside of him. He would never be able to get her out. She stirred and Furball stopped purring. Alex moved closer, wanting to just be near her, to feel her breathe in and out, which she did with a shuddery sigh.

"HEY," she whispered, turning her head to look up at him in the dark. His eyes had adjusted, but even if they hadn't, he'd know her face, every line, every crinkle, the way her lips barely moved when she spoke in her sleepy voice.

"Hi, sleepyhead."

He kissed her cheek and felt it move in a smile. She was warm even though she was on top of the covers ... or maybe that was him. He felt overheated. "I fell asleep."

"I noticed. I'm pretty observant like that. Looks like Furball took advantage of you."

She laughed quietly, and stroked the cat's back. Furball gave one meow and, clearly offended at the intrusion, jumped off of the bed. Lucy shifted herself around, almost kneeing him where he really didn't want to be kneed, and snuggled into him. She ran her hands over his arms as he kissed the tip of her nose.

Pressing her lips to his bare chest, she asked, "Aren't you cold?"

"Nah. I'm good. Were you waiting for me?"

"Maybe. How was your night?"

"Long." He pulled her tighter against him and she straightened her knees. The tip of his nose touched hers, and she continued to slide her hands up and down his body like she was soothing him, or maybe herself. "You okay?"

"Yes. I spent some time with my sister and Luke today. And Carmen."

"They're a nice little family."

"Yes. But I'm worried about them," she admitted, biting her lip and shifting her face. Her eyes almost glowed in the darkness. "Because of Carmen or because of them?"

"Why would you ask me if it was because of Carmen?" She asked, surprised.

Her body didn't stiffen, so he didn't think she was offended; still, he didn't want to say the wrong words. He rolled onto his back and pulled her with him so she was lying across his chest. The heat in the house kicked on, making the radiator stutter a few times. It'd be time to turn that off soon, he thought idly.

"She's a great kid. Sweet. Smarter than any kid I've met her age," he replied. "Have you met a lot of kids her age?"

"We do visits to the elementary schools—me and some of the deputies. Sam's fiancée, Anna, teaches grade two. She does this whole thing on community helpers. Not a lot, I guess. But enough."

"Enough to know she's different."

He hated that it wasn't a question and that her voice sounded sad when she spoke. He turned his face to her, but she was staring at his ceiling. When she turned to meet his gaze, her eyes were damp, but she smiled at him and then leaned in to kiss him.

"You arrest any bad guys tonight?" she asked.

Lucy held Alex's gaze, but her stomach wouldn't settle. She had started the conversation, but she didn't want to finish it now. His eyes watched her closely, like he could see too much.

"Actually, yes," he finally said. His eyes were tired but his voice hardened. "Our old pal Davey Morgan. He was causing a bunch of trouble out at The Catfish."

"Geez. The Catfish. I forgot that place was there. I guess some things never change," she murmured, moving so she was on her side again, her head resting on his bicep.

Despite the warmth in the room, she shivered a bit. Now that she wasn't sleeping, she felt a bit chilled.

"Yeah. Davey hasn't changed at all. We ended up throwing him in a cell for the night. He'll sleep it off and be at it again within a day or two. He had paint in his hair."

"What?" She sat up, pulled her knees up to her chest, and looked down at him. His hand came to rest on the small of her back as he continued.

"I noticed it at the bar when we showed up. When we got back to the station, with the light, I could see it was paint for sure. Blue. Like the blue that was all over the wall before the rec center burned."

"You remember the shade of blue?"

"Not really the shade, no. Just that it was a different kind of blue than your every-day dark blue or light blue. I asked him about it, and he said he was painting a friend's house."

"You don't believe him?"

"I don't believe a damn thing he says, but I can't do much when the only thing to go on is paint in his hair. I'll talk to the friend tomorrow, but my gut says it'll lead nowhere." Alex grabbed his water and took a long drink, like it could help wash away his frustration.

She took a sip when he handed her the water. "Why would Davey burn the rec center?" she asked him, passing him back the bottle. He put it back on the bedside table and shrugged.

"Damn. I don't know. Why would anyone? Davey's an idiot. Whatever stupid-ass choices he makes, I'm sure he has a rationalization for them."

He frowned and she could see the irritation coming off of him in small surges. She lifted herself so she could straddle his lap and put her hands on his chest. He leaned back to accommodate her, but his eyes were still troubled.

"You'll figure it out, Alex."

"What makes you so sure?"

"Because you won't stop until you do."

She leaned forward and kissed him gently before kissing each of his eyelids—hoping she could clear the worry from them.

"Do you have to sneak back to your parents' soon?" he asked, leaning up and threading his fingers through the hair at the nape of her neck. "I don't have a curfew," she chuckled, kissing him lightly.

"It feels like you do. You sneak away every night."

"I don't sneak. It's not a secret. And I come back."

"Yes. You do." She felt his smile against her collarbone as he kissed her there.

"Do you want me to stay?" she asked quietly. The words felt like they echoed in the silence of the room. The heat had turned off, making the hitch in his breath more audible. The sound caused a mirroring sensation in her heart. Which she tried to ignore.

"The answer to that will always be yes," he whispered, his hands sliding to her cheeks, his thumbs brushing over them as his eyes met hers, captured hers, and held them.

"Alex."

It was all she could say, because if she said anything else, it would be too much. Too much to say and too much to feel. Just as his face, the way he looked at her, made her feel too much, *want* too much—especially when she felt like she could keep doing this, being with him for a really long time. Lucy never did anything for a really long time.

"Stay," he murmured against her lips. "Always stay." His thumb was still on her cheek, making it easy for him to catch the tear that slipped from her eye. She nuzzled into him, realizing that she didn't feel panic at his words. Instead, she felt a slow, steady warmth travel over her skin and bury itself in her chest. She didn't know what to do with the feeling or what to say, so she kissed him. Kept kissing him, painfully aware that the warmth continued to spread inside of her, like it was part of her—like he was becoming part of her—like if she let it, let him, he could become the biggest and best part of her. The pressure in her chest increased, making her literally ache to get closer to him. To take more and give more before there was nothing left at all. Nothing but this ache and Alex.

CHAPTER ELEVEN

Since he booked and released Davey, two warehouses, the elementary school, and the wall behind Adam's Apples had been tagged. Four places in three days. The fire had been the most aggressive event, but it had been relatively quiet since. Now, someone seemed to be making up for lost time. Alex took a few more pictures as Nick swore under his breath beside him behind the grocery store. The smell of garbage was almost as oppressive as the heat.

"What's the matter with kids today?" Nick grumbled, stacking crates in a neat pile.

"We pulled pranks and acted like idiots, too, Nick. We just knew better than to throw it in everyone's face. We're going to catch the person doing this," Alex answered. He swiped his forehead with the sleeve of his shirt. The day was already long and hot, and it wasn't even noon yet. Stowing the camera, he took out a small, spiral-bound notebook and a pen. Nick swiped a cloth under his curtain of white hair to mop his brow.

"Anybody around lately that seems suspicious? Angry?" Alex asked him, the answer already in his gut like lead stones.

"You think someone is mad at me because I overcharge them on apples? Nah. You know I got no problems. Only person mad at me is my wife, and she's not even this good an artist," Nick answered, pursing his lips into a deep frown as he looked up at the brick wall. There were mostly swirls of color twisting into each other. They spiraled together to create a rainbow vortex. Some of the scrawling at the school had included words—stupid words that Alex figured

were this generation's curses. Words like "snap" and "frack." Words that seemed out of context and pointless to him.

"Alright, well, if you think of anything, anyone, let me know. I'm going to go print these out. You should call your insurance agent," Alex said around a large sigh.

"Yeah, yeah. I think they're probably pretty busy right at the moment, but I will."

He watched Nick go through the back door of his shop. Nick and Fiona would carry on as usual—as would the rest of the targets. What choice did they have until Alex could figure out who the hell had a grudge against the entire town? He walked back to the station, his shirt sticking to his back. Despite the heat, there was a breeze flowing, making it feel like hot air fans were blowing directly his way. He waved to the driver of a truck, who stopped so he could cross the quiet street. Opening the door to the sheriff's office, the push of cool air slapped him in the face. His dad was hunched over Dolores's desk, tapping his foot to the Taylor Swift song being blasted far too loud. The fact that he recognized the singer irritated Alex. Couldn't she play the classic rock station every once in a while? He was scowling when Dolores looked up, face flushed, and gave a little squeak.

"Well, hey there, Sheriff. How'd it go?" Her bright red lips smiled pleasantly.

His dad unfolded himself off of the front counter and turned to smile at Alex. Looking at his dad gave him a good idea of what he'd look like in thirty years. His dad was aging well, staying fit by hiking and running frequently. They shared many features—the height, wide shoulders, and dark, assessing eyes.

Something gnawed inside Alex's gut, but he couldn't pinpoint what.

"Hey dad. What are you doing here?" Alex redirected. Chuck's face looked a little flushed as he walked toward Alex and clapped him on the shoulder.

"Wanted to see my son. Most sons stop by and see their fathers, but if I want to see mine, I have to hunt him down," Chuck ribbed. Dolores held out a stack of pink sticky notes, despite the fact that Alex knew she had an unused stack of message pads. She preferred sticky notes in vibrant colors, and he often found them stuck to his desk, computer, or coffee pot.

"Mine is no better. Always off running with his friends or doing God knows what in his room," Dolores lamented.

"What about that art school he went to in New York?" Alex asked, trying to remember details as he looked through the sticky notes. Dolores talked so much that he didn't always remember the details.

"Well, I told him that staying with his daddy and his uncle wasn't going to turn out well, but what fourteen-year-old believes his mother? That fancy art program my ex promised him was nothing but a bunch of yuppie kids with nothing better to do than spend their parents' money. He came home after three months."

Alex looked up and saw his dad looking at Dolores, that same pink glow spreading across Chuck's cheeks again. *Christ. Don't go there, dad.* Alex moved toward his office with Chuck following behind. Dolores turned the music up a bit louder. Alex tossed the sticky notes down onto his desk, unstuck the ones that stayed on his fingers, and rubbed at his neck. Chuck seated himself on the battered wooden chair, unbothered by its lack of comfort.

"You look like shit," Chuck assessed, stretching out his long, denim-clad legs. "You're wearing cowboy boots," Alex replied.

"So?"

"So, when did you become a cowboy?"

"Never mind my choice of shoes. You sleeping at all? You got any leads? What's this I hear about you shacking up with Lucy Aarons?"

Alex swore under his breath and dropped into his chair. He rubbed his hands over his face and through his hair, making it stick up at odd angles. "Those aren't shoes. I'm not sleeping. I don't have any leads, and I'm not shacking up with Lucy."

His dad arched one eyebrow and waited. Chuck had been a good sheriff. Alex knew he had big shoes to fill, and at the moment, he wasn't all that fond of his father's cowboy boots.

"Hey, can I borrow your laptop?" Lucy asked, walking into Kate's room unannounced. Kate slapped the top of her computer closed and turned to face Lucy. "Ever hear of knocking?"

"Yes. I thought we outlawed it in this house. You looking at porn?"

"No! I'm not Char."

Lucy chuckled and flopped down onto Kate's perfectly made bed, giving in to the urge to stretch. For someone spending so much time in bed lately, she was really tired.

"Are you internet dating?"

"No. For goodness sakes."

Whatever she was doing, Kate didn't want to share. She opened the laptop back up but kept her body angled so Lucy couldn't see it from where she lay on her bed before she closed down what she was working on and passed the laptop to Lucy.

Still frowning, Kate asked, "Why don't you use yours?"

Eyeing her sister's pale blue shirt, wondering if she could borrow it, Lucy sat up, taking the computer. "Mine isn't connected to the printer, and it seemed like a hassle, so I thought I'd borrow yours. You look pretty. I like your shirt. Where are you going?"

"Down to city hall. There's a problem with the work permit for the reconstruction."

"I'll come with. We could grab dinner after. Maybe snag Char for an hour or so," Lucy suggested, opening the laptop as she pushed back on the bed so she could lean against the wall. Her head grazed the poster of Paris that hung over her sister's bed.

"I think her and Luke are having date night. She texted earlier."

Lucy listened to her sister as Kate puttered around her bedroom straightening books and talking about taking the lead on the reconstruction that, hopefully, would start next week. While she could repeat what her sister was saying, Lucy's attention was glued to Kate's browser history, trying to figure out Kate's weird mood. Being an older sister came with a snooping license. She opened the email.

"What are you printing?" Kate asked, eyeing her from the desk she'd had since they were kids. It still had boy band posters taped to the white-painted side. "Nothing. I'm reading your email now."

"What?" Kate screeched and scrambled toward Lucy. Lucy shut the laptop quickly and handed it over as Kate yelled, "What the hell, Lucy?"

"Why are you getting turned down for an internship at a fashion house?"

Kate blinked rapidly, yanked her computer from Lucy's hands, and set it on the desk. Her shoulders stiffened, and she didn't turn to face her sister. Lucy could smell whatever her mom was making in the kitchen, and her stomach rumbled audibly.

"Obviously, I'm not suited for the position. Duh."

"Duh? What are you, twelve? Why does a sociology major with a degree in social work apply for a fashion internship in New York?" Lucy scooted off of the bed. The breeze blew through Kate's open window, bringing in the scent of almost-summer along with the heat.

Kate turned to look at her, hands on her hips, voice firm. "It's nothing. Forget it. And don't snoop. I'm *not* twelve anymore, and this isn't you looking at my diary." Kate brushed past Lucy without meeting her eyes.

Lucy threw up her arms. "I did not read your diary! That was Char!"

Kate kept walking and Lucy scrambled after her, grabbing the rail as they went down the stairs. Glancing at the large, oval clock hanging over the fireplace, Lucy noted it was past six and wondered what time Alex would be home.

Whirling without warning, Kate looked up at Lucy and snapped, "I don't care. Just shut up about it, okay?"

Lucy froze, her fingers tightening around the banister. A lump formed in her throat. "Okay. I'm sorry. I just wondered what was up with you," Lucy apologized, keeping her own voice low. "I'm sorry."

Kate's face softened, but her eyes stayed heated. Kate looked just like their dad when she was mad; firm lips and angry eyes, but it never lasted long.

Alex crumpled a piece of paper and tossed it into the garbage can from across the room.

"I taught you that," his dad claimed when it went straight in. Alex laughed and picked up his mug but set it back down when he got a mouthful of cold coffee. Moving over to where his dad stood, glasses perched on top of his head—the only real sign that he had aged—they stared at the board in silence. Alex had posted pictures of all of the vandalized properties as a timeline.

They made a list of kids and jackasses known in Angel's Lake for causing trouble. Truthfully, there weren't that many, but they were all worth a second glance. Standing beside his dad, the knots in Alex's shoulders loosened. His dad had been a tough-love kind of dad, but he'd always been fair and brutally honest. The opposite of Alex's mother. So, Alex didn't mind going head-to-head with his dad over something. He valued Chuck's opinion.

"It's been a while since we had it out on the court," Alex replied, surveying the timeline, the list of names, the dates and frequencies. There were links between the incidents. Little things that hovered between them—all late night or very early in the day. Nothing mid-day.

"I can still take you, son, so don't go spouting off."

"Maybe if I go easy on you."

Alex picked up a mug shot of Davey. He was stupid enough, but Alex didn't see him painting buildings for kicks —he'd have to get off of his lazy, drunken ass to do it. There was a group home on the city limits for teen boys. None of them had caused Alex any trouble, but he had their shots from prior incidents, so he put them up on the board.

"How about we play a game of twenty-one? You win, I'll mow your lawn," his dad suggested. "And if you win? Not that you will."

"You tell me what's going on between you and Lucy."

"Shit, dad. I can do that anyway. We're just ... hooking

up. You know, while she's here." Chuck grimaced, shaking his head. "Don't make my mistakes, Alex."

Alex's jaw tightened—he actually felt the muscles there harden. "Do not compare her to mom. She's not mom."

"Gorgeous woman always looking for the next best thing? Can't stay in one place or put roots down?" Chuck pulled his glasses off his head and put them on.

"Don't compare them. I'm serious. They are nothing alike."

Chuck started to say more, but Alex gave him a look that stopped him. Rolling his shoulders, he walked to the water cooler. The air conditioning in the conference room of the station, where they'd been camped for hours, blew loud and weak. Alex felt the headache creeping back up his shoulder blades and into the base of his skull.

"Don't say I didn't warn you. Anyway, I need to get going. I'm going to head up to the cabin for a few days. I'll give you a call when I get back, and we'll play that game of twenty-one."

Chuck's eyes stayed on Alex—he could feel them assessing, waiting until Alex returned the steady gaze. "When did you decide to go to the cabin?"

"Just now. I need a break."

"From retirement?"

"Maybe. Or from my moody son."

Alex rolled his eyes and walked his dad out—past Dolores, who glanced up and gave a sickeningly sweet smile.

"Don't be a stranger, good-looking," she drawled, her fingers pausing over the keyboard. His dad winked at her, and Alex was grateful he hadn't eaten lunch. Shaking his head, he waved as his dad left. Turning back to Dolores, he waited until she made eye contact.

"You need something, honey?"

"Yeah. Don't flirt with my dad. He's a no-fly zone, and it's just weird."

He felt a wave of guilt at the crestfallen look on her face and he couldn't help thinking that he was missing something. Something right there in front of him.

Glancing at his watch, he decided he wouldn't leave until he had at least one piece, one part that could pull the case together. At this point, he'd settle for anything. He had a feeling he wouldn't be heading home soon.

"Okay. I'll call you when I get into town. No. I can only stay a couple of days," Lucy said into the phone. She heard Alex's front door open and close and felt a bubble of awareness, anticipation to see him, spurt up through her chest. The cat curled against her thigh on Alex's big, comfy bed. She smiled when he walked into the room, then frowned when she saw how tired he looked.

"I have to go, but I'll talk to you soon. See what you can line up for me. Okay. Thanks. Bye."

Alex was already ditching his shirt, making that bubble turn to more of a tingle that spread down through her stomach. "Talking to your boyfriend?" he asked, his voice laced with fatigue.

She closed her laptop, insulted Furball by pushing him over a bit, and patted the bed beside her. "No. My sugar daddy. Totally different."

Alex laughed, but the sound was empty. He sat beside

her on the bed, his hip touching hers as he leaned in to place a kiss on her forehead. "Obviously. This is becoming a habit, finding you in my bed at the end of the day."

"End of the night, really. You put in a long shift, Sheriff."

Their foreheads rested against each other, and Lucy closed her eyes. He was fast becoming her favorite smell. The mix of his cologne, his soap, and the heat of the day.

"Yeah. A lot of those lately. But I think I found something."

"Oh yeah? What?"

"Later. Tell me what your sugar daddy wanted," he said, kissing her nose and running his hand up her thigh. The cat jumped off the bed with a disgruntled sound.

"He misses me."

"Who could blame him? I'd miss you, too."

"Speaking of which..."

A dull, steady thump began in her chest, right under her ribs, at the look on his face. Everything slowed down. His hand came to a stop, and he retracted his head, distancing himself from her.

"You're leaving," he said, voice flat, his eyes darkening.

She tilted her head, told herself that it wasn't unreasonable for him to assume the worst. Even though she thought she had shown him that she wanted to be here. *With him*. She hadn't mentioned being anywhere else because, for the first time in forever, she didn't *want* to be anywhere else. She grabbed his wrist when he started to move off of the bed.

"Slow down, Captain Negative. I'm going to New York

for a couple of days. Then I'll be back. I was actually going to ask you if you want to come with me. We could stay in a pretty hotel and order room service. Get one of those big soaker tubs."

He blinked, his eyes still shadowed with a doubt that made the ache in her chest intensify. "Why are you going to New York?"

"I need to meet up with a couple of friends. I have to pick up the vouchers for the Mexico trip that we gave away at the town meeting a few weeks ago. And I've arranged to pick up some other big-ticket items. Kate and I have an old-school gala in the works, and we want to have an auction."

Even though Alex nodded in understanding and kept his gaze and his hands on her, she felt like he was too far away.

"I can't take off. But that all sounds great. You can't get them to just FedEx you the stuff?" His tone made it clear he thought she should be able to—that he was suspicious of her reason to go.

Irritation and a bit of hurt had Lucy moving off the bed. She walked to the chair that sat beside the gorgeous bay window, but she didn't sit. From his bedroom, when the blinds were open, you could look out on the sleepy neighborhood and watch it come alive in the summer and get buried in the winter.

"I could, but it seems kind of ungrateful to say, 'thanks for the thousands of dollars-worth of donations.' Wanna mail them to me'?" Alex stood and undid his pants. Lucy ignored the tightening in her belly and the urge to look at him.

"Okay. Good point. I'm sorry. I jumped to conclusions. But I still can't go. There's too much going on here."

"Okay. I'm leaving tomorrow night."

His reply was brittle. "That was fast."

She turned and bit the inside of her cheek to keep from sighing at the sight of his body standing in the dim light of the room. Wearing only boxers, he was running his hands through his hair, watching her watch him.

"It's not that hard to book a flight, Alex. And just so you know, it's not a one-way ticket. I booked a return flight."

He cringed at her tone and moved toward her. She bit her cheek harder, making her eyes water. *Better from pain than sadness.* He pushed his hands into her hair and covered her mouth with his, gentle but demanding. She gripped his wrists and held on, closing her eyes and letting herself feel. The hurt and the anger ebbed, leaving only longing and a bit of weepiness.

His forehead rested against hers. "Again. I'm sorry. I shouldn't have assumed."

"I do have a track record."

She looked down, even though he continued to hold her face angled upward. "Lucy. Look at me."

She did. Her eyes watered again, but she was no longer biting the inside of her cheek. "I should go." He shook his head, whispering, "Please don't." His breath washed over her.

"You're tired. You need sleep." She was caving.

"I need you. More than I wanted to. More than I should."

She moved one of her hands to the smooth skin of his

waist, then stepped closer. She lifted her gaze to his and squeezed the wrist she was still holding. "That's not one-way, either."

She closed the gap between them, showing him what she was too scared to say.

CHAPTER TWELVE

*L*ucy liked the quiet, but sometimes she found the noise of a busy city like New York more soothing than the chirping of birds or the rush of the river. It offered a different kind of noise—a different kind of beauty. She stifled a yawn and checked her watch. She was meeting Lola Okar at her art gallery on 5**th** Avenue in just under half an hour. She sidestepped a homeless man's outstretched legs and navigated around a yapping puppy on a leash. Her phone buzzed in her pocket, but she thought it would be better to check it when she stopped walking. There was more traffic on this one sidewalk in New York than in all of Angel's Lake.

The smell of fresh bread and garbage battled each other as the sun made its way higher in the slightly overcast sky. Horns honked and breaks squealed, but in Lucy's mind, she only heard Alex's voice: Telling her he was sorry for jumping to conclusions. Telling her she mattered. Telling her to come back. Telling her he needed her like air.

Pressing the button for the crosswalk, she put her other palm to her stomach, hoping the pressure would settle the butterflies dancing inside. There was a Starbucks just before the gallery, and she ducked in to check her phone and further unsettle her nerves with some caffeine. The text from Alex made her smile from deep inside.

Alex: *My bed is empty. I like it better with you in it.*

She typed back quickly, her thumbs not pausing.

Lucy: *I'm sure Furball would be happy to sleep with you.*

She waited, watched it send, watched the screen say 'read,' and imagined him smiling. Alex: *He hogs the bed and doesn't smell as good.*

As she waited in the line, she received a couple of funny looks when she laughed out loud. Lucy: *I think that's a compliment? It's only 2 nights. It'll give u a chance to miss me.*

"Can I help you?" The barista's voice was laid back, smooth, but his hand was already reaching for whatever cup Lucy wanted. She met his gaze, then wondered if getting his eyebrow pierced had hurt.

"Can I get a Pikes Place with cream and sugar?"

The studded eyebrow arched. Yes, she liked plain old coffee with all the fat and lots of sugar. She didn't need skinny, flavored, half-fat, whipped, or drizzled. Just some caffeine. Straight up. He shrugged as if her order were ridiculous, asked her name, and took her money. When she moved to the end of the counter, she glanced down at her phone.

Alex: *I already do.*

Her heart pinched. She exhaled a long breath and tried to ignore the roiling in her stomach. It felt like her dancing butterflies had turned to seasick rowers. It was discomforting to realize she missed him, too. She rarely got lonely on her quests. She liked immersing herself in the culture of whatever place she found herself in, and that rarely left time for missing people or dissecting her life.

"Lucy."

She thanked Studded Eyebrow Boy for the coffee and made her way to the door. She didn't reply to Alex's text. What would she say? *I miss you, too? I feel like crying? I wish you were here?*

Alex tucked his phone away when Lucy didn't respond to his last text. Pushing away from his desk, he shoved his hands into his pockets and walked out to the front counter.

Dolores had booked a few days off to visit her mother who was turning eighty. The lack of hip-shaking pop music was blissful. "You need anything, Sheriff?" Mick asked, glancing over the top of glasses.

"Nah. I'm going to head out to the group home on Perkins and see what those boys have been up to lately." Mick nodded, closed the newspaper he was reading, and rolled his shoulders.

"I was taking a look at the pictures you got up in the conference room. Nobody jumps out at you, do they?"

"No. But, in every photo we took of the tagged buildings, there's the same symbol kind of hidden within the work. I'm thinking that's not a coincidence." Mick scrunched his furry eyebrows together and moved around the front counter. "I was looking close, but I didn't notice a symbol."

They walked back to the conference room Alex moved to the white board and pointed to the red circles on each of the pictures that showed graffiti damage. It had taken hours of eye strain, combing through the pictures, but somewhere on each photograph—like a warped version of "Where's Waldo"—was a small series of woven lines. It made him feel a bit better that most of the designs were a series of intricate swirls. He wasn't unobservant; the tagger knew what they were doing—leaving a calling card, but only in an obscured way. Mick straightened his glasses and stepped closer to the board.

"What the hell you got circled here?" he asked with his nose almost pressed to one of the photos.

"Look. See how the top of these lines arches like a heart? Then it pulls down here like ribbons crossing over each other. They stem up from this line here like it's a balloon string or a tail," Alex explained, pointing it out in one of the photos, trailing his finger along the shape.

"That's just a b unch of squiggles. You seeing things, boy?" Alex gave a surprised bark of laughter.

"I don't think so. Look, see how the same shape is here, here. And here? Also, here."

Mick puckered his lips and pushed his glasses to the top of his head. He fisted his hands on his hips. "It's a good thing you're in charge, Sheriff. I wouldn't never have found that."

Alex clapped Mick's shoulder as the phone on his belt rang.

"Whitman," he answered. He motioned to Mick to follow him out of the conference room, and they made their way to the front desk.

"No…Alright…Calm down, Mrs. Bellamy…Yes, I understand that…Okay…I'm going to come over now, and we'll see if we can sort it out, okay? No…Don't do that…You wait until I get there…Okay…I mean it."

He hung up, hooking his phone back on his belt, and sighed.

"Now I bet you're wishing there was a fire or some graffiti somewhere, aren't ya?" Mick asked, his mouth turning up into a wide, toothy grin. Alex grabbed a bottle of water from the small fridge by Dolores's desk and grabbed the keys to the squad car as well. Mrs. Bellamy called about once a month complaining about her next door neighbor trying to steal her land, one little piece at a time. Today, Mrs. Bellamy insisted that Mrs. Netter was trying to take her trees, and if someone didn't come put a stop to it, Mrs. Bellamy said she would chop it down herself.

"A little," he admitted, making Mick laugh. Of course, the old man didn't offer to take the call for him and go check things out. No, instead, Mick sat down at the desk, opened up his paper, and gave Alex a mock salute indicating he'd hold down the fort.

"Give me another hug," Lola Okar purred. She didn't mean to, that's just how the model-turned-artist-turned-gallery owner spoke. Lucy was happy to oblige and equally happy that the gallery was still closed for a few hours so they could catch up.

"It's not right for anyone to look as good as you do," Lucy said, squeezing her long-time friend. They'd met when Lucy started photographing fashion shows and, in a sense, they'd come up through the ranks together. Lola was down to earth, loved pasta more than any model should, and had a rock solid work ethic. Her dark skin was flawless, and the camera loved her almost as much as Lucy did.

"Says the one who should have spent her life on the other side of the camera," Lola said. Her mocha eyes sparkled along with her melodic laugh. Lucy had always thought that if fairies existed, they would sound just like Lola.

"Not likely. This place is beautiful. Show me around," Lucy said, stowing her camera bag and her purse on the floor. Lola took her hand and led her through the gallery. Lucy could tell which images were Lola's. Always. There was sadness in every paint stroke that Lola made. It transferred incredibly to the canvas, and her work was both visceral and poignant. Having lost her mother at a very young age, Lola had created hundreds of pieces that showed variations of a young girl searching for her mother, seeing her in the images around her but never quite finding her. Though Lucy had seen Lola's work countless times, she felt teary as she looked at one of her latest. The black, grey, and white overlapped each other on the large canvas. A little girl, painted only in shadows, ran her hand along a rectangular stone. The subtle allusion to a gravesite made the emotion catch in Lucy's throat.

"This is incredible. One of your best," Lucy praised. Lola gave her hand a squeeze and then tugged her around a freestanding wall. The lump had loosened in Lucy's throat but she still couldn't say anything.

"Thank you, sweetie. You have no idea how happy it made me to know you were coming for a visit. I was going to send you pictures of the opening, but it is better in person, right?"

About fifteen of Lucy's photographs lined two freestanding walls, which created a hallway in the center of the main room in the gallery. Each black-and- white photo was of a different woman. The images were taken from different villages, cities, and countries around the world. Lucy could remember snapping every one of those shots.

"Lola. You asked if you could show a couple photos. I had no idea you were going to create a whole exhibit," Lucy whispered. She moved closer to each . Looked at them one at a time. Betra, an elderly woman from Kenya, who had taught her how to make the beads tribal women sold to earn money for their families. Lucia, a child activist in a small war-torn country near Somalia, who had shown Lucy the small school she and her friends had built. Every one of them had touched something inside of Lucy, made her feel like she was capturing something—someone—special on film.

"That was my plan, but I couldn't choose," Lola answered, looking closer as well. "Thank you."

"For what?"

"For showing my work in your beautiful new gallery like this. For believing in me enough to display my work in this way," Lucy said, turning toward her friend and meeting her indigo eyes that Lucy knew were contact lenses.

"Oh Lucy. None of us have trouble believing in you, my friend. It is always you. You need to see yourself the way you are seen," Lola told her, giving her a warm, quick hug.

They moved through the rest of the gallery. Lola put aside a couple of paintings that Lucy hoped would bring in some money at the auction she was planning. While they walked, Lola caught Lucy up on getting the gallery up and ready, the artist she was currently dating, and how she was thinking of taking some courses at NYU. Listening to her friend's voice and laughter reminded Lucy of the nights they used to stay up in each other's hotel rooms. The only difference now, other than their ages and the venue, was that a small part of her brain was wondering what Alex was doing.

Alex sat down at one of the two-top tables and nodded toward Danielle when she waved to him. He didn't need to pick up the menu before she wandered over.

"Hey Alex. You're all by your lonesome," she commented, taking out her pad of paper and a little pen with miniature cows all over it. She smiled at him and tilted her head.

"Yeah. That's okay sometimes," he said, even though he wished Lucy were with him. "You alright?"

They had been friends in high school—or maybe just *friendly*, as they had made out on more than one occasion.

But mostly, they'd been friends. Alex couldn't figure out why when talking to her now—her giving him a sweet, concerned smile—he felt a pang of guilt.

"I'm good. Just tired. Thought I'd grab a bacon burger and a coke before finishing my day," he replied, pushing aside the worry, reminding himself it had been ten years since high school. They were friends when Lucy had been off on her travels, and he didn't see Lucy as the type to take issue with him and Danielle being friends now. Still, there had been something between Lucy and her—some type of falling out. Alex didn't understand—the women had never been close in school—at least not that he'd ever seen.

Danielle scribbled on her pad before looking back up and speaking. "It's a good thing Lucy and her sisters are doing for the town. I've seen some of her photographs. They're beautiful. She did some family shots for my cousin, and they turned out gorgeous. Didn't even want money. My uncle runs the Home Depot in Little Falls, so Lucy took the photos in exchange for a discount on materials."

"She's got great ideas. She's actually in New York right now picking up some things for an auction she has planned."

"Yeah, I read on the Facebook page that there'd be a bunch of great items to bid on," Danielle said, a genuine smile making her face seem younger. She tucked the notebook in her pocket, along with the pen, then asked, "Do you think she'll stay?"

"I don't know. I hope so. But I really don't know," he said quietly, feeling the guilt build up in him again.

"She's not who some people think she is," Danielle

finally said after holding Alex's stare for a few seconds. The bell over the door rang, and a few teenagers shuffled in, laughing and giggling.

"Why do you say that?"

"Danielle! Order up!" Cal yelled from the kitchen, not at all worried about offending customers. Most of the regulars were used to Cal's bellow from time to time.

"She's just ... a really good person. I have to put your order in and grab that one. You look tired, Sheriff. Get some sleep." She walked away quickly, saying hello to the group of boisterous teens, treating them like she would any other customer.

Franny Mourtzin ran the group home for boys. She had been taking in teens from the ages of thirteen to seventeen for longer than Alex had lived in Angel's Lake. Rumor had it she had lost her own boy when he was twelve in a drowning accident. Alex had tried to pull the file one time when he'd been a deputy, but he couldn't find anything more than ten years old. She was a large woman, but sometimes Alex felt like it was more her presence than her body that took up all of the space. When she yanked the door open—Franny never did anything delicately or slowly—she blew the grey curls out of her eyes and smiled warmly at Alex.

"Well, hey there, Sheriff Whitman," she greeted in

a gravelly, singsong voice. "Hi Franny. How are you doing?"

He could hear some yelling in the background, and the smell of chili wafted through the open door. Someone was calling someone else a cheater in very colorful terms.

"Knock it off!" Franny hollered, turning her head over her shoulder. She turned back and laughed. "Those boys. It's like they don't realize it's just a game."

Alex nodded his head and shuffled his feet a little. Someone had just mowed the grass—he could still smell it in the air with the chili. Franny took good care of her property and her boys. He didn't think he'd find trouble here, but he had to check.

"Listen Franny, I was hoping to talk to the boys about some of the trouble in town," Alex began. "You think any of them have something to do with it?"

"Truthfully? No. You run a tight ship, and most of your boys are pretty good. But maybe they've got an idea of who *is* causing the trouble and why."

Franny pursed her lips as if considering. She was a practical woman, one that didn't jump to conclusions or get all bent out of shape over nothing. Alex really wasn't surprised that instead of being offended like many would have, Franny just moved aside and let him in.

Walking into the three-level home was like stepping into the seventies. The Mourtzins had been in Angel's Lake, or on the outskirts of it, for generations. Frank Mourtzin had built this house. Alex figured most of the decorating was what they'd originally chosen for their home. A small, funky-tiled entryway was separated from the living room by a half-wall that had built-in shelves. From the halfway stop, decorative, wrought iron bars made their way up to the ceiling, like the living room was a fancy jail cell that hadn't been completed.

In the living room, sprawled on the shag carpet, kneeling on a green-and-yellow plaid ottoman, and laying on the mustard orange couch were several boys. Alex knew a couple of them. He had dropped off Jimmy about six months ago when the boy had shown up at the station house, beaten. He hadn't said much even then, but when Alex brought him to Franny, she'd opened the door and pulled the boy straight into her arms.

"Uh-oh Jimmy. Sheriff knows you been talkin' too much," a dark-haired boy jibed. Jimmy smirked, nodded to the sheriff, and tossed a throw pillow at the speaker.

"Or he knows you've been trying to get into Lilly Simon's pants, Caleb," another boy, his blond hair tied in a ponytail that ran down his back, piped up.

"Mind your manners and turn off that racket," Franny instructed in a voice that Alex almost envied. She put her hands on her considerable hips. Alex wondered if Franny's dress was made from the same material as the ottoman. The boys straightened, turned off the television, to face him. Four of them all together, Jimmy being the only one he recognized.

"Hey boys. I'm Sheriff Whitman. I just came out to ask you about some of the trouble—the graffiti and the vandalism—that's been happening in town. Any of you know anything about it?"

He watched them, had been from the second he

entered the room. Body language often told more than words and, in Alex's opinion, none of them seemed truly worried that they were in any trouble. Jimmy's eyes darted back and forth between Franny and Alex before he cast them toward his bright white sneakers.

"We ain't done nothing!" the one who looked the youngest said indignantly.

"Nobody said you did, Tommy, so don't go giving the sheriff a hard time for doing his job," Franny objected. "I haven't seen anything, Sheriff," the one named Caleb said.

"How about you, Andrew?" Franny asked the dark-haired, dark-skinned boy who was tucked into a corner of the couch, a bag of chips on his lap. Andrew shook his head.

"No ma'am," he replied quietly.

Alex and Franny both looked at Jimmy, who was still staring at the floor. His straight hair was falling in his face, covering his eyes, but Alex got the impression he knew they were waiting on him.

"You got a voice, boy. Use it. You see anything?" Franny demanded.

"No." Jimmy looked up when he said it, and met Franny's gaze but not Alex's. *Something there.* Alex didn't think Jimmy had done anything, but he might know someone who did.

"You sure?" Alex pushed.

Jimmy looked at him. The eyes that had been empty and broken only six months ago were now full of sparks. His voice was steady when he said, "I didn't do anything."

"Never said you did. Can you think of anyone who

might be defacing and burning down property, Jimmy?" Alex asked again.

"Nope. Can't think of anyone off the top of my head," he answered, but his eyes shot back to his shoes, and Alex knew the window was closed.

Lucy's feet were dragging by the time she made it back to the hotel. As she waited for the elevator, she was thankful that Lola had agreed to ship the paintings so she didn't have to lug them around. Once she was in her room, she dropped all of her things onto the king-size bed, wished again that Alex had joined her, and then flopped face first beside her purchases and donations. Closing her eyes, she pictured the bath she would take. She would have lain there longer if her phone hadn't buzzed. She grabbed her cell out of her purse, scooted up the bed, and turned so she was lying on her back, resting on a pillow so comfy she wondered if she could fit it in her suitcase.

Alex: *Decided I don't miss you*

She frowned, but knew that Alex was joking or leading into something with his text. She typed back, a smile warming her cheeks and a second wind loosening her tired muscles.

Lucy: *Is this reverse psychology?*

Alex: *Maybe. I figured I scared u off earlier today.*

Lucy: *You didn't. It's too bad u don't miss me. I miss you. Enough to try sexting.*

Alex: *Is that the new version of phone sex?*

Lucy: *I guess it is. This way you don't have to get all breathy. You can just use emoticons.*

Alex: *I like when your all breathy, but I miss you enough to settle for the sexting*

Lucy: *LOL You start.*

Alex: *No way. You. Make it good. Hang on a minute. BRB*

She didn't know what he needed to do, but she used the moment to kick off her shoes, ditch her jacket, and curl back up on the bed. When her phone buzzed again, she felt bubbles of excitement burst through her, making her giggle. She was glad Alex wasn't actually in the room to see what a fool she was being.

You okay?

She smiled. Not as good as she was going to be.

Oh, I'm good. Tell me how good I am.

She frowned at the response.

Very good?

Finding it both endearing and disappointing that he wasn't good at this, Lucy texted:

That's too vague. Try harder. Say something sexy. Tell me how much u want me or wish I was there beside u, naked.

Lucy actually squealed out loud at the next text and finally looked at the name on the screen.

Mom: *Sweetheart, there is nothing wrong with enjoying our bodies, but it's really better to keep this kind of stuff private.*

She squeezed her eyes shut until they hurt, chanting, "No. No. No. Please tell me I didn't." She opened one eye, looked down at the phone. Sure enough. Mom: *Nothing to be embarrassed about, dear.*

The phone buzzed again, and Alex's name and screen popped up. Alex: *Sorry, wanted to get out of work clothes before we got started.*

Lucy texted her mom quickly, asking that they never speak of this again, said she loved her, and then dialed Alex's number. "Are you chickening out?" he asked, his voice thick and warm, making Lucy feel almost like he was there beside her.

"Uh, I kind of started. Only, with my mom. So I figured that had to be a sign that I'm not cut out for sexting," Lucy admitted and then waited, not amused by how hard Alex laughed. He apologized between fits of laughter, then immediately started up again.

"Are you done?" she asked. She was grinning when she said it, though; it was impossible *not* to when Alex laughed. Or smiled. Or reached for her hand when they were walking beside each other.

"I'm sorry. Really. I guess it's better your mom than your dad?"

"Neither would be the best option here."

"I'm not getting phone sex, am I?" he asked. Lucy shook her head at the sound of amusement lacing his voice.

"No. But I'll make up for it with the real thing when I get home," she replied, snuggling into the bed. Her heart fluttered at the word "home" because it was Alex's home that popped immediately into her mind.

"Speaking of home, you'll be happy to know that construction starts tomorrow. Sam was able to get a crew together that will volunteer their time. It'll be odd hours, as they'll be doing it around their day jobs, but that means any extra money can go into programs and other parts of the reno," he told her. She heard the cat in the background and could picture Alex shooing him off of the bed. Horns kept a steady rhythm outside of her own window, but it was easy to focus on the sound of Alex's voice instead.

"That's awesome! I'm guessing Kate knows, but I'll phone her tomorrow. Your pal Sam is pretty handy."

"Can be. He's a good guy, and he'll have chosen solid workers for this, so I think it'll get done faster than you would expect."

"How was your day?"

She liked listening to him tell her about his day, about routine callouts and interviewing people.

"Do you think Jimmy has something to do with it?" she asked when he told her about the visit to the boys' home. She rose to get a bottle of water but saw the $8.00 price tag and went to the tap instead.

"I think he might know something, but I really don't see him being part of it. It'll come together. What do you have planned for tomorrow?"

She took a quick swallow of water before answering him. "I'm meeting up with a couple more friends that I haven't seen in a while. I want to ... can you keep a secret?"

"I'm not a girl, so probably," he said. She could hear him shuffling around trying to get cozy. He probably wouldn't say cozy either. "That's sexist. And the only reason men can keep secrets is because they weren't completely listening in the first place!"

"What's that?"

She laughed as she crawled back into the bed, in just

her T-shirt and underwear. She pulled the covers up and yawned. She had lived in New York briefly and had spent her days running from one end of town to the other without pause. Lucy wondered if all of her time in slow-paced villages and her own little hometown was making her a lightweight.

"Anyway," she said, stretching out the word, "I snooped in Kate's email and found a rejection letter from a fashion house—a fashion house that I have connections with—and I wanted to talk to a friend there."

"I thought Kate wanted to be a social worker."

"Me, too. But, when I asked her about it, she got really pissed and clammed right up." Lucy pumped up the pillows and piled them on top of each other.

"I'm sure it wasn't because her older sister was reading her private email."

"Okay, a little, but still. She was really weird about it. I just want to talk to my friend, see if they have an opening for an internship, and then if they do, maybe she'll talk to me about it more."

She shrugged, even though he wasn't beside her. "But if they turned her down..." he began.

"This industry is 98 percent who you know."

"And who you sleep with?" Alex asked, the hard sarcasm not suiting him. "Sometimes. But I never worked that way, so I wouldn't know personally."

"I'm sorry. I'd still really like to meet your ex-ass-clown-boss."

The sky outside the window by the bed was dark, and if she closed her eyes and listened to his voice, it felt like she was beside him. "He's not worth it. I'm falling asleep, but I don't want to hang up."

She could hear his smile through the phone, which she realized didn't even make sense. But still, she could see him lying on his bed his lips turned up, his eyes half closed.

"The sooner you go to sleep, the sooner you'll be home. I want you home."

She was sure he meant it the way she had earlier in the conversation—home as in Angel's Lake—but hearing him say the word home made everything inside of her come to attention. Her heart stuttered, and her breath hitched a little on its way out. Her stomach danced. He was silent, and she wondered if he knew what he had said—what it had sounded like. If he thought it would scare her off again ... it didn't. If anything, it made her want things she hadn't thought or known she wanted. Maybe because, until now, she never had.

CHAPTER THIRTEEN

*A*lex waited until Kate was all the way out of her car before pushing open his screen door and wandering down his porch steps. The sun was behind her, but she still wore large-framed, black, movie star glasses. She pushed her bag higher on her shoulder as she walked down the path that lined the driveway.

When she noticed him, she shifted her sunglasses to the top of her head. He put his hands into his pockets and walked over his lawn. "Hey there, Sheriff."

Sometimes he wondered if anyone remembered his name. Lucy knew his name. Remembered it very well. *Don't go there right now.*

"Hey Kate. How was class?"

"How did you know I had class?" She looked at him, arching a brow in a way that only made her look cuter—in a strictly little-sister way—rather than suspicious.

"Well, I used my powerful super-sleuthing skills. College student. Backpack on her shoulder that looks a little heavy. I'm guessing that it has books in it. You're arriving home at"—he paused to make a show of looking at his watch—"eleven o'clock. I suspect you had a morning class. Do you see now why I'm such a good police officer?"

She laughed, sounding a bit like Lucy and hitched her bag farther up on her shoulder. "Here I thought it was just the sexy uniform."

"Brown isn't sexy on anyone. And I hardly ever wear my uniform. Listen, do you have a couple of minutes? I'd like to talk to you," he asked, changing his tone. Her brows drew together with immediate concern.

"Did she dump you?" Kate asked, touching his arm. He was surprised at the spurt of anger he felt at the immediate assumption. He pulled his hands from his pockets and stepped back.

"Why is that the first thing you would ask?" he demanded.

"Well. It's just..." she started but trailed off and looked at him as though her expression would finish her sentence.

"Maybe you don't know your sister as well as you think you do," he countered.

Her eyes widened, possibly at his tone, possibly at his words.

"Or maybe you don't. I love my sister—more than anything. But I see who she is. I know Lucy. I'm sorry. I shouldn't have jumped to conclusions, but you look sad. What did you want to ask me about?"

She walked toward her house and he followed, giving them both a second to smooth out the edges.

"I didn't mean to jump at you. I miss her. And that's

damn humbling to admit," he told her, giving her a sidelong glance. She nodded as if she understood, but he didn't think she really got it—he could barely wrap his head around how he was feeling.

"So, what's up?"

"First, Sam has some guys willing to volunteer with the construction, so you're going to be able to put some of the money to other uses," he told her. "That's wonderful!"

"I thought you would like that. Second, I know you had teens helping out with painting, setup, and organizing programs that would be offered. How well did you know the kids helping out?"

She stopped on the top stair of her parents' porch and looked at him. They were eye level now.

"I know their names and some of their history. They're not all willing to talk, but the ones that are, I try to listen. Offer advice without seeming like that's what I'm doing. Overall, I think a lot of them are good kids. Some aren't, some have earned their reputation and are helping out as part of their rehabilitation," she said thoughtfully. She shrugged again and pushed the screen door, holding it for Alex to follow after. She unlocked the white, heavy oak door with the glass panel revealing Julie Aarons sitting at the kitchen table.

"Hey mom," Kate greeted. Julie turned and Alex thought the genuine happiness on the older woman's face made her seem considerably younger. Even if it hadn't, it was easy to see where all three girls had gotten their attractive features.

"Hi sweetheart! Oh, hello Alex. How are you?" she

asked as she stood. She was a bit taller than Kate, but not by much. Also like Kate, she had smooth skin, dark hair, and happy eyes.

"I'm good, ma'am. It's nice to see you. Are you working on one of your books?" he asked, leaning down to give her a peck on the cheek when she leaned into him. She smelled like oatmeal cookies.

Kate unloaded her backpack on the table beside the laptop and papers scattered there. The scarred, wooden, rectangular table was huge and gorgeous. Since moving in, Alex had been trying to find just the right one for his kitchen. Kate signaled from behind her mother's back, shaking her head and slashing her hand across her throat. He chuckled, making Julie look back at her daughter, who froze before facing him again.

"I certainly am. It's about how to please yourself," she shared. He watched Kate close her eyes and shake her head sadly. "Uh..."

He didn't know what to say to that, so he put his hands back in his pockets and rocked back and forth slightly. The front door slammed, and Mark hollered out that he was home. Alex sighed internally—he just wanted to ask Kate some questions.

"It would seem you and my other daughter know very well about such things." Julie smirked and moved to the counter where she opened a cookie jar that looked like a giant bear. Alex felt the heat move all the way up his neck and was positive that if he looked in a mirror, he would be redder than the tomatoes Dolores prided herself on growing.

"Mom!"

"What?"

"Hello family! Hi there, Alex. I guess you kind of suit that label, too, don't you?" Mark asked, walking into the kitchen with the strap of his laptop case slung over his shoulder. He was dressed casually for a college professor—Khaki pants and a pale blue, striped polo. Mark waggled his eyebrows at Alex, but he didn't think he could go any redder. Mark moved toward his wife immediately and kissed her cheek with such obvious affection that Alex felt a gut-deep pang of envy.

"Stop it, you two. You're embarrassing him," Kate defended with a look that clearly said Alex had brought this on himself.

"As I said to Lucy, no reason to be embarrassed, dear. Here, have a cookie," Julie said, passing him a large, slightly warm oatmeal chocolate chip cookie. "Thank you," he mumbled like a teenage boy caught with his girlfriend. He was here on official police business. How the hell did this happen?

LUCY WAITED in the lobby of *Posh Magazine*. Waited was a generous term. Mostly, she sat on the luxurious leather sofa trying to not actually touch it with her body. She was essentially doing the most excruciating squat possible, because the couch looked like it had never been sat on before. Four women—who *had* to be models—sauntered by, and Lucy had the horrible image of leaving a wide bum indentation on the couch as she stood. The quiet clacking of the

keyboard was interrupted by evenly paced, heavy footfalls. She almost whimpered with joy when Kael finally joined her in the eerily still room. She stood, ignoring the cramp in her legs, and turned to see him. Immediately, she laughed and then was swallowed in a large hug.

"The expression 'sight for sore eyes' was made for when people like me get to look at people like you," he said in his low, gravelly, vibrato voice. He smelled like honey and felt warm like fleece. Kael Makhai was a hulking man who went against every stereotype the fashion industry could possibly have. He was also a brilliant designer, and some of Lucy's best photographs had been of his work.

"I don't even know if that makes sense," Lucy squealed, tightening her arms around his neck, one palm brushing the nape of his black buzz cut. He put her down but kept his hands on her shoulders, holding her at arm's length.

"Of course it makes sense," he chided, lowering his voice to a whisper before continuing. "I spend my day with women who avoid food so they don't get fat, avoid laughing so they don't get wrinkles, and avoid friendship so they don't get stabbed in the back."

She slapped his Hawaiian-shirt-covered chest and laughed louder than she should have, earning a glare from the pencil-thin, unsmiling receptionist, who looked like an ad for Business Management School. Snooty Business Management School.

"Don't be so negative. I know there're plenty of awesome people in this industry," she said, following along as he guided her across the gold-flecked tile flooring. "In fact, I saw Lola yesterday."

"You should have called me. We could have all gone to lunch. Like old times."

"I didn't stay long, but it was good to see her, and it's good to see you."

He didn't walk so much as shuffle along as his size allowed. He wore canvas shorts and sandals. Not one person, in all the time she had known him, had ever guessed his occupation correctly. It always amazed her that this brusque, large-framed man with hands the size of her head could create the most delicate, intricate designs favored all over runways in Europe.

"Good to see you, too, my girl. It has been too long."

They made their way past racks of clothes, half-naked women, doorways leading to design rooms, photo shoot rooms, unused lunchrooms, several bathrooms, a fitness room, and a lounging area. Off of the lounging area, Kael led her into an open room with a wall of windows. Heading straight for them, she gave a small gasp.

"You can see all of New York from here," she said in both awe and envy. There was nothing like a good view of New York on a perfectly clear day. *Except maybe the view from a mountain on an equally clear day.*

"Pretty close," Kael laughed, coming up beside her. "You know, they're looking for a photographer here. I could put in a good word. We could work side by side again. Two thirds of the dream team." Along with Lola, they had made quite the crew: designer, model, and photographer—a trifecta of friendship. A lifeline at times.

She crossed her arms over her chest, grateful she had worn a purse that could be slung across her body effortlessly. Lucy looked up at her friend, his tanned skin on his round face stretched smooth. She bumped his hip casually with her own, or tried to, but she was considerably shorter.

"That would be pretty amazing."

"But? Tell me this doesn't have anything to do with that ass or the Africa assignment?"

Eyes wide, she unfolded her arms and began looking around his chaotically organized space. "You heard about that?"

"I heard a bullshit rumor and figured the rest out for myself."

"Yes, well, I guess I'm not always wanted just for my great photography skills," Lucy tried to joke. She ran her hand over his design table, careful not to touch the actual page that showed some sketches of a dress he was designing. She eyed the way the delicate curve of the neckline created folds and ruching as it came down to curve over the chest. It cinched at the waist and then simply exploded in extravagance. A wide, intricately designed skirt—for which she knew he would use some sort of delicate material—flowed out like the ripples of the creasing had burst into a river of fabric.

"Don't do that. It pisses me off," he said, bringing her attention back, shuffling to his desk and opening up his laptop. "What?"

"Your photography speaks for itself. Yes, you're gorgeous. But you get work based on your talent. Vincent is well known for being a sick bastard. That has nothing to do with you, and your reputation isn't in question. Don't doubt that. It pisses me off," Kael repeated. Lucy shrugged and moved to his back counter where shelves lined the wall. He had fabrics laid out, sketch books open, and dozens of pencils scattered. She loved looking at his space—imagined having her own little spot where she could line her cameras along the shelves and hang her shots. She pushed the thought aside.

"Anyway, you turned my sister down for an internship," she said without censure.

He looked up at her in surprise, his dark eyebrows arching, wrinkling his beautiful skin.

"What? First, I didn't know you had a sister that wanted into fashion. Second, when? I get hundreds of applications a day. Most of them, I don't even read. I get my assistant to do it."

"Well, to be honest, I didn't know Kate wanted to be in fashion, either, but she applied for an internship, and when I asked her about it, she got defensive and shut down."

Kael grabbed a pen and a small notepad before leaning over his desk. "What's her name?"

"Kate Aarons."

"So, she shut down and then asked you to pull some strings?"

Lucy tilted her head and narrowed her eyes in his direction. He put up a hand and laughed at her expression. "No. She doesn't know I'm here. I want..." She didn't know how to finish the sentence.

The moment of quiet seemed unsettling and when the phone rang, she was grateful for the interruption. She moved back to the window and took in the skyline again, savoring it and locking it away.

"You okay, Luce?" Kael asked from behind her. She heard his feet shuffling away and looked back to see him closing his office door.

"Yeah. It's just that..." she started. She turned to face him and sat on the thin window seat. "Since I've been home, I've started to realize how much I've missed. How much I haven't been a part of."

"Because you've been part of something else. Many something elses. You've traveled all over the world and taken some of the greatest photographs I've ever seen."

"Thank you. And yes ... but at what cost, K? My baby sister is graduating from university. My older sister just had a baby. My oldest niece is five now. Something is up with my mom. And being with my dad makes me realize how much I missed him. Them. They all take care of each other—"

"Do you want them to take care of you?"

She felt tears stinging her eyes and shook her head, unsure of how to explain or even of how she felt. "No. I guess. I don't know. They take care of *each other*. I want to be part of that. Both ways."

Lucy wiped her eyes with the heels of her hands, rubbed her hands on her jeans brusquely, and stood up, smiling too brightly.

"You want to do something for your sister. Even though she isn't ready to confide in you," Kael summarized, reading her as well as he always could. She nodded her head and bit the inside of her cheek to stop any further tears from falling.

"Alright," he said, moving back to his desk and picking up one of his cards. "Tell her to email me directly when she's ready and remind me that she's related to one of my favorite people."

She laughed and skipped toward him, making him laugh when she threw her arms around him. Or part of him anyway. He squeezed her back and placed an affectionate kiss on the top of her head.

During conversation over an impromptu lunch with Kate and her parents, Alex realized none of them knew Lucy would be back early the next morning. No one knew her flight times or arrangements. When they'd said good-bye to her, they figured she'd be back again or she would be in touch. Kate knew she had gone to New York to secure some items for the auction but little else. *Why don't they question her? Wonder when she'll be back? A coping mechanism maybe?* For him, it wouldn't work. He crawled into bed early that night and texted Lucy, confirming her flight time. She said she would see him after he got home from work. Told him, she'd be fine getting herself home from the airport. She hadn't seen reason to trouble anyone in her family with the details.

Because she expected no more of them than they did of her. When she was here, she was here, and when she wasn't, she wasn't. But it wasn't good enough for him. At all.

"You still don't know you matter," he said to himself after texting that he missed her and looked forward to seeing her the next day. She texted back smiles and hearts and then a bunch of jumbled symbols that he guessed were meant to be X-rated, making him laugh.

"But you will. You need to realize you belong. Here. With me."

He fell asleep with that thought in his head and a smile on his face.

Lucy navigated the airport with the ease of a well-traveled person. The routine was as common to her as getting ready in the morning. Exit terminal, head to baggage, then customs if necessary, and find the cab stand. She yawned behind her hand and pulled her travel bag onto her shoulder more securely as she made her way toward the baggage claim. The air conditioning made her grateful for the dark grey, oversize, cable knit cardigan she had picked up in New York. It wasn't frivolous if it was useful. It was early, but hundreds of travelers were milling about, rushing around as overhead pages rang out from speakers. Some people were laughing, others crying. One man was at an airline counter demanding a full refund and emphasizing his request with a slam of his fist. Two security officers moved in quickly, flanking the irate traveler on either side. Lucy side-stepped a little girl pushing a huge baggage cart, full to the brim, and smiled at the dad who gave Lucy a well-meaning shrug. She could smell coffee and pastries and wondered which one she wanted more at the moment. *Both, obviously.* Then she stopped short and stared. To her utter mortification, she burst into tears and covered her mouth with her hand.

Between inelegant sobs, she wiped at her face with the sleeve of her hand. Alex walked toward her, a coffee in one hand and a pastry bag in another. He looked uncertain, a half smile on his lips and his eyes bright with concern. She moved then, straight to him, ignoring the coffee and the pastry, and put her arms around his neck, almost strangling him in her need to get closer. His arms came around her, despite being occupied, and she could feel the strength of his biceps as he crushed her to him.

"Are these good tears?" he whispered into her ear. She nodded against his shoulder. She leaned back her cheeks wet, and put her palms to either side of his face.

"No one has *ever* met me at the airport," she whispered fiercely. Then she sealed her mouth to his, pouring everything she felt into the kiss. He backed them out of the aisle of foot traffic, his lips never leaving hers. She came up for a second of air when she heard a thud and felt his hands on her skin, pushing under the back of her sweater and T-shirt.

"What?"

She looked down at the trash can where he'd just deposited her coffee and treat and back at him. "Hey!"

His hands gripped her tighter before he wove one hand into her hair, tangled his fingers at her nape, and brought her mouth back to his. "I'll buy you more. As much as you want," he said hoarsely against her lips.

She grinned and tightened her arms around his neck again, absorbing his heat and strength, the feel of him against her, surrounding her, comforting her and driving her crazy at the same time. She had no idea how long they kissed, devouring each other, and gave no thought to those that passed them. All she could think, feel, and see was him. It was him that pulled back finally, his hands on her face while hers were wrapped around his waist, tucked under his lightweight coat.

"Did you miss me?" she asked, no longer crying. He gave a short, harsh laugh. "A little bit."

She burrowed into his arms, absorbing the feel of him. Savoring the fact that he was here. His hands came to her shoulders before one hand trailed down her arm until it found her hand. He wove his fingers with hers then touched his mouth to hers, one more time. They walked toward the baggage claim, and Lucy couldn't keep the smile from her face. Her cheeks were aching with it, and she wrapped her other hand around his arm, snuggling into his side.

"I can't believe you met me at the airport."

"I can't believe no one ever has."

The luggage was starting to drop from the conveyer belt as they approached. She looked up at him. "I didn't know it mattered to me. Maybe it didn't. Until you."

His face tightened and he looked like he wanted to say something, his eyes holding hers captive just as his hand did. Not that there was anywhere else she wanted to be. He kissed her forehead, making her close her eyes and sigh. When she opened them again, he was still watching her with an intensity that made her heart stumble and her throat dry up.

"That's how I feel about most things when it comes to you," he finally said. She saw her bright purple suitcase from the corner of her eye and moved to retrieve it before Alex could. She pulled the handle up and rolled it over to him. She wondered if her face showed all of the turbulent emotions swirling in her stomach and chest.

"I believe you owe me coffee and a pastry. Then I think we should head home. To your house," she correctly quickly, her heart skipping one quick beat. He smiled at her and once again took her hand.

"Sounds perfect. If I remember correctly, you promised me the *real thing* when we get there." He grinned, tugging her through the crowd. She laughed, but in her mind, she thought, *doesn't get much more real than this.* The thought, which would have terrified her months ago, made her more eager to get back to his home.

"We can grab coffee in a drive-through," she insisted when he made to stop at a stand in the airport. "God, I missed you," he laughed as they both quickened their pace.

CHAPTER FOURTEEN

*A*lex didn't follow the thread of Lucy's conversation. She was telling him about New York and, he thought about his favorite songs and how he could listen to them repeatedly. Lucy's voice was like that for him—knowing the words was irrelevant. As he took the overpass out of the airport parking lot, he covered her hand with his and smiled in her direction.

"Have you ever been?" she asked.

"To New York? No. I've been back to Chicago a few times to see family, but I'm not really much of a traveler," he replied. She smelled like vanilla and hotel soap. He wanted to yank her closer and wished he had a bench seat instead of buckets.

"I don't think I could live there anymore. I have to say, that surprised me when I realized it," she said, tracing her fingers over the back of his hand. Traffic was fairly light at this time of day. Shoulder checking, he merged onto the freeway and relaxed, somehow rebalanced just by her presence.

"Did you like living there?"

"As much as I liked any place, I suppose. I never really attached to one place more than another. I had friends there, so I think that made a difference. I enjoyed the freelance work I was doing. But it's too busy now."

He looked toward her and caught her profile as she stared through the windshield. Her hair was tied back but falling loose. He couldn't wait to get his hands in it. Ignoring the burst of hope he felt, he teased, "Careful. You'll end up craving a small town like Angel's Lake."

She looked over then and their eyes met before he put his back on the road. She leaned a little so she could rest her hand on his thigh. His hand slipped to hers.

"Somehow that doesn't seem as terrifying as it once did," she said so softly he thought he might have heard her wrong. He cast a fast glance and saw she was still looking at him.

"Oh yeah?" He kept his voice measured, but his heart was battering his rib cage.

"It's got a nice view. It's not far from major cities. There's a Starbucks..." His lips quirked as he nodded. "And a brand new cinema."

"I do like movies." She laughed.

After a bit, he pulled off to follow the sign for food and beverages. They drove in silence, their hands on each other. Alex could feel her watching him as he kept his eyes on the road. He was trying to keep all of the emotion he was feeling locked down. He'd missed her—that was all.

Nothing wrong with missing the woman you were seeing when she went away for a couple of days. Just because he felt like he could breathe again didn't mean he was in way too deep. Once he had her home, in his bed, this swirl of emotions would settle. It would go back to hovering instead of eating away at him with an intensity he hadn't faced before. Maybe she was feeling overwhelmed, too. Maybe he wasn't the only one drowning. He wished he knew what was going on in that gorgeous head.

"Mom, food," she said when he pulled up to a drive-through.

Lucy hated nervous fidgeting, but it was exactly what she felt like doing. She was forcing herself to keep her hand still on Alex's thigh. The unspoken words and obvious lust filled the cab of the truck like water slowly rising to the top of a tank. Only a little bit more and she wouldn't be able to breathe. When Alex pulled up to the speaker, he gave their order before she could even say what she would like. As she listened to him order her two cinnamon buns, a large coffee, and a water before ordering his own apple fritters and coffee, she realized he knew her. She let people see parts of her, but never the whole. *Not even family*. Because if anyone saw too many of the pieces, they would see she didn't fit, didn't fully belong. Sure, apply a little pressure and it seemed like she could cram her way into an empty spot, but if someone looked closely enough, they'd see that she was a fraud.

He passed her both coffees wordlessly and she realized that he not only saw the pieces—he didn't care how they fit. He passed her the bags, paid, and said, "thank you." She tucked the coffee into the drink holders while he got them back on the highway.

What did it mean when someone saw all of the pieces and wanted you anyway? Her heart jackhammered with the realization that she *knew* what it meant. What it meant for him to know her coffee order, to pick her up at the airport, to be so *happy* to see him. How had she missed him so much? *It's only been a couple of days.* That didn't seem to matter to her heart, and the more she thought, the more she felt, and the higher the water rose, submerging her completely. Instead of panicking or feeling like she would drown, she chose to dive deeper.

"I think I'm in love with you," she whispered. She wasn't even sure he'd heard her, but the car stopped at a light and he stared at her. He'd definitely heard her. She refused to avoid his wide-eyed gaze or have a panic attack. Saying it felt right.

"You *think*?" he asked, his voice husky and low. The light turned green. Alex continued to stare at her, and she wasn't surprised when a horn honked behind them. He accelerated and her nerves pushed harder; it was like thousands of butterflies beating against her rib cage.

"I do. I really do think I am. Maybe I shouldn't have said it, but I... I really feel like I am, and I thought, well, if I feel it, I should say it, but maybe I shouldn't have, not like this. Just because I thought it doesn't mean I just have to blurt it out—"

Her increasingly hysterical babble was halted by Alex pulling off of the road and onto the shoulder. Maybe she was wrong—maybe she couldn't swim so well after all. She certainly couldn't breathe. He turned the car off, but she couldn't face him. She watched the cows standing in a field, munching grass as the sun shone on their backs.

"Can you look at me?" he asked. She heard the trace of amusement in his voice, and it steeled her spine. She gave him a haughty frown to combat his teasing tone. He reached out to take her hand and asked, "Say it again."

Lucy wasn't sure if she could get enough air into her lungs to actually speak. It was one thing to say it while he was focused on something else. But she was done running away.

"I think I'm in love with you."

"I *am* in love with you," he replied. Her heart fell like a water balloon thrown from a tall building. When it landed, it simply burst, and emotions scattered everywhere. She bit her lip to keep from crying. God, when had she become such a crier?

"You are?" she whispered. He put his palm to her cheek and used his thumb to release her lip from her teeth. "Yes. More than I ever thought possible."

She smiled and her heart picked itself up, put all of its pieces back together, and drummed happily, ecstatically, against her chest. "Say it again," she asked, feeling inexplicably shy.

"I am in love with you, Lucy. I love you," he replied easily, as if the words had always been waiting, right there on his tongue. She leaned forward and met his lips, which were already seeking hers, and undid her seatbelt at the same time. Wrapping her arms around him, she felt his hands grip her sides and yank her toward him. She couldn't get close enough to him with the console between them. Kissing him, knowing that he loved her, made her want him more—need him more. Those tears she had tried to keep back tumbled. Just a couple, but she tasted them as their mouths met over and over again and he whispered the words.

"Alex," she said, pulling back only slightly. His hands were gripping her head, holding it close to his. His breathing was ragged and hers was shallow. He tried to kiss her again, but she put her hand up between them. "Wait. I'm done thinking."

"What?" he asked, giving a half laugh.

"I'm done thinking," she repeated, enjoying his look of confusion. It seemed perfectly fair given the way he baffled her with his kindness, his humor, and now, his love.

"I love you. I don't just think I do," she finally said. He grinned down at her. "Took you long enough," he said against her lips.

LATER, as the moon sent streaks of light through the bedroom window, Alex kissed the underside of Lucy's jaw and breathed in the sweet smell of her soap. He pressed a kiss to her neck, adoring the way she stretched and sighed contentedly. He didn't think he would stop smiling anytime soon. He ran his hand over the smooth curve of her waist, her soft stomach, up and over her breasts, and cupped her jaw, turning her face toward him. She smiled, shifting her body so they were face-to-face.

"I guess this means we're going steady, huh?" she joked, pressing her lips to his. When she would have pulled back, he held her and continued kissing her, wondering if he would ever get enough. How was it possible to feel this much for one person?

"I think I still have my jacket from high school. Do you want to wear it?" he asked between teasing her lips.

"It's getting too warm for jackets. I was thinking I would just write our initials in a heart on the side of the school," she replied, pushing at his chest until he was on his back. He gripped her hips as she lay on top of him, looking down at him, her hair falling around her face, brushing his shoulders. She nuzzled

his neck, under his jaw, then trailed her way up to his ear, placing soft, playful kisses along his skin. He had never wanted anyone like this and knew that he never would again. She shifted, purposely, making it more difficult to be playful.

"That would work. You do that, and I'll make you a mixed CD with sappy love songs on it. You could play it over and over and drive your family nuts," he offered.

His breath snagged when he felt her teeth graze his neck. He was done playing. Gripping her and moving swiftly, he shifted their positions so he was over her.

"That's good. I like that one. I've never..." she trailed off. Raising his eyebrows, he waited. "You've never?"

She bit the inside of her cheek, making him curious. He

leaned in and nibbled on her lip before tracing his tongue over it.

"I've never ... gone steady or, you know... The love stuff. I might mess it up," she mumbled, keeping her eyes on his chin. He was humbled by her admission and overwhelmed by this gift.

"You won't. *We* won't. We might not get everything right, but the love stuff will take care of itself. There's only a couple of rules," he told her, happy when her eyes lifted to meet his.

"Rules?"

"Mmmhmm," he murmured, moving slowly against her, kissing her softly. "You have to say it every day."

"Okay," she replied, her breath accelerating slightly. "I can do that."

"You should be naked when you say it," he continued. She laughed, her hands moving restlessly over him. "So now would be a good time?"

"Actually, there's no bad time. It's just better when you're naked," he told her with a wide grin. Her hands trailed down his back, making him lose his own train of thought.

"Have you ... said it a lot?" she questioned, and his heart twisted at the smallness of her voice.

"I've said it," he admitted. He would always be honest with her. "But I have never felt it like this for anyone. Only you. You've had my heart since I was twelve years old."

Her eyes were damp as she beamed up at him. "That doesn't count," she said, laughing.

"I've loved you for more than half of my life. That counts."

"I said it first," she reminded him. He laughed and closed his mouth over hers. "That counts, too. More than you know."

Lucy groaned a little when Alex shifted in the bed. Her arm was around his waist, and he was pushing it away. "Don't," she grumbled. He gave a soft, muffled laugh and kissed her lightly.

"I heard something. Move your hand sleepyhead," he said. Her eyes launched open in the darkness. His face was close, and she could make out the features she'd memorized in the soft moonlight that came through the cracks in the blinds.

"Heard what?" she whispered, heart hammering.

"I don't know. That's why I need you to move your arm," he replied, also in a whisper. "You're going to leave me here?"

"Honey, I'm just going to look out the window. I'll be right back," he replied, moving off of the bed and leaving the cool air in his space. He pulled on his shorts, which he'd dug out earlier when they decided they had better eat something. Lucy was surprised that they had slept so soundly. She rubbed her eyes and scooted herself into a sitting position. Alex opened his side table and took out his gun. Lucy straightened, coming fully awake.

"You're taking your gun?" she squeaked.

"Just stay here. Everything is fine," Alex assured her and walked from the room.

Lucy looked around, her eyes adjusted to the darkness, and saw that it was almost three-thirty a.m. She hadn't been home yet. She and Alex had barely surfaced from his bedroom to eat. She knew her family wouldn't be worried, but now, thinking about someone prowling around, concern for them had her wondering if she should get up. She also had to pee, but she was too nervous to move.

"Alex knows what he's doing. He's very good at his job," she told herself, shivering.

"Yes, he does and he is," Alex agreed, coming back into the room and making Lucy squeal. Alex laughed and put his gun back in the bedside drawer. "You scared the hell out of me," Lucy spat, getting out of the bed.

"Where are you going? I didn't mean to scare you," he soothed, reaching for her.

He ran his warm palms up and down her skin, pushing the thin strap of her tank top back onto her shoulder. "There's no one outside. Nothing that I can see. The street is quiet. Get back in bed," he yawned.

"I have to pee," she said, then, when he laughed, she added, "Why is that funny?"

"It's not. Just, it's a good thing I heard something so you could get up and pee. Do you want me to come stand guard?"

"Shut up," she suggested, walking toward the bathroom.

When she returned, he was kneeling on the window seat, looking through the cracks of the blinds. "I thought you said everything was quiet," she whispered, coming up beside him.

"It is. I was just checking from here. Want me to carry you to bed?"

"You're a real comedian in the middle of the night," she commented then laughed loudly when he dramatically scooped her up into his arms. "Yes. But that's top secret. Only the woman I love can know that."

She laughed as he tumbled them both down onto the bed. She knew they were being silly, like lust-filled teens, but even in high school, she had never felt this carefree, this full of hope and possibility. If the price of that was some cutesy banter, it was definitely a worthwhile bargain.

CHAPTER FIFTEEN

Alex whistled as he strode through the parking lot toward the back of the sheriff's office. The sun had risen over the Messabi Range, which the locals called Giant Mountain, only forty minutes ago. Alex felt ready to conquer crime and fight bad guys. He laughed to himself as he unlocked the back door and went through. More than likely, his day would be conquering paperwork, arranging schedules, and returning phone calls.

"Morning," Cam greeted when Alex walked into the small back room that mostly served as a lunchroom. Cam, his uniform perfectly pressed, was making himself a cup of tea, and Alex was in such a great mood he didn't even feel the need to razz him about it. Cam still lived with his mom, and the guys often gave him a hard time about her cutting his hair military style, pressing his clothes, and making his lunches.

"Good morning, Deputy Stevens," Alex replied. After unzipping his jacket, Alex hung it on the wall in the break room and noted Cam's arched eyebrows. Being the new guy, Cam didn't comment on Alex's obvious good mood. Mick would have called him on it in a second.

"Everything quiet so far?" Alex asked. Cam picked up his tea, sipped it, and followed Alex out to the front where Elliot Peters was sorting files at his desk. Elliot had been working as a police officer in Angel's Lake for five years. He was a good cop—quiet and thorough.

"Been deader than a cemetery, Sir," Cam replied.

"Quit calling me sir, Cam. Morning Elliot," Alex said.

"Hey. How are you, Sheriff?" Elliot asked, picking up a ridiculously large cup of coffee and taking a long swallow. The only person at the station who liked coffee more than Alex was Elliot.

"I'm good. We've been missing each other on shifts. Things alright?"

Alex came around the counter, glanced at the files Elliot was reading through—cold cases that he couldn't let go of—and picked up a stack of messages, blessedly written on message pads. He thumbed through them and glanced at Elliot, who tossed down the file he held and scrubbed his hands over his weathered face. With somewhat shaggy hair and a goatee he was a little too proud of, Elliot seemed more like a dark-haired surfer than a cop. But he had cop eyes that noticed details and paid close attention.

"Good. Gina didn't show to pick the kids up last night and it was a long one. Both girls are having nightmares lately. But mostly, things are good," Elliot answered. Elliot and his ex-wife, Gina, shared custody of their five-year-old twin daughters. Mostly, Elliot did all the work, and Gina popped in when it suited her to take on her *share*. Elliot rose with his coffee cup and clapped Alex on the back. "Saw your dad last night. Waved to him, but I guess he didn't see me. Looked right at me and ducked into his house."

Alex stopped looking through the messages and glanced up. "My dad's out of town." Elliot shrugged and walked past, saying, "He must be home. It was him."

Cam tuned the radio to a classic rock station and sat down at his own desk. Alex frowned at Elliot's retreating back and started for his office. He turned, looking at Cam.

"Dolores still out of town?" he questioned. Cam looked up and nodded. "Said she'd be back by Saturday. She's having a good time with her family."

Alex took his messages to his office and tried to shake the snake of annoyance that had slithered into his morning. Why would his dad be back early? Had he imagined sparks between his dad and Dolores? *Sometimes it's better not to know.* He opened the blinds and the window in his office.

Putting a French Silk coffee into his machine, he sorted his messages by order of priority. He needed to contact a lawyer that was calling him as a witness, the mayor wanted to meet, and a reporter called to ask about the vandalism and get a statement. He pulled the last message from the pile and looked at it. *Stacey Whitman Traverse Moore.* Did she think that Alex would forget who she was if she didn't leave her full name? He had no plans to return his mother's phone call. Wadding the paper, he tossed it into his trash bin and willed the coffee to hurry up.

Lucy jammed the last of her clothes into the washer

and hoped it didn't explode. Kate came up the stairs as Lucy pressed start and exited the laundry room. The sun was slanting through the sunroof, casting diagonal spotlights over the hardwood floor and banister. Little specks of dust danced in the light.

"Hey. How was New York?" Kate asked, backpack on her shoulder and laptop case slung over her chest.

"It was really fun. I have the most amazing art pieces from Lola's gallery. Plus, I was able to pick up the travel vouchers and a few other little things. How was class?" Lucy, clad in pajama bottoms and a tank top, followed Kate to her bedroom where she unloaded her bags.

"Four more. Of this one, anyway. Four more weeks in total. Then I am a college graduate," Kate said without enthusiasm. Lucy bit her lip, uncertain if she should bring up the internship. Kate unzipped her hoodie and hung it behind her door. Crossing the room, she yanked out her hair tie and tossed the elastic onto her busy desk.

"Speaking of which," Lucy said, taking a chance, "I have a unique graduation present for you." Kate smiled over her shoulder as she dug out running clothes.

"Is it money?"

"No. It's something money can't buy," Lucy teased. She pulled a book off of Kate's shelf: *Fangirl* by someone named Rainbow. She held it up and asked, "This any good? Who names their kid Rainbow?"

Kate laughed and walked into her small, walk-in closet. "Someone who sees the best in all situations or knows that things will turn out bright. That book is one of the best I've ever read. Actually, it's about a relationship between sisters.

How even when you need them, they can be really annoying."

Lucy read the jacket flap and smiled. "That rule must apply just to younger sisters. I'm borrowing this. Do you want to know your gift or not?" Kate came out of the closet dressed to run. "Yes," she said.

"It's an internship at Posh Fashion. With Kael Makhai," Lucy blurted, unable to keep the excitement off of her face. Kate continued to stand there, her face blank, as if she was waiting for Lucy to tell her the punch line.

"What did you do?" she finally whispered. Kate shook her head, her face pale. Lucy's heart stalled and then rebooted in high gear. She set the book on the bed and moved toward Kate.

"Kael Makhai. He's won Fashion Designer of the Year three times. We don't even know anyone who can afford to buy his clothes. Kate, this is huge. I know you didn't want me to say anything, but—"

"Stop. Stop talking," Kate snapped, shaking her head more vigorously. Kate began pacing the length of her room. She walked to her desk, and Lucy saw her close her eyes and inhale deeply several times.

"Kate. I know you want this," Lucy whispered, unease tickling her skin.

"Of course I want this. Who wouldn't want this?" she demanded as she whirled and stalked up to Lucy. "But I can't have it. Which is why I put it aside. And now you're throwing it in my face and calling it a gift."

"Everything okay girls?" Julie poked her head in the room. Both girls flinched and turned her way.

"Everything is fine, mom," Kate assured, her voice even, as though it hadn't been laced with accusation and anger only seconds ago.

"Are you trying to make your sister do your chores again, Lucy?" Julie joked. Lucy wasn't in the mood to walk down memory lane and be reminded of how she used to con Kate into making her bed and cleaning her room.

"Yes. Because I'm still twelve," Lucy snapped, immediately regretting her words. "Don't take it out on her," Kate said, giving Lucy an icy glare.

"Girls, what is going on?" Julie asked. She came into the room. Her brown hair was tied back loosely to the side. She wore a thin, flowing sweater that was slightly longer in the back over a pair of black leggings. She looked very earthy, and Lucy's fingers twitched for her camera.

"Nothing mom. I was just borrowing a book from Kate," Lucy said, picking up the book off of the bed. She looked at Kate. "I thought maybe I had one she would like. I was wrong."

Kate crossed her arms over her chest and looked down as Lucy walked past. Julie stopped her with a hand on her waist, and Lucy placed a kiss on her mom's cheek.

"You look really pretty, mom," she said quietly.

"Thank you, sweetheart. I'm going to make some lunch. Do you want some?"

"Nah. I'm not hungry."

Julie looked back and forth between her girls, assessing them with that mothering eye, her hand holding Lucy still. "Me neither," Kate claimed.

"I have some errands to run, and then Char is bringing

the kids over. Do you need anything?" Lucy asked to the room in general.

"I have some items I need from the store. Your dad was going to go, but this will save him the trip. He's monitoring exams, so I'm sure he'd appreciate it," Julie answered. Lucy nodded and looked back at Kate, who was still looking at the floor.

"I was going to do some yoga. The breathing and calming poses are very good for restoring your balance and energy. Do you want to join me?" Julie asked, looking back and forth between them, ever the peacemaker. Lucy gave her mom a one-sided smile.

"How about later? We could do it on the porch?" Lucy suggested, using her own ability to assess. The porch was certainly big enough, and most of it was covered and screened. Studying her mother's face carefully, she noted that her jaw tightened, her lips opened, closed, and then drew into a firm line.

"Actually, I have a DVD I use, so I need to do it in the living room," Julie said, looking at Kate. Lucy bit her lip. Something made a steady pinging noise in

the washer. "Okay. Sure," Lucy agreed. Her heart ached as she looked at both women—neither of whom she could help. She shook her head slightly and left the room. She was pretty sure she could handle the laundry without messing things up, so she figured, for now, she'd stick with things she understood.

When the call came in for a two-car accident about twenty minutes from town, in the general vicinity of his father's house, Alex told Cam and Elliot he would cover it.

He left through the front of the station, grabbed one of the three department cruisers sitting in the lot, and made his way to the town's edge. Drumming his fingers on the steering wheel as he drove, he tried to think of why his dad would come home early. Why it was bothering him that he had. Something wasn't sitting right. He'd just drop by and ask Chuck how his time at the cabin was after he dealt with the accident that he already knew had no serious injuries.

"Ah, boss?" Cam's voice crackled through the radio. Alex shook his head at the deputy's ability to make him feel like he was ancient. "Yes, Cam?" Alex answered back.

"You—uh ... well, you know—"

"Spit it out, kid!" Mick's voice boomed through the radio instead, making Alex chuckle. "What's up, Mick? And what are you doing there? It's your day off," Alex said.

"I picked up some supplies for the lunchroom and was dropping them off. You know someone's done some shitty artwork on your truck?" Mick asked, breaking into a fit of coughing.

"What? What are you talking about?"

Alex pressed the button to lower the window, letting the fresh air and smell of trees push out the stale air and mingling scents of cigarettes and sweat. "Your passenger door. I parked beside you, was bringing in a couple cases of soda. There's a bunch of squiggles and shit all over the door," Mick replied. Alex tightened his grip on the steering wheel, then banged his fist on it.

"No. I did not know that," he ground out. *The noises last night.* "Listen, I've got to deal with this accident report first. I need to swing by my dad's. Take pictures for me, okay? I'll be back within a couple of hours."

Mick agreed, and as Alex pulled up on the accident site, he tried to get his head focused on one annoyance at a time. Two teens were leaning against the hood of a white Honda Civic. A girl with long, loose braids leaned on a boy's shoulder. Beside them, another girl with hair darker than the asphalt was pacing back and forth, texting on her cell phone. Alex sighed as he pulled the cruiser up beside them. *One thing at a time.*

Lucy glanced over at Julie, who was bouncing the baby in her arms and cooing something unintelligible. Carmen was staring intensely at the cards in her hand while Lucy watched in amusement. They were on the carpeted floor of the living room. Jake and his Neverland Pirates were singing a song that Lucy knew would be stuck in her head later. Carmen eyed Lucy over her cards.

"Do you have any fours?" she asked.

"Go fish," Lucy said, unable to stop the smile. Carmen sat ramrod straight and puckered her lips. With her brows drawn, she looked serious and older. She picked up a card from the scatter of them on the floor and gave Lucy a toothy grin, looking her age again.

"Success!" Carmen laid down her pair.

"Cookies are almost ready," Julie said between trying to make Mia laugh, or at least smile.

"I was thinking we could go for a walk after we have a snack. Your mom brought the stroller. We could take your sister," Lucy suggested to Carmen. She looked over at her mom. "What do you say, Grandma?"

"Grandma doesn't like to go outside," Carmen said. Lucy and Julie both whipped their heads toward Carmen. Looking back at her mom, Lucy saw that her cheeks had reddened. Lucy felt bad for continuously pushing but was happy that the obvious had been said by someone who likely wouldn't receive Julie's anger.

"That's not entirely true," Julie said quietly, bringing Mia over and handing her down to Lucy. Lucy took smiling Mia into her arms and kissed her forehead. Julie sat down beside Carmen, who hid her cards.

"Don't look, Grandma. And mommy and Auntie Kate say that you don't like outside. But that's okay. I don't like it that much, either," Carmen said. "What about the park?" Lucy asked, trying to take the heat off of her mother, even though she'd intentionally thrown it at her.

"There are a lot of germs at the park. But I like the swings. It's your turn, Aunt Lucy," Carmen stated.

The buzzer for the cookies sounded and Lucy could smell the warm chocolate. Her stomach growled at the same time Mia began to fuss.

"We'll put the park aside for another day then," Lucy said, looking at her mom and seeking forgiveness with a small smile. Julie nodded and rose to grab the

cookies.

By the time Char and Luke picked Carmen and Mia up, Lucy had lost at Go Fish four times, eaten six cookies, and been spit up on twice. Char looked tired when she shuffled in through the back door of the Aarons' house. Carmen continued to focus on the cards, even when Char kneeled down next to her.

"Hey. How's my favorite five-year-old?" Char asked.

Luke kissed Julie's cheek when he came into the kitchen where they had been sitting. Lucy's family was fond of food, so they generally ended up in the kitchen.

"I'm almost six," Carmen said.

Char smiled. "True. Say hi to daddy." Carmen tried to shuffle the deck. "Hi daddy."

"Hey sweet girl," Luke said, kissing Carmen noisily and coming to steal Mia from Lucy's arms. "Hi other sweet girl." Lucy put a hand to her chest and tilted her head in jest. "Aw, Luke, you're so nice. Oh, did you mean Mia?"

"Nah. You're kinda cute too," he said.

"How did everything go?" Julie asked. She had been typing something while Carmen drew pictures and Lucy cuddled Mia. Luke and Charlotte exchanged a glance.

"It was good. We found out a lot of helpful information," Char said cautiously, her eyes not leaving Luke's. Luke shook his head, a seemingly frustrated gesture, and began to pack up the girls' bags.

"We can discuss it another time," Julie offered, closing her laptop.

"Yeah," Char agreed, looking from her mother to Lucy. "How's it going with Sheriff Hottie?"

"Nice," Luke snorted.

"Shut up," Lucy replied.

"Shut up isn't a nice thing to say. I'm not allowed," said Carmen.

The adults laughed, which startled Mia and saved Lucy from having to answer.

Alex was greeted by two smells when he let himself

into his house. Something burning and toast. Furball met him at the door and brushed his legs.

"Hi there. Do we have company? Is she hot?" Alex asked, bending down to pick up the cat. He carried him into the kitchen, where he found Lucy standing at the sink, washing her hands. Her hair was loose and flowing down her back. It looked a little damp, as though she'd just gotten out of the shower, and he felt a stab of regret that he'd missed out. She was wearing an almost see-through T-shirt and a pair of cropped pants. Her feet were bare, and he could see her toes were brightly colored. Watching her in his home, knowing she loved him, uncurled a need and tenderness in him that he hadn't known was lying dormant in his heart. It scared him to think that she could become—could already be—everything to him.

"She is hot," he murmured to Furball.

"Hey," she greeted, turning off the tap and grabbing a hand towel from his stove. Two plates sat on the island counter, laden with toast and scrambled eggs, which didn't look burnt.

"Hey yourself," he said, rooted to his spot, unable to do more than just smile at her. She came to him, pet the cat, then reached up on tiptoes to kiss his lips. He leaned in and took the sweet greeting she offered. He put the cat down and pulled Lucy in for more, enjoying the feel of her arms winding around his neck, the feel of her breath on his face, and the weight of her body leaning against him.

"You made breakfast," he murmured.

"Dinner. Well, breakfast for dinner. I warned you I could only handle eggs."

"There's toast."

She laughed.

"Yes, and toast. Though I burnt the first slices."

"I like eggs and toast," he said, taking the kiss deeper, until he felt her sink against him; into him.

"Did you have a good day?" she asked, pulling away and grabbing the two glasses of milk she had poured. Other than the tagging, paperwork, missing her, and not being able to check in with Chuck, he figured it wasn't a bad day. Alex took the plates, charmed to see that she had already set the small table by his kitchen window with cutlery and napkins.

"I should have been more thorough in my check last night when I thought I heard something," he said, sitting across from her. She took a long swallow of milk—almost half the glass—and he arched his eyebrow. She shrugged sheepishly and set her glass down.

"Why?"

"My truck was tagged. The idiot painted up the passenger door. Mick noticed it when he parked beside me at the station," Alex told her, taking a large mouthful of eggs.

"Do you think it's the same person? Or people, I guess it could be."

"Definitely. There's a symbol on all of the tagging that my dad and I noticed, and it's on my truck."

"Hmm. What's the symbol?"

"Some heart thing. I'll show you after dinner. Which is good, by the way," he said. "Yeah, my talents know no bounds," she answered and took another bite of her eggs. "I agree." He winked at her, making her laugh.

"I watched my nieces today. It was fun. Tiring and somewhat humiliating when I lost at Go Fish repeatedly, but fun."

"Go Fish is a tough one."

"Shut up. Oops, Carmen told us 'shut up' was not nice to say," she said, laughing while pulling the crusts off of her toast.

"She's not wrong. Just wait until she finds out there's worse. Where were Luke and Char?" he asked, taking her crusts and popping them into his mouth.

"They went to a meeting about autism. Char seemed to think it was good, but Luke seemed kind of reserved about it. We didn't get a lot of details, but I'm glad they're realizing that they'll need help with Carmen."

"Can't be easy. Admitting that something might be wrong with your child. Facing that must be breaking them a bit," Alex said quietly.

"I think it is. But if they don't face it, what good does it do Carmen? Or them? She's still their little girl. It doesn't change that or how much they love her. It just helps them find the best way to support her," Lucy returned, finishing up her last bite of eggs.

"True. All true. But it still must be hard. Did you tell Kate about the internship?" Lucy groaned and rose from the table, clearing her place.

"That bad?" Alex followed her with his plate and glass. Furball meowed at their feet. While Alex loaded the dishwasher, Lucy grabbed the cat food out of his pantry and shook some into the cat dish, earning Furball's everlasting adoration.

"She was seriously pissed."

"That seems weird."

"It's occurring to me that my family is a bit weird. I thought I was the only one," she remarked, and Alex laughed loud.

"Did you think you cornered the market on strange? I don't even think you *are* that strange. You seem pretty normal to me, and so do the rest of the Aarons'. You're all pretty good in my book," he said, still laughing. He saw her face tighten when she turned from the pantry.

"I'm not just like them. I'm ... missing pieces of what makes them, *them*."

He didn't like the sound of her voice when she spoke as though she were on the outside looking in—her tone was vacant, far away. He walked over and took her hand, pulled her into his arms, and hugged her, happy that she returned the embrace immediately.

"Kate's probably just in shock. Give it some time. And from where I'm standing, I think you have the best parts of all of them," he said, trying to reassure her.

"Not all of them," she murmured into his chest. He kissed the top of her head. "What does that mean, Luce?"

She shook her head, leaned back and looked up into his eyes. Hers were clouded and he wished he could clear them. He wanted to tell her everything would be okay, but how could he know for sure?

"Nothing. It doesn't matter. Right now, all that matters is this. Us."

"Oh yeah? I like the sound of that."

"Surprisingly, so do I. I didn't see this—see you—coming."

"Sometimes the things most worth having are the things we aren't prepared for. If it helps, I didn't plan on you, either." He kissed her lips, then trailed his mouth to her chin, bending his knees to scoop her up against him.

"But you love me anyway?"

"I really do. I love you. I don't think I'll ever get tired of telling you," he whispered against her ear. He felt the small shiver go through her body, and his own body tightened with need for her. She kissed his neck and ran her hands over his chest—restless, needy. Her fingers moved quickly, tugging at his buttons. Alex pushed her hair off her neck, touching his lips to the spot that made her sigh. His hands touched and explored, lowering over the curve of her hips, greedy to pull her as close as possible.

"I'll never get tired of hearing it, either," he encouraged. He felt her smile against the skin of his chest.

"I love you," she whispered, walking backward, leading him through the kitchen. He smiled at the sly smirk on her face and the way her eyes danced in the dim light of his house. "I love you," she repeated, then turned and ran toward his room. He did what he'd been doing since he was twelve—he followed Lucy, heart on his sleeve. Only this time, hers was there, too.

CHAPTER SIXTEEN

"Okay. If this is a regular occurrence for you, I will happily become a photographer," Kate said, a swooning lilt to her voice as Sam, Luke, and a two of Alex's deputies joked around, shirtless. Lucy had asked them to toss a football around for now, to lighten up and relax. None of them were particularly shy, except maybe Cam, but it still wasn't common practice for guys to meet up and take off their shirts.

Lucy and Kate were both enjoying the view, however. She had received permission to use one of the empty rooms at the town hall for the day. It was open, with good light coming through the wall of wide, long windows. Kate had grumbled about helping her set up the lighting Lucy had also borrowed.

"Worth carrying some lights?" Lucy joked, clicking from a distance, trying to let the boys have their fun. They were teasing Cam about his lack of chest hair, and Lucy almost felt bad for him, but the slightly embarrassed smile on his face was making for some great shots.

"I'll say. Poor Cam. He's so sweet," Kate crooned.

"He's also quite cute. Even without chest hair. He's your age, right?"

"Hmm. Yes. We graduated together. I think the surprise of the day is Elliot. Those are some serious abs he's got going on."

"Alex says he's got two little girls," Lucy commented, moving in a little closer.

"Maybe he does sit-ups while lifting them," replied Kate. "Luce? We about done here?" Luke called.

Elliot shot the football right at him, but Luke looked in time to catch it.

"What's the matter, Davis? Too much work for you? You should get him a calculator, Lucy. Maybe a desk," Elliot goaded him good naturedly. In return, Luke, good-naturedly, suggested where Elliot could put a calculator.

"You should just get rid of these clowns. I've got all you need, Lucy," Sam told her, flexing his appealing, muscled arms. Toned and defined described most of the men, like they spent their free time playing sports or staying active. Only Elliot looked like he put effort into sculpting his body, but not in an overdone way.

"I leave you alone for one morning, and I find you with a roomful of half-naked men," Alex said from the doorway, getting Lucy's attention. She smiled at the sight of him. He had needed to go to court that morning to testify and, as such, was dressed in a dark navy suit with a lighter blue tie. His hair was brushed to the side a little, making him seem both sexy and boyish. Her heart flip-flopped. She was turning into an absolute sap.

"She's probably just bored with your lack of skill, Whitman," Sam said.

"I hope she's not looking your way then," Alex replied easily. The guys laughed.

"Okay, water break, I guess. Then we'll slick you boys up with some oil and get the good shots," Lucy said. "Oh! I want that job!" Kate jumped up and down a little while all five of the guys gaped at Lucy.

"Wow. I should take a picture of the look on all your faces right now," she said, and did before telling them, "I'm joking about the oil. Relax."

Alex walked to her and kissed her lightly, his grin playful. He tugged on a lock of her hair that had fallen out of the loose bun she'd made at the back of her head.

"I don't think I like your job," he said quietly, humor lacing his tone.

"I know. It's tough, but I'm muddling through," she replied. "How was court?"

"Fine. Everything went as expected. So do I get a private photo shoot later?"

"Hmm. I'm not sure. Can I make you pose any way I want to?"

He arched an eyebrow, pretending to consider it. "Will the photographer be naked?"

"Unlikely."

"Then no."

"I'm trying to eat here," Kate muttered, a pile of potato chips in her hand and a few in her mouth. Alex snagged one and shoved it in his mouth. "Sorry. Didn't know there were little ears around," Alex said, earning a smack from Kate.

"Okay, enough. I need to get these shots, then I want to do individuals," Lucy said, laughing.

Alex went to chat with the guys for a few minutes while Lucy got Kate to help her set up a dark backdrop. She'd found an old wooden chair. She wanted simple. She was also going to see if any of the men wanted to advertise along with the calendar. A small caption with their photo would give them extra business and, hopefully, the town a little extra cash.

"You seem different," Kate commented, looking at her as she pulled down the dark screen. "Different how?"

"Like both of your feet are firmly planted in one place," Kate said carefully. "That's because they are. Maybe you should cut me some slack."

"I just thought you'd be gone by now. You're always gone by now."

"Maybe I didn't have the right reason to stay," Lucy commented, then realized what she'd said. She saw the hurt flash across Kate's face, but it was replaced immediately with a blank nod.

"Fair enough."

"Kate. That is not what I mean. It's complicated. I always thought it was better for everyone if I was somewhere else," Lucy tried to explain quietly. The guys were still laughing and eating the snacks she and Kate had put out for them.

"That's stupid. You belong here. With your family. And, I guess, with Alex."

"It took me some time to realize that. I wasn't ready before, but right now, there's nowhere else I want to be. I think I needed to go all of the places I went to find where I belonged," Lucy said, more to herself than Kate. Kate walked back to the small cooler bag she had brought and took out a water, offering Lucy one as well. Lucy sat on one of the upside down crates and took another chance.

"Kate. Holding yourself back will never help you find the place you're meant to be."

Kate drank her water, her dark eyes seeming far away. Recapping the bottle, she turned another crate upside down and sat carefully, testing its strength.

"It's not that easy, Luce. Mom and Dad paid for my education. They wanted me to go to school and not have to worry about working. I can't repay them by saying, 'Oops, made a mistake. I don't want to be a social worker. I want to be a designer.' It just doesn't feel right. How can I tell them that they wasted money they didn't have on me?"

A part of Lucy was happy to know that she hadn't been completely off about Kate's unspoken desires. While she might not have been here physically, she kept in contact with her family, frequently checking in via whatever modes were available. She hated feeling like maybe she didn't know Kate as well as she thought. It made her feel guilty, like the time away had affected more than just herself—which of course, it had. She had been naïve, and perhaps a little self-absorbed, to think that it wouldn't. Knowing that Kate wanted something that Lucy felt like she could give her meant that she could start mending fences that she hadn't realized were becoming weathered.

"Education is never a waste of money," Lucy said gently, taking Kate's hand. "It is if you don't have the money."

"Mom and Dad have the money," Lucy countered. With their dad having tenure at the university and their mother putting out anywhere from one to three books a year, Lucy had always known her family to be financially comfortable. Even when economic times had taken a hit, people still went to university, and they still bought books. Kate closed her eyes briefly and shook her head. She pulled her hand back from Lucy's.

"No. They don't, Lucy. When you stay in one place for longer than a week, you'll find things aren't always what they seem," Kate said, standing and moving away from Lucy.

Lucy stared after her, puzzled and frustrated by her sister's continued references to her staying power. It was starting to wear on her nerves. "You okay, honey?" Alex asked, walking toward her. She looked up, standing too fast and swayed a little.

"Okay, seriously," Alex said, steadying Lucy with his hand on her arm. "Are you okay?"

"Yes," Lucy said and then laughed lightly. "Just stood too quick." He continued to watch her for a moment, his hands tight on her shoulders. She still felt light-headed, but didn't him to worry, so she stepped into him and put her arms around his waist.

"I'm fine." Lucy hoped it was true, but right at that moment, she didn't feel that way.

Alex popped the top off of a couple of beers and passed one to his dad. "Thanks for helping me with this," he said, taking a drink of his own.

"Happy to. It still feels a little strange to have you working on your own house. You got a good deal here," Chuck said. They picked up their beers and headed toward the back deck. Alex could have easily stripped and stained the deck himself, but inviting his dad over served more than one purpose. Still early afternoon, Alex had taken the rest of the day off after he'd testified in court that morning. He had to drop his truck off to be painted, which still pissed him off, but the guys had the station covered and he had some questions he needed answered.

"I'm happy here. I knew I wanted to buy a house, but I didn't think I'd enjoy fixing it up so much," Alex said, grabbing the large pail of deck stripper. "You and Sam did a hell of a job on that kitchen. I'm thinking of redoing the kitchen at the cabin. Needs some updating," Chuck replied. *Perfect opening.*

"How was the cabin?" Alex asked. Chuck set his beer down on the rail and shrugged. Alex opened the deck stripper and poured some into two paint trays. "It was good. Nice to relax. Caught a couple fish. Released them. You know what the cabin is like," Chuck replied, opening the package of nylon brushes.

"When did you get back?" Alex asked. He wanted to know if his dad would lie to him to his face. The thought of it made his stomach turn. Chuck met Alex's eyes as he accepted the paint tray his son passed him.

"I told you. Last night."

Alex held his stare, but Chuck didn't flinch—didn't shift his eyes or his weight. He looked Alex dead in the eye and lied. And that realization struck Alex harder than if Chuck had physically hit him. The air in his lungs was replaced by an unexpected fury.

"Oh, right. You did say that. Must have forgot," Alex said, his words clipped. He moved to one side of the deck, tray in hand, and began to brush the stain on the peeling strips of wood. They painted in silence on opposite sides of the deck. Alex felt the warmth of the day through his T-shirt as he tried to focus on covering all of the worn parts of the beams. *Why would he lie?* Slapping stain in wide strokes, he moved back on his knees to cover more ground.

"You keep slopping that around, it's not going to rinse off properly," Chuck commented from a similar crouch on the other side. Alex said nothing and continued to apply it his way. He wasn't good with games. He hated them.

"Elliot saw you two nights ago. Said he waved to you, and you ignored him and rushed into your house," Alex said, putting the brush down and turning so he faced his dad. His knees were aching in his crouch, but he stayed where he was, forearms resting on his jean-clad legs. Chuck's mouth scrunched up, the only sign that he had heard Alex. Placing his brush down with exaggerated care, he rose and looked down at his son.

There had been times growing up that Alex had hated his dad with a teen's jaded view, but for as long as he could remember, Chuck had been straight with him. Or so he'd thought. Feeling like his legs were going to cramp into the position permanently and not liking the height difference, Alex rose to face his dad.

"You got something to say?" Chuck asked. "I think I just said it."

"Parents don't answer to their children. I'm entitled to have a life of my own," Chuck said, his shoulders stiff and his eyes hard. "Having a life of your own includes lying to me?"

"Lying and not giving you the details of my private life are two different things." Alex shook his head. He walked to where he'd left his beer and took a long swallow. Slamming the bottle back onto the railing, he chose his words carefully.

"I don't see those two things differently if whatever is happening in your private life makes it necessary for you to lie to me," Alex told him. Chuck looked out over Alex's back lawn, recently trimmed and edged with trees. Alex pictured backyard BBQs with friends and family, which is what had gotten him started on the deck in the first place.

"It's nothing that concerns you. When I'm ready to talk about it, you'll know," Chuck said with less heat. His shoulders dropped a bit, and Alex had the quickest flash of recognition that his dad was older. He never saw him that way, but the look on his face right this minute showed his age, and Alex didn't care for it.

"Until then, you'll just lie when it suits you," Alex replied. He leaned back against the railing and shoved his hands into his pockets so he wasn't tempted to toss his beer bottle against the side of the house.

"Every now and again, you remind me so much of her. God, you're stubborn. Just like she was. Once you think something, there's no swaying you. Your way or no way." Chuck pulled his keys from his pocket and tossed them lightly in his hand.

"See, now, that's funny. I've always appreciated how different you are from her. But right now, your parenting styles seem to match perfectly. Lying, evasion, and to complete the hat trick, I bet you're going to leave," Alex replied coldly. Anger skittered up his spine and made him want to lash out. *What the hell is he hiding that is worth this fight?* Chuck's fist snapped tightly around his keys.

"You're right, I am. You need to get your head on straight, and if I stay any longer, I'm likely to smack it in the right direction. Not every person in your life is hiding some God-awful secret. Maybe everything isn't about you," Chuck said, his teeth clenched and his graying eyebrows drawn tight. "Wash this stain off before it dries, or you're going to ruin this deck."

With that, he shoved past Alex into the house. A moment later, Alex heard the front door slam. *That went well.* Sighing heavily, Alex picked up the paint brushes, itching to hurl them far and wide, and took them inside to clean. He'd do the deck another day. He wasn't feeling much like backyard BBQs or family get-togethers right now.

"Hey dad. Can I come in?" Lucy asked, knocking lightly on her dad's study door. He was sitting at his desk, grading papers. In his light grey cardigan with leather elbows, he looked every bit the college professor. His smile was warm and inviting, and his eyes focused on her the minute he heard her voice. She wondered how many of his students had crushes on him. Had he ever acted on any of them? She couldn't imagine it, but then, she liked to keep her head nestled in the sand rather than face reality sometimes. Preferably the sand of another continent.

"Of course you can. You don't need to ask," he said, leaning back in his leather chair. She moved into the room, lit by wide panes of glass and a gorgeous window seat like the one in Alex's bedroom. From this spot, she could see the side of Alex's house. Or would be able to if it hadn't grown dark. She'd waited until her mom had gone to bed to talk to her dad.

"You okay?" he asked, picking up his cup, which probably had some sort of herbal tea that her mother swore by.

"I'm alright. I'm good, actually," she replied honestly. She studied the wall of built in bookshelves. They were filled with history and political science books, family photographs, and family albums. On one shelf, there was a collection of miniature items that Lucy had sent or given him. She picked up the gold Eiffel Tower replica, smiling because he still had it after all of this time. Lucy placed it down between the tiny bust of Shakespeare and the six-inch Statue of Liberty.

"You still have all of these," she remarked when he came to stand beside her. He put his arm around her shoulder, pulling her into his side. She rested her head and wondered how it was that one person's arm could provide such an anchor—a feeling of safety, stability.

"I certainly do. For starters, I love them. I think every one of them is great," he told her, picking up the palm-size blue crane that was the South African national bird. "But also, as you well know, I'm a bit of a sap when it comes to my girls. I think I have every Father's Day card ever made by all three of you."

Lucy laughed, but it did nothing to ease the ache in her chest. Did he *really* feel no different toward her than the other girls? He'd never treated her differently, so why was it so hard to believe that?

"Dad, are you and Mom okay financially?" she asked. She hadn't meant to be so blunt. He looked surprised for a split second then dropped his hand from her shoulder and returned to where he'd left his tea.

"Why are you asking?" he countered, picking up his mug.

Because I checked mom's book sales, or lack thereof. Because she's had dismal releases for the last three books, and no one has mentioned it. Because she's stopped doing book signings and author visits. Because Kate is going into the wrong career just to please you.

"I'm just curious. I'm not a kid anymore. You can talk to me if you guys are in ... a tough spot. I've always just put my paycheck in the bank, except what I needed to travel or live. But I've never needed much—"

"Stop," he said in a tone that left no other option. "I realize that you make a considerable amount of money. I'm very proud of you for doing so well. But your mother and I have never needed help taking care of our family. I'm not sure why you think we do, but I can assure you, we are just fine."

"I wasn't trying to insult you, dad," she said, wishing she had pockets so she could shove her hands into them. He set his mug down, and by the time he walked over to her and pulled her into a hug, his face had softened.

"I know, sweetheart. There's nothing for you to worry about. We manage just fine when you're not here, and the fact that you're home doesn't change that," he replied.

Lucy frowned, easing out of the hug. "It's good to know that everyone does perfectly well when I'm not here. Perhaps I should go so I stop stirring things up and trying to change things." He hadn't meant anything by it, but she was tired of feeling like she had to defend herself. She started to walk out of the study.

"Lucy Marie Aarons. You come back here this minute," her father said. She would have laughed when she turned around, but the expression on his face was not one of humor. She stayed where she was but kept her eyes level with his. He stepped closer to her, so that her space was filled with the smell of lemon tea and Old Spice.

"We are fine when you're not here because we have no other choice, and I am not talking about finances. When you have a child that wants to roam the world, you have no choice but to accept it," he said, his tone both stern and wistful.

"Dad," she interrupted.

"I am not done. Make no mistake, we are fine when you

aren't here, but we are *better* when you are. All I meant was that you do not have to take it on your shoulders to come home and try to fix everyone's problems," he explained. Lucy's heart cracked when she realized that he had come as close to confessing that they *were* having problems as he ever would.

"But I *want* to. It's what you guys do for each other. It's what families do. If you guys are having trouble, I *want* to help. Let me help. Let me be part of this family the way everyone else is," she pleaded, her voice wavering. She put her hand on his arm.

"You are part of this family, Lucy. But remember, families also back off when someone asks them to. So unless you want to start answering some questions about your relationship with Alex, I'd quit while you're ahead," he said, but this time he smiled. He turned her gently, and they walked to the kitchen.

"That's totally different," she said.

"Not from my perspective. Families confide in each other is what you're saying, right? How about confiding to your dear old dad what your intentions with Alex are," Mark said and then laughed at the look on Lucy's face.

"Okay. You don't want my help? Fine. I'm going to bed," Lucy said. She backed away from her dad as he plugged in the kettle. "To your own bed?" he asked.

Every inch of her body turned red with embarrassment. Her parents didn't say much about her not spending nights in her room. Which, she realized, was a blessing.

"Goodnight, dad."

"Goodnight, dear. Let me know if you want to talk about anything," he said.

Lucy groaned audibly and took the stairs two at a time. *How did he turn that around so quickly?* In her room, she closed her bedroom door quietly and changed into pajamas. No reason to tell her dad that Alex was working through some issues with his own dad tonight. She was an adult—she didn't need to talk about her relationship. *And they don't need to talk about their personal issues.* Maybe some boundaries were a healthy thing. But Lucy didn't like the feeling that the boundaries for her were more visible than for her sisters. Like they kept her back just a little further. Obviously, Kate knew that they were having financial difficulties. As she pulled back the covers, she thought that Char probably knew as well. They didn't want to tell Lucy anything because they figured she'd be off on another trip soon. She plumped her pillow, wishing she were in Alex's bed, and lay down with a sigh. Her family was just going to have to get used to her sticking around. To her meddling. To her being a part of the good and the bad. If Lucy was beginning to deal with the idea that she might be staying for good rather than for now—then they would just have to do the same.

CHAPTER SEVENTEEN

Lucy grabbed an apple from the dish on the table as her mom came into the kitchen. Julie was dressed in a pink robe and fuzzy slippers, her hair piled on her head and her eyes still sleepy.

"Hi. You're up early," Julie said, yawning and heading straight for the coffee pot. "Yes. I'm setting up for some family photos I agreed to do. You remember Ginny?"

"Mmhmm. Sweet girl. She's just about due, isn't she?" Julie asked.

"Yes, so I want to get some pregnancy shots before she pops," Lucy said, taking another bite.

"Is that all you're having for breakfast?" Julie asked, grabbing two coffee cups from the cupboard. "Yes, mom," Lucy said in a monotone voice.

"Perhaps you should worry more about having a healthy breakfast than whether or not your mom and dad are doing okay," Julie suggested, her eyes more alert. Lucy felt a moment of awkwardness. She hadn't thought of her dad going right to her mom.

"Geez. You guys tell each other everything?"

"Yes. It's called marriage, honey," Julie said with a smile.

Don't say it. Don't ask. It's in the past, and it doesn't matter. Let it go. Trying to wrangle her thoughts, she grabbed a bottle of water from the fridge.

"I'll eat more after the shoot. I'm fine and I'm also allowed to worry about and care about my parents," Lucy replied, grabbing the milk for her mom's coffee.

"Thank you," Julie said, taking the carton. "But we're fine."

"So I've heard. But, if you're willing to at least listen to me, I do have some ideas for book promotion," Lucy said slowly. Julie looked at her and started to protest.

"It doesn't involve leaving the house. I know that ... isn't your favorite thing. It's all things you can do from home. Are you on Twitter?" Lucy asked. Julie's features went from irritated to relaxed to confused in a split second.

"The bird thing?"

That answered that. Lucy laughed, kissed her mom's cheek, and picked up her purse and her camera bag. "Yes. I'll explain later. It's painless. I promise. Love you," Lucy said as she walked out of the kitchen.

She walked across the lawn and realized that with all of the time she was spending with Alex, she hadn't had to knock on his door in a while. She hoped he was up. She quietly checked the knob first, but Mr. Safety First had it locked up tight. She rapped three times and waited.

When he answered the door in low-slung lounge pants, a sleepy scowl on his face, and his hair at odd angles, she felt such a powerful rush of love, she questioned her own sanity.

"You don't have to knock," he grumbled, rubbing his hand over the stubble on his chin. He walked away, leaving her to shut the door and follow after him. "I do when it's locked, Mr. Safety," she said, still smiling at the sight of him.

"I'll get you a key," he said as he went for the coffee beans in the freezer. Lucy's heart flipped over in her chest. Alex stopped with his hand on the freezer door and looked at her, his eyes widening a little. "If you want. You don't have to have one. I could just leave the door unlocked."

Just like that, her heartbeat evened out. He knew what to say, and his ability to say the right thing calmed the panic inside of her.

"That doesn't sound very safe," she said, pretending to consider it as she unloaded her purse and camera onto his counter. She turned to face him. "I'll take the key," she said quietly.

His eyes lit up in slow degrees like his smile, one notch at a time, as he realized what she'd said—what she'd agreed to. The panic was pushed aside by another unexpected spurt of "this feels right." He kissed her forehead before going to grind the beans.

As the grinder growled and churned, Lucy took a look at the photos that Alex had laid out on his table. He really needed a bigger table for this room. She picked up one and saw the painted words and pictures on the side of the elementary school. Another had the damage that had been done to his truck.

There were over a dozen photos scattered across the surface. Each one had a bright red circle drawn in sharpie. The smell of coffee filled the air, but she didn't feel like a cup. Looking over, she saw Alex pouring water into the machine.

"It's an odd symbol for a tagger, don't you think?" she asked. He looked her way, pressed the on switch, and came over to look. "I don't know. I can't figure out if it's a signature or what. Those two curves there could be an M."

He pointed to the spot, and she could see why he would say that, but it wasn't what she saw. She took her phone out of her purse and pulled up Google. "What are you doing?" he asked, looking over her shoulder.

"Checking something," she answered. She typed in "symbol for loyalty." The search turned back hundreds of hits, so she switched to images and scrolled through until she found one that matched the circles in all of the pictures.

"Son of a bitch. How did you recognize that?" he asked, taking her phone from her hand and looking closer.

"A friend of mine has a tattoo of this symbol. Only inside of the heart, she put her boyfriend's name. Right before he broke up with her," Lucy said. "Loyalty. What the hell? What does loyalty have to do with defacing property?"

"I don't know, but clearly the symbol is meaningful to whoever it is," Lucy said. He looked at her and nodded. She could see his mind at work in the steady set of his jaw and his eyes, now awake and sharp, as he looked through the other photos and held her phone up against them.

"Uh, I kind of have to go," she said, laughing at his sudden intensity. "Okay," he said, kissing her absently.

She grinned, holding out her hand. "My phone?" He looked at it, then back up at her. She just shook her head. "I'll pick it up later," she said, sighing exaggeratedly. He pulled her in, kissing her sweetly.

"I'll trade you a key for the use of it. And dinner."

"Maybe I should buy you a Smartphone for your birthday, seeing as you might be the last person on earth without one," she said. She didn't want to admit, to herself or him, how the idea of coming back later to dinner and her own key made her feel ... whole. Found. When she hadn't realized she was lost.

"Maybe. But for now, I'll borrow yours, since it's in my hand."

She just laughed and picked up her things. As she started to leave, he called her name. "I love you."

"I love you, too."

As she got into her mom's rarely used car, Lucy realized that the more she said it, the more it felt true.

Alex swung by the recreation center on his way to the station. He wanted to see the progress and make sure no one had caused any damage. He was pleased by what he saw; the construction was going well. The framing was done, the walls were up, windows were in, and with the weather holding up, they would have it finished reasonably soon. Part of Alex thought that it was a blessing to start from the ground up with the center. Lucy and Kate were planning an elaborate affair in a few weeks, complete with an auction and dancing. As he got back into his cruiser, Alex hoped that he would have all of the answers by then.

Dolores was at the front desk, talking to someone on the phone, when Alex walked into the station. With her hair teased up several inches, her cherry red lips, and her black mesh shirt, Alex could see why the eighties went out of style. *Don't be such an ass.* She hung up the phone.

"Hey there, stranger," she said, her eyes ... seeking. *Seeking what?*

"Hey, Dolores. Good to have you back. How was your visit?" Alex asked. She was already pulling sticky notes off of her desk to hand to him. Lime green ones this time.

"It was really nice. Caught up with my mama and my aunties. Played some cards. I had a great time," she said.

Her perfume scented the air when she came near. She hesitated before patting his arm. Even with her mile-high boots, she had to look up at him. Her eyes were sad.

"Listen, Dolores," Alex said, looking around the empty station to make sure no one else was around. "I was a jerk to you last week. I'm sorry about that. This case is getting to me, but that was no reason to take it out on you."

Dolores looked surprised and slightly uncomfortable, making Alex wonder if he'd actually hurt her feelings. She moved back to her desk and kept her head down.

"Water under the bridge, sugar. One thing had nothing to do with the other," she answered with a nonchalant wave of her hand. The phone rang and Dolores practically jumped on it.

"Angel's Lake Sheriff's Department," she said in her

honeyed voice. Maybe his dad was right—maybe he did see secrets underneath everyone's words. He might be suspicious, but it didn't mean he was wrong.

He and his dad rarely fought. There wasn't much need. If they didn't see eye to eye, they stopped looking at each other until the moment passed. Still, when they did get under each other's skin, a bit of space generally solved things. Alex didn't think a couple of days was enough, so when Dolores came to his door and told him that Chuck was on the phone, he simply scowled at her.

"Tell him I'm busy," he said shortly.

She frowned at him and put her hands on her generous hips.

"I will do no such thing. Good Lord. There is nothing more stubborn than a man. You don't want to talk to him, you pick up the phone and tell him, or you hang up on him yourself," she said, her voice a little pitchy at the end. She turned and stomped away.

"I'm not stubborn," he called out. Her reply was less than ladylike. Alex picked up the phone and pressed line one. "What?"

"Nice greeting," Chuck barked. "Hope your attitude improves when you get here."

"Why am I coming there?" Alex asked, rubbing at the back of his neck where it was beginning to ache.

"Because it's your damn job. Some punk broke all the windows in my shed and painted the hell out of one side," Chuck said. "When was this?" Alex asked, sitting up and grabbing a pen.

"Now how would I know? If I had been here, it

wouldn't have happened," Chuck said. "I'm on my way," Alex sighed.

As he grabbed the keys and told Dolores where he was heading, he knew there was no denying the obvious—this was becoming personal.

Chuck Whitman's house was about twenty minutes from the center of town. Alex hated the house when his mom had dropped him off there—he'd seen the two-story Victorian home as just another place he wasn't wanted. True, it had felt good when he arrived to find that his dad had prepared a room for him. They had talked on the phone once Chuck had returned to Angel's Lake, but he didn't see him. Chuck had told him that he always had a place waiting for him, but Alex had never wanted to leave Chicago. To a ten-year-old boy, friends and baseball were all that mattered. Now, as he drove down the quiet roads that still looked more like lanes, he couldn't imagine living anywhere else.

WHEN ALEX PULLED up to Chuck's house, he noticed that the lawn had been freshly mowed. He could smell the newly cut grass as he unfolded himself from the cruiser. Chuck came down the three wide steps from the porch, where he'd been standing.

"Hey," his dad greeted. Alex didn't want to fight with him, but he couldn't swallow the irritation of knowing his dad was keeping secrets.

"Hey," Alex replied, sidestepping the lawn and heading down the long gravel driveway that led to the shed, which looked more like a guest house since Chuck had added siding and redone the inside to make a workshop for himself.

"I was out running errands. Came back to this," Chuck told him. Knowing Alex would need to take photos, his dad had left everything as it was: glass glittered in the gravel, both large and small shards. Each of the white-trimmed windows had been smashed, probably with a rock, from the look of it. Alex pulled the small digital camera out of his pocket and began to take photos.

"Did you check inside the shed to see if anything was taken?"

"Yes. Bastard took *my* paint to deface the siding."

When Alex wandered around to the side that was painted, his stomach took a dive. Not only was the loyalty symbol in the far right corner, but it was painted in the same blue that had been part of the other tagging. The same blue that had been in Davey's hair. *Is there only one shade in this town?* If the answer to that was yes, then it made sense that his dad had the same blue paint. If it wasn't, it seemed like a hell of a coincidence. There were other colors mixed in—Alex could see that the tagger was running out of spray paint from the way the letters faded away near the edges. The word "fucker" was darker at the beginning than it was by the time the R trailed off.

"This one seems more direct," Alex said quietly. "I noticed the same thing."

"You piss anyone off?" Alex slid his dad a sideways glance.

"Besides you?" Chuck raised his eyebrows and crossed

his arms over his chest. The smell of grass continued to waft through the air and mingled with the scents of someone grilling. Alex saw Mrs. Weatherly peek out from her living room window next door, and he put his hand up to wave hello.

"Yeah. Besides me," he replied when the curtains next door closed abruptly.

Alex took more pictures, stepping lightly and carefully. The door to the shed was open.

"This is the same paint from most of the others," Alex said, looking at his dad over his shoulder.

"Yes. Now you're going to ask why I have it. I got it from a friend. I'm making a couple of plant stands. I'm painting them this blue," Chuck replied. His voice was defensive, but Alex knew that he understood the line of questioning.

"Hell of a coincidence," Alex murmured, echoing his earlier thoughts. "I'm going to send one of my deputies out to take statements. See if your neighbors— maybe Mrs. Weatherly—saw anything."

"Listen, Alex. About earlier," Chuck said, his gruff voice gentling a little.

"Not now, Dad. Unless you think that whatever secrets you're keeping have something to do with this, then not now."

"Fine. But later then."

"Later."

Alex continued to take pictures while Chuck filled him in on the details. He hadn't been out much more than an hour, he didn't see anyone, and there hadn't been any trouble in the neighborhood lately. Mick showed up shortly after Alex called him and said he would canvass the neighbors. Chuck asked Alex if he wanted to come in and have something to eat. Alex declined, needing to get back to the station, but also because he still wasn't ready for "later." When his phone rang, he hoped it was Lucy. He could use some Lucy right about then, but remembered he had her phone. Instead, it was Kate.

"You okay?" he asked instead of saying hello.

"I'm fine. Listen, can you come by the high school?" Kate asked. He could hear the noise in the background, making it clear she was already there.

"Everything alright?" he asked, signaling to Mick that he was taking off and waving briskly to his dad. For good measure, he turned and waved to Mrs. Weatherly, who, once again, snapped the curtains closed.

"Yes. I'm helping with the job fair. I mentioned it a while ago? Thought maybe you could drop by and talk to some of the kids about being a police officer," she replied, telling someone to wait a minute.

Shit. There were too many things going on to keep track of. In the back of his mind, he remembered a conversation from a while back about taking part. "I'm on my way." What was one more thing?

Lucy parked her mom's car in the driveway and figured she would run into her parents before heading over to Alex's. Since she was staying, she should probably find a place of her own. A place with a little room where she could spread out her work, her cameras and equipment, and line the walls some of her favorite photographs. *Alex's place is plenty big.* Lucy grabbed her bag and headed into the house. *Too much. Too soon.*

Leaving her bag in the kitchen that still smelled like hamburgers and fries, she went to find her parents. They were cuddled on the couch, watching The Voice. Her dad looked up and smiled.

"Hey honey," he said. "Hey."

"Hi sweetie. Have you eaten?" Julie asked, sitting up a bit. Her dad paused the show.

"Not yet. I was going to see if Alex has eaten," Lucy answered, flopping into the recliner beside the couch. Julie sat up a little straighter and looked Lucy up and down.

"Are you feeling alright? You looked tired and a little pale," Julie commented, leaning to put her hand to Lucy's forehead. Lucy laughed and shifted away. "Mom! I'm almost thirty. You do not need to check my forehead."

Julie huffed and picked up the glass of water that was sitting on the coffee table. "Suit yourself. You should be taking vitamins. Are you taking vitamins?"

"Julie," Mark interrupted, his voice thick with amusement and tenderness. Genuine tenderness that made Lucy's chest constrict. How they felt about each other was so visible in every look, every touch. Lucy wondered what had happened all of those years ago—twenty-eight, to be exact—that had caused that foundation to shift, to crack. And how had they managed to repair the damage so seamlessly?

"I am allowed to take care of my children. While they're here," she said, arching her eyebrows at Lucy. Lucy stood, afraid that if she stayed longer she'd either fall asleep or ask questions she wasn't ready for answers to.

"I want to go over my ideas for book promotion tomorrow, okay?" Lucy said, looking down at her mom. Julie was wearing striped pajamas with a tank top and a soft, pale blue cardigan. Leaning over to give her a quick hug, Lucy inhaled the scent of lavender, and her heart constricted once more. So much had changed while she had been gone, but not everything and, for that, Lucy was grateful.

"Don't pressure your mom, Luce," Mark said, turning the show back on.

Lucy frowned. She was recognizing how serious her mom's boundary was, but she was also on the outside of the situation enough to realize that *someone*

had to push a little. Taking a deep breath, she leaned over her mom to give her dad a kiss on the cheek as well. "I'll see you guys tomorrow," she said.

Her dad chuckled. "Say hello to Alex."

"And be safe, dear. Even if you —"

"Mom!"

Lucy covered her ears as she walked away from them, but she could still hear them laughing at the singers on the television.

The door was unlocked when she crossed the yard and arrived at Alex's. She did knock, but she checked the handle at the same time and found it open. Something smelled delicious, and her stomach growled loudly. The lights were dimmed, but Lucy could hear soft music playing in the kitchen, so she left her things at the door and followed the scents. She heard Alex humming and smiled. Her feet stopped moving when she saw him in the kitchen, draining pasta into a large colander. Candles flickered on the table that was set for two. When he turned to grab an oven mitt, he saw her. Or maybe he heard the heavy, fast thud of her heart as she watched him.

"Hey," he said, smiling. He was dressed in a pair of jeans and a soft grey T-shirt. His hair was wet, like he'd just showered. He walked to her and kissed her gently. Teasingly. Once. Twice. And then not so gently. She moved her hands to his chest and wound them around his neck, grabbing on to the moment as much as him. Pulling back, she couldn't stop the wide smile.

"Hi. You expecting someone?" she asked. He grinned, kissed her nose, and released her. "Yes. I invited a girl over. But you got here first, so you can stay."

"Very funny," she replied, coming in to peek at what was simmering on the stove. Jealousy wasn't something she was familiar with. Not since her senior year in high school when she'd caught her prom date, naked, with none other than Danielle Peterson. At eighteen, Lucy had been naïve and was rewarded with a heavy dose of humiliation. But she was an adult now and could separate one feeling from another. The thought of Alex being with or wanting another woman, turned her stomach so fast, it could only be labeled as possessiveness. He was hers. And for once, she wasn't letting go.

"How was your day?" he asked her as she stuck a spoon in the spaghetti sauce and took a taste. "Mmm. Did you make this?"

"I did. I told you I would cook for you. I should have done it sooner."

"If I'd known you could cook like this, I probably would have made you," she said, taking another bite of the sweet red sauce that held just a touch of heat. "Uh-oh. Now I've done it."

She laughed and watched him put together the rest of their dinner, chatting with him about their respective days. As they sat down to dinner, the candlelight shimmering, Alex raised his glass.

"To you," he offered. "To me?"

"Mmhmm. For coming home."

He clinked her glass and leaned in to give her a gentle kiss. When he rose, she was happy to have the moment to breathe and calm the tidal wave in her stomach. How could he make her feel so much? When he came back to the table, he was holding a square box wrapped with pretty pink paper. When he handed it to her, she found it had some weight.

"What is this?"

"Open it."

She smiled, feeling excitement push through her and settle the waves in her stomach. She untied the ribbon as he sat down and watched her take the lid off of the box. Inside, nestled in white tissue paper, she found a beautiful, perfectly square photo album. The black leather cover was cool, smooth, and soft.

Delicate, silver lettering was etched across the front: **Live Laugh Love**. Lucy felt ridiculous for the tears that fell as she ran her hand over the slightly embossed lettering.

Alex passed her one of the linen napkins, making her give a watery laugh.

"It's beautiful. I'll fill it with pictures of us. Of you," she said. He smiled, cupped her jaw with his hand, and kissed her. "That was the idea, actually. Great minds. Open it."

She opened the cover to reveal pockets for 4x6 photographs. In the first pocket, there was a silver key. She looked up, locked eyes with Alex.

"As promised. If you want it," he said softly. She closed the book, hugging it to her chest before setting it on the table. She stood and moved to his lap, wrapping her arms around him and hugging him tightly.

"I want it. I want you."

She kissed him, surprised again by the intensity with which her words rang true. He tightened his arms around her and stood. "Great minds," he repeated. She laughed and looked down at their plates.

"What about dinner?" she asked, running her fingers through his hair and kissing his neck.

"It reheats well," he replied. He bent slightly so she could blow out the candles before he carried her to his room.

CHAPTER EIGHTEEN

For someone who had lost their job, Lucy was extremely busy. Even more surprising was that she was happier than she had been in a long time. She'd managed to sign her mom up for a Twitter account, though she wasn't positive that Julie understood the process. She'd also started a Facebook author page for her mom, which was instantly liked by several of her own friends, boosting Julie's self-confidence. While they were looking at some of the simple ideas that Lucy had for boosting sales, Julie shared her publisher's website. It had a link to Julie's bio, but as far as a web page was concerned, her mom hadn't taken that step.

Lucy had done some research, mostly through Julie's agency's website, to find out effective ways for authors to market themselves. Lucy planned to walk her mom through blogging and blog tours, but she didn't have time today. She had promised Kate she would help supervise some of the teens that had agreed to help paint over the graffiti on a couple of the buildings. They were starting with Mr. Kramer's back wall.

The air was cooler today even though the sun was making scattered appearances. The snow line on the mountains had lowered, adding a bite to the soft breeze that blew. It wouldn't be the first time the month of May had brought a cold front to Angel's Lake, but Lucy preferred the warmer weather.

"Alright angsty teens, line up," Kate said to the motley crew that was assembled in sweaters, baggy jeans, and a mishmash of hats. There were more boys than girls. Almost all of them were holding a takeout coffee container, making Lucy salivate a bit. The teens gave Kate their attention, and Lucy realized that she really did have a strong rapport with them. They connected with her—maybe it was her age, her demeanor, or a combination of both. *Maybe she is meant to do this.*

"What's angsty mean?" a boy with a plaid shirt over a long-sleeve Henley asked. He ran his hand through his shaggy blond hair, but it fell back into his eyes immediately.

"Moody," said a girl with a condescending curl to her lip. Lucy didn't think she was actually mad.

"We here, ain't we?" asked another boy. He had an enviable afro growing that looked like a planet intricately perched atop his head.

"You are," Kate replied, a clipboard in her hand. "And I'm not only glad, I'm grateful. Before we go over the plan, I want to introduce my older sister." Lucy waved and gave a smile, but the teens barely acknowledged her with a glance.

"She'll be helping, but she'll also be taking photographs. She's an amazing photographer, and her work has been featured in *National Geographic*, *Elle*, *Vogue*, *Esquire*," Kate shared. Lucy's gaze must have registered the astonishment she felt over Kate knowing so much of her resume because Kate tilted her head in a what-did-I-say? gesture. The kids, however, continued to stand impatiently, their expressions settling between bored and tired.

"I did a *Maxim* shoot as well," Lucy offered with a weak smile. If Kate could win them over, so could she. It worked. The boys' heads whipped in her direction with comical synchronicity.

"Dude. That is sick," one of the boys said. His shadow of a goatee moved oddly when he spoke or smiled, but Lucy was pleased by the recognition. "That means cool," said the girl who knew what angst meant.

"Yeah. I know that much. Anyway, I'm taking your pictures because I'm putting together an exhibit for the opening of the new rec center. If you don't want to be photographed, please just let me know," Lucy told them, taking the elastic off of her wrist to tie her hair back.

"Will there be photography lessons offered at the rec center?" asked another girl. Her eyes were quiet, and she barely moved when she spoke, like being still mattered in her world. Lucy smiled gently and hoped the girl, who couldn't be more than fifteen, was just nervous. Kate looked at Lucy and pursed her lips.

Lucy answered the girl, since Kate hadn't. "Uh. I don't know. I think Kate is planning the activities and courses that will be available. I'd be happy to offer lessons, though"

Lucy said, more to Kate than the kids. The kids were starting to fidget, and Kate pulled their attention back by tapping on her clipboard.

"Okay. More about what we're offering later. Let's get ready to paint."

Kate gave them sections to work on and put them in teams. Lucy decided to take pictures before she grabbed a roller. Kate, never one to sit on the sidelines, kept everyone's paint trays full and pitched in when needed. Lucy crouched to get a profile shot of everyone working on the wall.

"Pretty clever, challenging them like that," Lucy commented as she worked. Kate had told the kids that the first group that finished their section to her approval would get out of cleanup.

"It doesn't take much. They're really good kids. They've made mistakes, but they're atoning for them. I hate the thought of them being pigeonholed because of what other teens are doing. If it even is a teen," Kate said, dipping the roller before applying it to the brick.

"You're really awesome with them. Like, really," Lucy said, standing and lowering the camera. "I'm sorry that I've been pressuring you. You will make an excellent social worker."

Kate lowered the roller, took a quick inventory of where the kids were at, and then came to stand in front of Lucy. One of the kids turned on their iPhone so music sounded out of his jeans. A couple of the other kids sang along with the words, making Lucy laugh.

"I love working with these guys. I truly do. But if you think I don't want what you're offering, you're wrong. I'm not trying to be mean. I love you so much—"

"But," Lucy said stiffly.

"But, we're not all you. We can't all just take off and see the world and do whatever we feel like, Luce. I'm trying to be responsible. I'm trying to do what is right. They paid for my education. I will not slap Mom and Dad in the face by taking off," Kate said in a hushed tone, glancing back at the teens.

Lucy's grip tightened on the camera until the grooves were digging into her fingers and palm. "We're almost done, Kate!" one of the teens shouted.

"Keep going. I'll check in a minute," Kate hollered back. Her eyes looked sorry, but Lucy couldn't hold back.

"Wow. Well, I really appreciate you being the responsible one in my absence. While I've been running around the world, selfishly living it up, I'm so glad to know that Mom and Dad can count on *you*."

"Lucy. I didn't—"

"You had your say. Several times now. It's interesting to me that you can spend your days working with these kids because you believe they can change— they can grow and become someone different than you expected them to be. But you can't see that in me. Staying home for Mom and Dad is a cop out.

You're scared. You're scared to leave, and you're scared to try. And maybe I'm not the responsible one—the one all of you can be really proud of—but I'm here. And I'm not going anywhere. To me, that's as scary as leaving is for you. But I'm doing it anyway. That makes me brave."

Lucy's voice shook on the last few words. With her hands equally unsteady, she put her camera away and grabbed her bags. "Lucy. I'm sorry. Please don't go," Kate said quietly, putting her hand on Lucy's arm.

"Don't worry, I'm not running away. I have some sessions booked. You can finish telling me what a disappointment I am as a sister and daughter when I get home."

"Lucy."

Lucy turned without saying good-bye to the kids and walked down the alley before the tears slipped down her cheeks. She swiped them away and ignored Kate calling her name.

Mad or not, Alex wasn't going to let his dad take care of the cleanup of his driveway and shed himself. With gloves on their hands, Alex and Chuck tossed the shards of glass into a large bagster, an invention Alex hadn't even known existed. It was a heavy duty bag in the shape of a mini dumpster. It saved them time hauling while Sam punched out the rest of the glass to replace the windows in the shed. Chuck had decided he wanted new frames as well, rather than just replacing the glass.

"Damn mess. I should probably remove most of this gravel," Chuck commented.

"Some of it, for sure. I can get one of my guys to bring the mini excavator over this weekend. They'll take a couple of loads out, and then you can replace it with fresh stuff," Sam offered. Alex nodded in thanks but said nothing.

"Maybe I should just pave it," Chuck said, standing up and surveying his driveway. He looked at Alex. "Don't look at me. Ask him," Alex said.

"It's a bigger job, but I think you'd be happier with it," Sam replied.

Chuck mulled it over while they worked. Alex and Sam talked baseball and weddings, which surprised the hell out of Alex. He'd never seen Sam as the type to fall head-over-heels-crazy-in-love. He was happy for his friend—thrilled, but it was still amusing.

"Who would have thought you'd know the difference between silk and satin? Or whatever the hell chiffon is," Alex said, taking a break to drink some water. His back was aching and damp with sweat. If they were going to get an excavator, this seemed like a waste of time. Alex walked over to hold the window in place while Sam grabbed his drill.

"You'll see, man. I go home at night, grab a beer, put my feet up, and Anna curls into me with a fucking binder full of stuff she wants an opinion on," Sam told him. Alex laughed and shook his head, but it didn't really sound so bad.

"Do *you* know the difference between white and vanilla?" Sam asked as he held the drill steady and secured one side of the window. "Nope. And I'm okay with that," Alex answered.

"He doesn't get it, Sam. Save your breath," Chuck chimed in.

"Oh, here we go. Because you're the expert on

weddings? Do you know the difference between white and vanilla?" Alex asked, moving so he and Sam could switch sides.

"It's not about white versus vanilla, dumbass. It's about listening to a woman and making her feel like she matters. Took me way too long to figure that out. It's good you've already learned that, Sam," Chuck said. He sat down in one of the lawn chairs he'd opened when they started and drank his water.

"The right woman makes it easy. Speaking of which, Anna's asking to do a double date. You good with that?"

"Sure," Alex said. Agreeing seemed like the easiest solution, and it actually did sound like a good idea. He should probably bring Lucy over to properly meet his father, too, since they were headed in that sort of direction. While they finished up the windows, and Chuck watched, Alex poked around the shed. He'd taken the paint into the station to compare it to the photos.

"Where'd you say you got this paint again?" Alex asked.

"I didn't," Chuck replied, looking up from under the brim of his cap. "Dad. I need to know where you got the paint."

"I bought it."

Alex swore and exchanged a look with Sam, who shrugged his shoulders. He'd sent evidence into the Minnesota crime lab, but petty acts of vandalism hardly rated in comparison to what they dealt with daily. Stalking over to where his dad was far too comfortable, he knocked Chuck's boot with his own.

"There's a good chance you're holding up the investigation. Whoever gave you the paint could be part of this. It may not seem like much, but the incidents are escalating and becoming personal," Alex said, hands on hips. His dad *knew* this. Chuck stood so they were eye to eye.

"So haul me in for obstruction. But know this, I can personally guarantee you that the person that gave me the paint is not who you are looking for," Chuck told him. His voice was steady. Years of being a good cop kept his tone even and sure. But years of being Alex's dad kept it sincere as well.

"How can you know that?" Alex demanded, knowing that he could water-board his dad and still get nothing. If Chuck Whitman didn't want to talk, he didn't talk.

"Jesus, kid. Can't you trust me?"

Chuck stomped off and Sam whistled low behind Alex. Alex hung his head and tried to take a deep breath, but the words "I don't know" kept running through his brain.

Lucy didn't feel like being at home. But she knew that she needed to resolve things with her sister, and she *wasn't* irresponsible, so she was waiting in Kate's bedroom when she got home later that day. When she walked in, Kate was holding a gigantic Slurpee. Lucy's gaze locked on it as she tried not to convey how very badly she wanted it.

"Mom said you were up here," Kate said softly. Lucy nodded.

"I thought we should talk," Lucy said, pulling her gaze from the drink that looked like the perfect blend of ice and pop. "You can stop drooling. I bought it for you," Kate said, handing it over.

Lucy took a slow, careful sip, avoiding brain freeze. It

was sweet and syrupy—the perfect mix. Kate was sorry. Kate hated convenience stores. She claimed they weren't very convenient when everyone went to them. If she went into 7-11, poured a Slurpee, and waited in line to pay, she was definitely sorry.

"Thanks," Lucy said, feeling the ice slip down her throat.

Kate slipped off her shoes and sat down beside Lucy on the bed. "I'm sorry."

"I know."

"I am scared. I'm terrified. New York is really far away. I know I hurt your feelings. I'm sorry," Kate said. Her voice lowered, and she laid her head on Lucy's shoulder. Lucy tilted her head so it rested on Kate's and continued to sip her drink.

"It's not that far."

"When I criticized you for traveling the world, part of it was because I'm jealous that you're brave enough to do that. To just go out on your own."

Lucy shrugged, dislodging Kate's head. She turned and crossed her legs on the bed, choosing her words carefully. Kate didn't need to know why Lucy always felt the need to stay away, to skirt around the edges and hide behind a plane ticket. Even if she wanted to tell her, it wasn't her right. Was it?

"It's scary. Every trip, every village, every plane ride has been scary. Anything new is scary."

"Then why do it?" Kate asked, mirroring her sister's position.

"Because there are amazing things to see and do and be

part of outside of Angel's Lake. And because when you're done seeing and doing, or even if you're not, you can always come home."

"What if I'm no good? It's a silly pipe dream. I like to sketch, but that doesn't mean I should be in New York," Kate argued without heat.

"It's not all about the fashion part of it. Some of this is about taking a risk and following your dream. Taking an opportunity that not everyone gets."

Kate took the cup from Lucy's hand, stirred the contents, and took a sip of her own before passing it back.

"It feels wrong. Cashing in on who my sister knows, leaving Mom and Dad, and not following through with social work. Then there's the center," Kate said. She got up, went to her desk, and pulled open the bottom drawer that was covered with an NSYNC poster. She pulled out a brown, faded leather book. It had a leather cord wrapped around it twice. She ran her hand over it and came back to the bed.

"It's not wrong to use connections if you have them. Especially in New York. Especially in this business or any other like it. Sometimes, that's the only way to get in. Mom and Dad will understand and support you. Having a degree in social work will never be a bad thing. And the center will be fine. It'll be great. And you did that. Because when you wanted something, you went after it and made it happen," Lucy said softly, encouragingly. She stood to set the Slurpee down on the dresser, sensing that Kate was about to share something precious. She sat back down and waited while Kate stared at the leather bound book.

Finally, with a mix of emotions in her eyes, Kate looked back up at Lucy.

"Be honest. From the minute you open it, I'll know from your reaction whether or not I was meant to do this. Either way will be okay. I'll be okay. But your reaction will be a sign," Kate declared.

Lucy gave a short laugh. "No pressure."

"None. But you can't hide anything. Your face is so expressive.," Kate said, still holding the book. "Hey! I can hide my feelings," Lucy countered.

Kate arched her eyebrow and stared. "If you say so. But I can see through you." She handed Lucy the book, and the simple act of trust, faith, and hope pushed any lingering hurt aside and left only room for how much she loved her little sister.

Undoing the leather binding by pulling one string, she carefully unfolded the book. The thick pages were a cream color and filled with enough beauty to stop Lucy's breath in her throat. With it trapped there, she couldn't speak. She looked up from the images and into Kate's eyes. Lucy watched her sister tear up slightly and give a one-sided smile.

"You really like them," she whispered. Lucy could only nod because there were no words that described how much, and the air was still caught. So she turned the pages, nodding in awe at the secret her sister had kept for who knew how long. Finally, she found her voice when she stumbled across a gorgeous dress in an array of shimmering colors that could be dressed down or up. The thin straps and scooped neckline gave it a summery feel, while the cascading folds of fabric made it elegant.

"Kate. I had no idea you were so talented."

When a tear slipped down Kate's cheek, Lucy leaned over and hugged her hard, still holding the book on her lap. "You have to help me tell Mom and Dad."

"Deal."

CHAPTER NINETEEN

"And she can *really* draw, Alex! It was amazing. She had hundreds of design ideas sketched out in all of these notebooks she kept in her desk," Lucy said excitedly while he nibbled his way down her neck. She was as cute as she was hot, and he found it quite an irresistible combination.

"Mmhmm," he murmured, running his hand up her smooth thigh until he hit her shorts. They were stopped on a bench overlooking a spring that came from the mountain as if by magic. The air smelled like wildflowers and trees and Lucy. Her camera was on one side of her, more appendage than machine. The warm breeze shifted over them. She made him ache. Sometimes, he still couldn't believe she was right here, letting him touch her whenever he wanted.

She was *his*.

While he was getting lost in her scent—vanilla and flowers, her taste—peppermint, the feel of her against him—

mind-blowing, she giggled. Amusement crowded his lust but didn't diminish it. He looked at her with mock annoyance and raised eyebrows.

"I can honestly say I have never had a woman laugh while I'm trying to seduce her," he said. He couldn't keep the smile from spreading as she threw her arms around him. He wrapped his around her and held her tight, breathing her into every piece of his soul.

"I felt like I had no place. Here or in anyone's life. Now I feel like there's nowhere else. No other place that would fit," she said hoarsely. The first couple times she had cried, it had torn little pieces inside of him, but now he knew that the hint of tears he heard were happy ones. She leaned back and looked at him, cupping his face in her hands like he did to her so often. "I feel like I'm part of something. Not just on the outside taking pictures. I'm going to help Kate tell my parents tonight. I honestly think they will be okay with it. They've always been supportive of our choices."

"They're amazing people. And a really wonderful couple. With extremely excellent and beautiful daughters," he smiled, kissing her. "You are more than just part of something, Lucy. To me, you're everything."

It was the complete truth, and though he wanted this—a life with Lucy, with everything in him, it scared the hell out of him. If she was everything, would he be nothing if she left? *She's not leaving.* To secure himself in the moment, he took her mouth—hard and sure—making sure she felt something. He needed her to feel the way he did.

She put her camera into its bag and then threw one leg

over him, straddling him on the wide, wooden bench that looked like it was an extension of the tree they sat beside. With the water rushing and the sun shining, they were secluded in their own world. He ran his hands up her sides, moved them over her shoulders and down the front of her slowly, watching her eyes heat and her lashes lower. He could feel her skin through the thin material of her tank top. She inhaled sharply when his hands covered her breasts, and he nipped at her ear with his teeth. Her legs tightened around him.

"You drive me crazy," he whispered. It was the most intelligible thing he could think to say before her mouth found his and he couldn't think at all. He'd never had sex outside—other than in a tent, and that didn't count—but he was trying to figure out how to make that happen when his phone rang. It took her a moment to resurface, to let him ease away, which gave him a surge of satisfaction. His voice was husky and not so steady when he answered.

"Whitman."

She continued to move on his lap and laughed noiselessly at the way he narrowed his eyes, promising payback. "I'm on my way...No...I'll be there shortly."

He hung up and the moment, unfortunately, was gone.

"Is everything okay?" Lucy asked, getting up. Alex stood, pulled her camera bag onto his shoulder, and took her hand.

"Yeah. Couple of the boys from Franny's got caught shoplifting at Wal-Mart. I've got a better rapport with them than Mick," Alex said, leading the way out of their secluded spot on the trail. The sun was warmer when they left the cover of trees.

"At least they didn't graffiti anything," Lucy said, attempting a smile. "Small blessings."

He opened his newly painted passenger door for her, stopping her just before she got in. Winding his hand into her hair, he pulled her in for another kiss that would have to hold him over for the night.

"I wish you could come to the birthday party tonight," she told him, winding her arms around his waist.

"Me, too. Wish Carmen a happy birthday for me," he said, kissing her forehead and heading to his side of the truck.

"I signed the card for her present from both of us," she told him when he got in. She fiddled with his radio as though she needed direct eye contact with it to make it work. He understood that meant something to her, for them. Every little step that Lucy took toward him tied another knot in his heart strings, securing them to her. And while he didn't mind her pulling every last string and tying an unbreakable bond, he couldn't help but wonder how he'd ever get the knots undone if she were to leave him.

"That's like triple-platinum couple status," he said, trying to lighten the tension. She laughed and finally met his eyes when he backed out of the spot they'd taken at the foot of the hill.

"You've earned it," she murmured, taking his hand into hers and squeezing.

It was very rare for Lucy to be home on someone's birthday. She never forgot even one, but typically, she would send a gift early enough to arrive and, if she was lucky, managed to Skype on the day. She was elated to be here for Carmen's sixth birthday. She spent her life trying to capture the true essence of a moment in one photograph. She'd caught many. But she'd missed out on her family's to catch those moments somewhere else. No more. She was where she wanted—needed to be. She blew up balloons in silver and blue, Carmen's favorite colors, while her mom hummed under her breath and checked the cake.

"I've reached almost five hundred likes on my Facebook page," Julie said, pulling the round cake out of the oven. The smell of chocolate made Lucy's mouth water. She tied the balloon and swatted it toward the living room.

"Mom, that's awesome! It's a great way to connect with your readers. The more you connect with them, the more likely they are to buy your books," Lucy said, stretching another balloon.

"Yeah. My agent was quite pleased by my progress. She's been talking about this social media for a while, telling me I needed to get on board and make some changes. But I was scared to do it. I guess I'm what you call 'old-school,'" Julie told her.

"Aw. Yeah, I guess you kind of are. But there's nothing stopping you from coming into this century. And I'll help you," Lucy said, then puffed her cheeks up and wrapped her lips around the end of the balloon.

"While you're here," Julie said. The air deflated from both Lucy's cheeks and the balloon. Julie looked over her shoulder and met Lucy's eyes. "It's like not one of you can have a little faith in me," Lucy said quietly, standing and gathering up the balloons.

"Oh, honey, I didn't mean to hurt your feelings. It's just hard to believe you'll really stay. But I'm sorry. That was passive aggressive," Julie said, coming to put a hand on Lucy's.

"It was and it seems to run in the family. I'm here. Why do all of you doubt me?" Lucy asked, hating how small her voice was.

"Sweetie, we don't doubt you. But you can't deny you have a track record," Julie said softly, removing her hand from Lucy's on the table. Lucy clenched her jaw and shoved balloons back into the bag that was suddenly too small.

She tossed the bag and the balloons down onto the kitchen table. "Okay. So how long do I have to be here to set a new record? How long until this counts?"

Julie's lips tightened. "I didn't say it doesn't count. You know we're happy to have you here. Especially me. But quite honestly, this is a new record. You've been moving around since you were eighteen years old and it's hard to just let that go because you're back for a couple months. The past doesn't just fall away, you know."

Something inside Lucy snapped. No, it didn't fall away. It stuck around, hovering until you couldn't move. Couldn't breathe. Couldn't escape it. Despite all the good happening in her life, how happy she felt and how sure she was about Alex and her decision to stay, Lucy couldn't keep pretending she didn't know the truth. She'd tried to push it away, bury it, block it out. Hell, she'd run from it for years.

But being home had changed Lucy's knowledge of her mom's indiscretion from a scar to an open wound.

"Lucky for you, Dad doesn't feel the same about judging people based on past actions," Lucy snapped. Her mother's face paled beyond possibility. Lucy looked away, refusing to feel guilt. If she were going to continue to be judged for every mistake she'd made, shouldn't the rest of her family be judged by the same measure? Why could Mark forgive Julie but Lucy couldn't have the same forgiveness from her family? From her mom? *You're her mistake. That's why you've stayed away.*

Tears burned in the back of Lucy's eyes, more so since she saw them rimming her mom's eyes as well. She turned and stomped up the stairs. She had a present to wrap, and she clearly wasn't needed. They'd handled plenty of birthday preparations without her. Wound up and overwhelmed, Lucy wrapped Carmen's gift and then lay down on the bed. She closed her eyes, pretending that would make everything better.

Lucy didn't scream when she opened her eyes to see similar ones staring into hers, but she came close. Carmen regarded her with a maturity that surpassed a normal six-year-old's. Lucy could feel her heart thumping against her ribs, but she attempted a smile.

"Hi. Happy birthday," she said, her voice groggy. She hadn't meant to fall asleep.

"It's not my actual birthday. That's on Tuesday," Carmen replied, still staring. Lucy stretched and sat up. "Well, I guess I should wait until then to give you my gifts," Lucy teased. Carmen frowned and considered this.

"No. You can give them to me today because this is the day we are celebrating," Carmen replied. While sitting, Lucy thought she'd take her chances. "That sounds good. So, are you too old for a birthday hug from your aunt?"

Carmen thought about it. A concerned smile tilted her lips. With a serious expression, she shook her head. Lucy's heart stuttered and she put her arms around her niece slowly, letting her adjust to the contact.

Despite the stiffness in Carmen's arms and embrace, her small hands gripped Lucy's shoulders. "I'm a very good hugger," Carmen said. Lucy laughed, everything in her lightening. "You most certainly are," she agreed.

They went downstairs together, joining the noisy group. Mia was laying on the floor on a blanket, giggling at Kate. It was the sweetest sound. Almost as sweet as the hug Lucy had just received. Her dad was reclined in his chair while Luke and Char sat on the couch. Her mom came in from the kitchen with a tray of cheese and crackers.

"Oh, good. You got your aunt Lucy up," Julie said, avoiding Lucy's gaze. She greeted everyone and sat on the floor. Carmen picked up her book and began to flip pages while Kate tried to make Mia giggle.

"Mia laughs for me because she thinks I'm funny," Carmen said without looking up. "She's a wise baby," Lucy said.

"Babies can't be wise. They just copy what we do," Carmen replied.

Julie asked Kate to help her with bringing in the gifts, and they spent time watching Carmen open them. After each gift, Char and Luke reminded her to say thank you and to look at the person who gave her the gift when she spoke. Lucy was warmed by the genuine smile that lit Carmen's face when she opened her *National Geographic Book on Sharks*.

"Did you photograph any of these?" she asked. "No," Lucy replied, picking up some of the paper. "I still like it."

She chuckled, knowing it was high praise. Mia started to fuss, so Char went to make a bottle. Luke asked Kate if she wanted to play cards, and Lucy joined in. Mark and Carmen looked through the book Lucy had given her. Julie puttered back and forth between the kitchen and the living room, obviously happy to have her family all together. Lucy didn't want to feel bad, but she hoped her mom wasn't avoiding being in the same room with her. After a while, she came in and sat with Carmen and Mark, looking at the sharks and listening to Carmen's detailed description of each one. After Kate and Lucy had lost at crazy eights twice to Luke, Julie asked them to clear the table.

"Time to set the table for the birthday girl's dinner," Julie announced.

While Kate and Lucy set the table, they communicated silently, and Lucy could see the nerves pushing their way to Kate's surface. Carmen had wanted chicken, potatoes, and blue Jell-O for dinner, and it was a long-standing tradition that the birthday person could have whatever they wanted for their birthday meal. Lucy wondered what she would ask to have for her own birthday.

"The next big celebration will be your graduation, Kate," Char said, putting squares of Jell-O on Carmen's plate without letting it touch any of the other food. Lucy kicked Kate under the table.

"Ouch," Kate glared at Lucy, and the two of them earned strange looks from the rest of the family. "Yes. Speaking of which, I've decided to take a break before applying for any jobs to become a social worker."

Lucy watched her parents' faces. Her dad frowned slightly but nodded. Julie froze, staring at her youngest. Luke asked for more potatoes. "What will you do?" Julie asked.

Lucy saw Carmen balance her Jell-O on her fork to watch it wobble. Her mother's eyes never left Kate's face.

"I'm going to New York. Lucy has arranged an internship at a prestigious fashion house for me," Kate said, exhaling loudly as though all the words had been sitting inside of her lungs. Julie set her fork down with a clang.

"It's a great opportunity. Do any of you know how incredibly talented she is? How well she can draw?" Lucy said, breaking the silence. Carmen piped up, but kept her focus on her food. "I do. She draws with me when she comes to babysit. Right Auntie Kate?"

Kate smiled gently at Carmen, who kept her eyes on her fork.

"Why have you never expressed an interest in this before, honey?" Mark asked.

"It felt like a hobby. Then I saw this ad for an internship, and I just ... I don't know, I wanted it. Badly," Kate said. She pushed the potatoes around her plate. Luke took a drink and then raised his glass.

"I think it's great. I've seen some of the dresses she's

drawn with Carmen," Luke said. "To Kate. To a new adventure and following your heart." Lucy lifted her glass immediately in a show of support. Carmen raised her fork with Jell-O. Slowly, the others joined in, but Lucy had a feeling the conversation was far from over.

They sang "Happy Birthday" to Carmen and watched her blow out the candles on her shark-shaped cake. They ate quietly and Kate fidgeted with her fork, with her hair, with her cake. Luke stood and picked up the birthday girl.

"Char, why don't you stick around, and I'll take these monkeys home and get them ready for bed," Luke suggested. Char leaned in to kiss him and he met her halfway. Lucy, who had her camera on her lap, taking random shots, pressed the button and captured the moment.

They had been to a couple of information sessions on what was called ABA techniques. According to Char, applied behavior analysis looked at how behavior was influenced by environment. Using strategies, such as positive rewards, they could encourage the behaviors they wanted to see from Carmen. Luke and Char were still uncertain, but they were more united and had an idea of what they needed to do to help their daughter. It eased the pressure in Lucy's chest to see this.

The three girls sat in the living room while their parents spoke in the kitchen. It reminded Lucy of the time she and Char had snuck out to a party and Kate had followed them. They hadn't known she was following until they were already there, and they immediately had to come home. They'd received a long lecture on setting positive examples and thinking through their choices.

"Why didn't you tell me?" Char asked. Lucy understood the hurt in her voice. Being blindsided with information hurt. Especially when something was purposely withheld.

"It wasn't something I had planned to pursue. It was more like a whim. Until pushy-nosey-pants here read my email and decided to take matters into her own hands," Kate replied, tossing a pillow at Lucy, who sat on the floor.

"I was trying to help. To do something for you," she replied, throwing the pillow onto the couch.

"Why are we waiting in here for them to scold us? We're not children. You can go to New York if you want," Char said, standing and putting her hands on her hips.

"She can. Likely, she will. But I'm sad that you all feel like you have to go behind our back and make plans that you then just spring on us," Mark said, startling Char into turning around. Mark and Julie came into the living room together. Char came to sit beside Lucy.

"We understand that you are not children, Char, but we're family. We're a family that depends on each other and genuinely likes each other, so you'll understand why, when you keep things from us, it's not only a surprise, but a shock," Julie said, sitting beside Kate on the couch. Mark sat on the arm of his recliner, close to Char and Lucy.

"I wasn't trying to keep it from you, Mom. I really didn't think this was a possibility," Kate said, taking her mom's hand. Julie's eyes welled up. "I just get one back and now another is leaving," she whispered.

"Julie," Mark said, his voice so tender it made Lucy wonder how they had fixed it. How had they moved past the hurt that must have been there? As a child, she couldn't fathom the details...and she'd spent the rest of her life pretending not to know the truth by ignoring it. What had happened all those years ago? Sitting with all of them—her family—the need to know was scratching at her from the inside, leaving deep welts on her heart.

"You girls can tell us anything. I'm not happy you're going. I hate when any of you are anywhere but here," Julie said, staring intently at Lucy. It felt weird not to be the one leaving. "But we can't be a real family if we don't face things together—if we hide from each other."

Her words were a direct kick to Lucy's stomach. Lucy lost her breath while inside, her heart hammered. *If that's true, where do I fit?* Her mother's words felt hypocritical. She hadn't come home to make things worse. She'd come home to heal. But if she was staying, if she wanted to move forward, she couldn't listen to words like that from her mother and bite her tongue at the same time.

"I agree. We shouldn't hide from each other. Or what any of us are facing," Lucy said, curling her legs under her. She looked at her mother. "You have agoraphobia. You are scared to leave the house."

Julie's face blanched for the second time that evening, and Kate's hand flew to her mouth in what would have been a comical gesture if there was anything at all funny about it.

"Jesus, Lucy. There is just no pot you won't stir, is there?" her dad asked, standing. The anger in his tone surprised her. He went immediately to sit by Julie and take her hand, and for some reason, this sparked her own anger.

Char covered Lucy's hand with her own, and Lucy looked at her older sister, surprised by the gesture. And so overwhelmingly grateful. She needed the boost of strength.

"Lucy's right. I've been researching it, along with applied behavior analysis therapy," Char said hoarsely, squeezing Lucy's hand so tight it sent a shot of pain through her wrist. "Because ... Carmen has Asperger syndrome."

Tears ran down Char's face, and Lucy pulled her closer. The others said nothing because they knew. They all knew. And knowing hurt. But it also helped. "You'll be able to help her so much more by facing it," Lucy said quietly into Char's ear.

"I know. But Luke doesn't want to believe it. He thinks we can just fix her, and I don't think we can. I think we can only help her," Char said around her sniffling.

"We will all do whatever we can to support you," Julie said. Lucy looked at her mom.

"Same goes for you, Mom. You've trapped yourself in this house. It's silly for us to ignore that. You need help." Lucy said gently but unwaveringly. "You are not here to fix everything, Lucy. Not everything *has* to be fixed. You cannot come home, stir everything up, and then fly off to some unknown

destination again while all of us deal with the fallout." Mark stood and moved toward the window, his hands clenched. Their dad rarely lost his temper. She wasn't trying to hurt him. She'd never do anything to upset any of them on purpose. But she was suffering too.

"I am so tired of all of you ignoring the obvious fact that

I'm staying. So what? I traveled for some years after high school. Not one of you recognize *my* talent, *my* accomplishments. I'm an award-winning photographer. I've done good things. But instead of saying anything about that, all of you throw the fact that I've left in my face every goddamn opportunity you get," Lucy growled, pulling out of Char's embrace and standing. She stalked over to her dad. "The worst part is, you don't even realize I did it for *you*! So you wouldn't have to look at me every fucking day and face the truth.."

Lucy's dad whirled and faced her, utter shock replacing any anger he held. She didn't expect the sob that escaped her throat, but in truth, it had been lying in wait. Julie jumped to her feet.

"Do not swear at your father, Lucy! What has gotten into you?" Julie yelled.

"He's not my real father," Lucy raged back. "And I've spent ten years running from that. Eighteen knowing it. So don't tell me what to do, Mom. Don't tell me about being here for each other and supporting each other and being truthful. Not unless you actually plan to follow through."

Lucy glanced at Kate and saw that her eyes were wide with shock. Char's mouth literally hung open a bit as she looked back and forth between her parents and Lucy. Julie's face crumbled, and she covered it with her hands, silencing the tears Lucy knew fell.

"This," Lucy whispered, backing up slowly. "This is why I've stayed away. Because I didn't know how to pretend. I'm sorry." She looked at her dad. He stood still, staring at her, and Lucy lost any chance at composure when tears slipped down his masculine cheeks. Lucy wasn't sure if any of them heard her say she was sorry again. The sound of her heart breaking might have interfered. She ran from the room, grabbing her purse from the hook by the door.

Running is what she did best. Only this time, she had somewhere to go.

CHAPTER TWENTY

*A*goraphobia   [ag-or-uh-foh-bee-uh]   [noun]
Psychiatry.
an abnormal fear of being in crowds, public places, or open areas, sometimes accompanied by anxiety attacks.

Lucy stared at the definition on her iPad screen from her cozy position on Alex's couch. The shades were drawn, she had a fleece blanket she'd found in his linen closet wrapped around her, a cat at her feet, and a box of Kleenex by her side. She wasn't wrong. The definition jumped out at her from the screen. If she wanted to, she could press the speaker icon and listen to the voice sound out the word. She didn't need to, though. She knew how the word felt on her lips and in her heart. At the moment, she even understood how it could happen. The absence of crowds, the public, and open areas were comforts to Lucy right now in the cocoon she'd created for herself in Alex's dimly lit living room.

She had called him, tears making her words difficult to

understand. He'd apologized for not being able to come to her, to come home. He told her to stay, like he still thought she had the option to leave. Furball meowed and looked up at her. She leaned to stroke his soft fur. Yes, she could stay here in Alex's house and never leave. Or so she told herself. But she knew that she'd crave the outside world soon enough. Which was what surprised her about her mother.

Julie Aarons was a force. A beautiful whirlwind that made others laugh and feel good about themselves. She could charm any man or woman and give them advice at the same time. Lucy had watched her mother at book signings, seen her speak at conferences and give workshops to aspiring non-fiction writers. Trying to figure out how that had changed was giving Lucy a headache.

She threw off the fleece, put her iPad aside, and ignored Furball's irritated protest over her movement. She needed water. And possibly chocolate. Copious amounts of chocolate. Did Alex keep chocolate in his house? If not, she was going to see that he started. Her phone rang on the way to the kitchen. She answered when she saw it was Kael.

"Hey. How are you?" she answered, rooting through Alex's cupboard. "I'm good. Really good. Busier than hell, though," Kael said.

"Hell probably is a pretty busy place," Lucy considered. She found several chocolate bars in one of his cupboards and mentally reminded herself to kiss Alex for being such a good man.

"I bet it is. Filled mostly with New Yorkers," Kael said, laughing loudly. "I need your help, *hoapili*."

Lucy smiled into the phone. She loved when he used

Hawaiian terms of endearment. Another contradiction to who he seemed to be on the outside. "Tell me," she said, unwrapping a Kit Kat bar and breaking it along its lines.

"Delilah had an intern in mind. When I said I had found one, she blew her lid," Kael said. Lucy bit into the rectangle of chocolatey wafer and held back vocalizing how much she enjoyed it. It wasn't a surprise that Delilah Montgomery blew her lid. It was only surprising that she still had a lid to blow. With multiple plastic surgeries to perfect her Barbie look, it was amazing she could even show expression. Nobody lost their temper like Delilah. She was both feared and revered in the fashion industry.

"So? What else is new?" Lucy asked, grabbing another piece and thinking milk would go wonderfully with the rest of the bar.

"We made a deal. There's a huge shoot coming up. We're getting all of the Oscar nominees for best actress in the last five years. In one room. It's the spread of a lifetime. She hasn't selected a photographer because she wants perfection. She wants you. I said that I could get you," he confessed. Lucy choked on the chocolate she'd swallowed too quickly. Kael waited patiently for her to finish coughing.

"What? Are you nuts? One, I don't do those kinds of shoots anymore. Two, that's a huge job, and my last assignment was in a tiny African village shooting tribal life. And I got fired!"

"It doesn't matter what your last shoot was, Lucy. She doesn't care, so I didn't even bring it up. And what do you shoot now? Birthdays and weddings?" Kael asked, his voice more panicked than angry.

"Actually, townspeople and nature, mostly, but I would love to do a wedding. My wants have changed. I don't need to be in the center of it all anymore, Kael. I don't need to be far away to do what I love."

"Okay, well, if you want the sister you love to get the internship, I need to deliver on my promise to D-Day or she's calling her niece twice removed. What does that even mean?"

Lucy's stomach churned. The milk no longer seemed like a good idea. "Dammit, Kael. You should have asked me first."

"I'm asking you now. Come on. It's a week. All expenses paid, I'll make her foot the bill for a luxury hotel. It's within a couple of weeks."

Lucy's mind twisted and twirled with details and timing. Kate would be done with school. She could help her get settled. It was a week. A finite amount of time. The exact opposite of what she had always looked for in a job. But the only reason she was able to accept this one.

"Okay. For Kate. And for you. Because I love you both. But it better be a kick ass hotel. Downtown. And I'm going to try to convince Alex to come with me."

"Oooh, someone's got it bad. I want to meet him. Don't tell him I'm nice until after I interrogate him. Let me have some fun," Kael said, laughing that enormous laugh that suited him perfectly.

They talked for a couple more minutes and ended the conversation with Kael promising to get back to her with flight details. He would see that Kate's details were taken care of as well. It would be nice to have some money go into her bank account. Not that she was anywhere near trouble, but she hadn't been paid for any of the work she was doing in Angel's Lake. Everything had been in exchange for work or money for the center. Which was nearly done. Funny how, when she'd arrived, she hadn't thought she'd see the end of the project. She'd thought she'd be long gone. Her laugh echoed in the quiet house as she headed for Alex's bedroom. She was long gone, alright. Just not in the way she expected.

Alex stood on the paved walkway looking at the Aarons' house. The kitchen light was on. It was late, and he should just head into his own house, where he knew Lucy would be curled up on her side, in his bed, with the cat not far away. She had been so sad when he'd phoned to say hi, and he couldn't make out most of what she was saying. It stripped him raw to hear her hurting and not be able to go to her and comfort her. It also fueled every protective instinct he had, which left him standing on the walkway, wondering if he should speak to her parents. He sighed heavily, wearily, and turned back toward his house.

The porch light turned on just as he made it to his stairs. Mark came out into the darkness and Alex waited.

"Another late night," Mark commented. He had on a U of M sweater and a pair of track pants. Alex couldn't make out his expression in the dark.

"Yeah. Some kids were shoplifting, among other things. Another day at the office," Alex said rigidly. He didn't know what the fight had been about, but he sided with Lucy, regardless.

"My girl was pretty upset when she went running to your house."

"I know. I called her to say hi and couldn't make out much of what she said through the tears," Alex said, unable to keep the condemnation out of his voice.

"She has every reason to be upset. I'll let her tell you what she wants you to know. But when she's done crying— when she breathes long enough to listen— can you do me a favor?"

"Maybe."

Mark rocked back and forth on his heels and nodded his head.

"I like that you're looking after her. Just let her know that there isn't anything that could change how much I love her," Mark said, his voice cracking. Alex wondered what the hell had happened in the Aarons' household that night.

"Sounds like something you should tell her," Alex commented.

"And I will. Every single chance I get. But she won't be ready to hear it from me for a while. She'll hear you. Because she loves you." Mark looked up at the night sky then back at Alex. "She loves you."

"And I love her," Alex said, in case there was any doubt.

"I know you do, son. Otherwise, I wouldn't trust you to relay words that matter so much."

Alex nodded and watched as Mark went back into his

house. The porch light went out and he went to find Lucy—to see what the hell she had faced that night without him.

She wasn't curled in his bed as he'd thought she would be. She was curled on his couch, tucked into one corner with a blanket thrown over her and the cat at her feet. His heart twisted and he realized that every time she was there, he breathed a sigh of relief. He wanted her there. Always. He unloaded his weapon and put it away. He debated taking a shower, but instead changed out of his clothes and put on some lounge pants and a T-shirt. She mumbled when he put his arms under her to lift her.

"Alex," she said, her eyes snapping open when he stood up with her. "Nope. Prince Charming."

"Hmm. Pretty close."

Alex snorted and shook his head. He carried her to his bedroom and laid her on the bed. When he moved to extract himself, she clung to his neck.

"I was going to go shower, Sleeping Beauty," he whispered, kissing the tip of her nose. She threw her leg up to pull him into her and knocked him off balance.

"Oops. You fell. You must be really tired," she said, her arms still like a vice around him.

"Either that or I'm really clumsy," Alex said, laughing and smoothing her hair away from her face. Her eyes fluttered open and shut, and finally, locked steadily on his.

"I'm a tornado," she whispered, her eyes welling up.

"What are you talking about, sweetheart?"

"I came in unexpectedly, stirred up all the bad, and left nothing but devastation," she told him. The strings of his heart tightened. Another knot.

He scooped her up again and then settled himself on the bed so h e could have her on top of him while he soothed her and dried her tears. She told him about their dinner. About their fights. About their truths—her truth. She undid him completely when she dried her tears and took a few deep breaths to steady herself.

"I'm the one that doesn't belong. I'm not like the rest of them, Alex."

"That's just not true, Luce. Your family *loves* you. Blood is about the least important element of truly being a family. Sharing all of the same DNA does not guarantee that a person will always be there for you. That you can count on someone. That there will always be a home for you to come to. There's nothing that could make you any less to them. Your dad loves you so much and doesn't see himself as anything other than your dad."

She nodded her head as if she were trying to believe him—wanted to believe him—but she nestled her face in the crook of his neck, and he felt her body shake with more tears. He held her tight, hoping to take some of the pain—absorb it somehow so she didn't hurt so much.

"The thing is, I'm a reminder of what must have been the worst part of their marriage, Alex. She *cheated* on him. I can't even comprehend that, never mind the fact that she got pregnant with me and he *forgave* her. How can he not resent me?" Lucy asked through her tears. Alex let her cry, stroked her hair, and passed her Kleenex. When it seemed like she couldn't speak, he went to get her some water. Handing it to her, he sat beside her.

"Maybe you're looking at it wrong," he said, watching

while she gulped the water like she'd been in a desert. She handed the glass to him and tilted her head.

"How is that possible? What is the right way to see adultery and deception?"

"What if you're what saved them?" Alex asked. She stared at him blankly.

He leaned against his headboard and pulled her astride him. He held her hands in his and kissed them before he continued.

"I've seen your parents together. There's no faking that kind of love, that kind of commitment and connection. I don't know what happened twenty-eight years ago, but obviously, something did. But you aren't what cracked that foundation, sweetheart. I think you may have been what repaired it. Raising you. Loving you. Whatever tore them apart, it's possible that you stitched them back together."

She was looking at him with so much hope and surprise, he hoped to God that what he'd said had a chance of being true. Lucy Aarons would not be able to stomach being the cause of someone's grief. He knew that and so much more about her. She'd stayed away ten long years to make sure that her very presence didn't cause upset. She would rather bear that burden than watch those she loved suffer. It was one more reason he absolutely adored her, but it also reminded him how much she needed to know she was loved, believed, and needed. She needed to know that, regardless of anything else, she belonged. And she did. With him. And he would prove it to her. He already had a few ideas of just how to do that.

For now, he whispered to her softly, telling her he loved

her. He laid her down on her back and placed kisses along her delicate, soft skin. He ran his fingertips along her, trailing repeatedly over the spots that made her shiver. He traced his tongue and mouth along the path his fingers had taken. He told her he needed her and that he always would. He breathed in every sigh and swallowed every gasp. He stared into her eyes as he hovered over her until she was pulling him down to her, into her, so there was nothing between them. Until they were completely and utterly connected. Every last heartstring tied together. Knotted.

CHAPTER TWENTY-ONE

The real benefit of traveling—Lucy figured out over the next couple of days—was not being around during or after family arguments. The Aarons had had their share over the years. Char wanted a tattoo at fifteen. Kate had spent a week during sixth grade refusing to go to school because she'd gotten a bad perm. Then there was the prom that Lucy chose not to attend, which apparently embarrassed her whole family. She could laugh about petty arguments, or even the odd blow up, from the other side of the globe. But from across the yard, it was much harder to throw herself into her work, keep her head down, and pretend nothing was wrong.

Her dad had taken to weeding the stone pathway that separated the yards. Very slowly. She looked out the window a few times and saw him watching the house. Of course, her mother wasn't going to come over. Kate and Char had texted and asked if she was okay, but since the answer was no and the question was stupid, she didn't reply.

"You could go out there, you know," Alex said from behind her. He wound his arms around her waist and kissed the side of her neck. She was looking out the dining room window to the area her dad was now weeding.

"And say what? Sorry I blurted everything out? Sorry I called my mom a freak, caused a big fight? Oh, and thanks for raising me when I'm not yours?" Lucy asked. Alex chuckled and she whirled on him. "How is this funny?"

"It's not. But you're being a bit dramatic. Things get blurted out in fights. Except by guys, because we don't blurt, we shout. Your mom is not a freak, and you did not say that. And your dad loves you. Go talk to him," Alex replied, stroking her hair. When he did that, something uncurled inside of her chest and spread little waves of contentment through her. She sighed, angry at him for being right and rational and much calmer than she felt.

"Is that what you're going to do? Go talk to your dad?"

"Trust me, sweetheart, if I could get my dad to talk to me, I would. I've threatened to charge him with obstruction, and he still won't tell me where the damn paint came from."

"I'm sorry. I'm being all moody and emotional, and you have stuff going on, too," she said, putting her arms around his waist. Furball brushed between them.

"We need a date night. I need to take you out. How about tomorrow? We'll go to a movie," he suggested, kissing the crown of her head. "Ooh—"

"Something funny. Without subtitles," he added quickly.

When Alex left for work, she realized she couldn't stay in his house all day, staring out the window. She grabbed her things and headed back to her parents house. Both of them were in the kitchen when she walked in. The three of them stayed still, looking at each other, all of their words trapped in the silence.

When Alex pulled up to his dad's, he parked behind a work truck that read "Clay's Concrete." A couple of guys were smoothing out the cement. Finishing the driveway would spruce things up a lot and make parking easier. Sam had done a good job fixing up the shed. Alex walked over the lawn and up his dad's front steps. He knocked twice then opened the front door and called out.

"Back here," Chuck answered.

Alex made his way through the sparsely decorated, masculine living room. Wandering through the house he knew as well as his own, he found Chuck just where he'd thought he would—in his office, working on one of his maps. His dad had a lifelong fascination with cartography.

A few Christmases ago, Alex had bought him a massive map of the world that took up one entire wall of the decently sized study. Chuck was at his desk, glasses perched on his nose, sketching on thin parchment paper. It was only in the last year or so that his dad had taken up drawing the maps. It was tedious work that would have driven Alex nuts, but it was interesting to look at. Chuck put his fine-tipped pencil down

"You're becoming a regular," Chuck said, stretching his neck to each side.

"You phoned me. I'm stopping by like you asked. Driveway is going to look good," Alex said. He wasn't trying to be stiff and formal—he just couldn't stop being irritated with his dad. Chuck stood and came around the wide-planked teak table that he used as a desk. The table would look good in Alex's dining room.

"You're right, I did. Let's get a drink. I'm thirsty," Chuck replied, moving out of the room, leaving Alex to follow. "What are you mapping?"

"An old route between England and Spain that wasn't found until after a number of voyages had already failed."

Chuck grabbed two cans of soda from the fridge and tossed one to Alex. They both tapped the tops a couple of times and cracked them open. Alex took a long swallow and set his can on the counter. He had helped his dad do the backsplash in this kitchen and, looking around now, he realized they had done a pretty good job. It was a beautiful house and, overall, Alex had been happy growing up here. His dad was a stubborn son of a bitch, but he was fair and, usually honest. Which is part of what was bugging Alex so much right now.

"So what's up?" Alex asked. "Your mother phoned me."

Alex was glad he had put his drink down. If he'd been mid-swallow, he probably would have choked. If he'd been holding the can, he would have crushed it. "What the fuck?"

"Watch your language, boy."

Alex smacked his hand against the countertop. "Okay. What the fucking hell?"

Chuck shook his head and carried his pop to the living room. *Jesus. Stay still. Talk already.*

"You know what sucks about having kids?" Chuck asked, settling into the corner of one of the leather couches.

"When they want you to be honest?" Alex said. His thoughts flashed to Lucy, and he felt a pang of regret for what she was going through.

"Smart-ass. No. What sucks is when they have certain traits that annoy the hell out of you and then you suddenly realize that they got them from you."

"At least you're accepting the blame."

"See," Chuck said, gesturing toward Alex with his can. "That's what I'm talking about. No one can talk to you about something when you've made your mind up. Your mother wants to talk to you, Alex. If I can give the woman a chance, so can you."

Alex's heart fell to his stomach and twisted inside out.

"What do you mean 'give her a chance'? What kind of chance are you giving her?" Alex demanded, glad he hadn't sat down. His fists clenched at his sides and his breath froze, making his chest tight.

"Shit, Alex! Not that kind of chance. She's called a few times over the years. I'm not mad at her anymore. I think you should work on that," Chuck said. "Oh, yeah. Why should I do that?"

"Sit down, Alex," Chuck said in a tone that demanded he did. Alex sat on the edge of the couch, feeling fifteen again. Like he'd been caught sneaking out and Chuck was going to give him a talk that would make him wish he hadn't been so stupid.

"I don't want to do this. She didn't want me sixteen years ago, I don't need her now," Alex said.

"Maybe not. But one day, she'll be gone, and all you'll have is your stubborn, bruised heart," Chuck said gruffly.

"My heart is just fine, thanks."

"No, it's not. Not that piece of it, anyway. She wrecked a piece of yours the way she did mine. We can either hang on to that and let it fester, or we can let it go. There's a hell of a lot of relief in letting it go, son."

"There's nothing to let go, dad. I'm fine. I don't need to reconnect with my mother."

"She's got cancer, Alex."

And just like that, his heart twisted again and pushed its way upward to lodge in his throat, painfully. Alex said nothing. He looked at his father, trying not to let it matter. Three seconds ago, she hadn't mattered.

"Her prognosis is good. She's already had surgery. She's not calling to say good-bye or anything morbid like that. I think she realizes that we only get one shot at this. She messed up a good portion of it. You can't go back, but you can move forward. She just wants to move forward."

Alex still said nothing. How could he when his heart was stuck in his trachea? He stood and walked to the window. He could see the guys pouring concrete. The thick, heavy liquid dispensed slowly. Someone smoothed it out, and then they left it to move to the next section. If anything got caught in that concrete, it would stay there, essentially, forever. Unless someone made a conscious effort to change what had been imprinted in the cement.

"What kind?" Alex asked.

"Breast cancer. She's doing well. They caught it early. She was a shitty mother. A shitty wife. But she's a good person, Alex. She's your mom."

Alex shook his head. He didn't have the words. He didn't know what he felt or what he wanted. Obviously, he didn't want her to have cancer. He hadn't thought he'd care about anything connected to her, but he knew, in this moment, he didn't want her to have cancer, he didn't want her to die, and—son of a bitch—he didn't want her to die without him ever having a chance to talk to her again.

"Do you want some tea? I have some chamomile. It's calming," Julie said, puttering and fidgeting with the kettle, the tea bags, and taking out cups. Mark stayed where he had been sitting when Lucy had walked in.

"No, thank you," Lucy answered, unsure where to look.

"How did you find out?" Mark asked, surprising Lucy. She looked up at him. Her heart seized. She loved him so much. She didn't have his nose or his height or his blood, but he was her *dad*. A cup clattered onto the counter. Julie picked it up and put it away.

Lucy thought back to that night so long ago. She had vague memories, snippets, of her younger sister being sick off and on, but as a kid, she only knew what her parents told her. "You were having an argument one night. Char was at a sleepover, and Kate came to sleep with me. She was stealing all of the covers, and when I went to shove her out of the bed, I realized that she was burning up. I came to get one of you."

Julie gave a small, strangled sound that was half gasp, half whimper. Lucy sat down at the table across from her dad. Julie turned to face them but stayed with her back to the counter.

"We didn't keep it from you because we didn't want you to know. We didn't want you to feel what you feel now," Julie said quietly. "What's that?"

"Like you're not mine. How the hell can you think that you aren't mine?" Mark asked, sitting up and banging his fist on the table. Lucy jumped and wondered if she had gotten it wrong all those years ago. Words were failing her as her breathing quickened.

"What? Are you ... do you mean ... are you my dad?" she asked, hating the tears in her voice.

"It depends on what you call a dad," Mark said. His eyes were heated—the way they were when he gave a lecture that he felt passionate about. "Biologically, no. I am not. But that doesn't change one damn thing, Lucy. I'm surprised at you."

He shook his head and Lucy felt like hers was spinning. How could he be mad or surprised at *her*? She stood, suddenly wanting a drink and needing something in her hands. She went to the fridge to grab some apple juice.

"Mark. Don't be like that. She's shocked. Honey. What your dad means—"

"What I mean," Mark interrupted, "is your first word was Santa. You pronounced it Sa-Sa. You were eleven months old when you took your first step. You fell headfirst into the coffee table, and I just about had a heart attack. I taught you how to ride a bike. I told you the truth about Santa Claus and the tooth fairy, and I held you when you cried over the first idiot boy who broke your heart."

Lucy shut the fridge with nothing in her hands. Her dad stood, all but vibrating with his energy and passion and all of the conviction that made him, *him*. He moved around the table, glancing at Julie, who smiled encouragingly at him. The sweetness of the exchange just about broke the fragile grip Lucy had on her emotions.

"I helped you study for your Spanish test in eleventh grade. I hated Spanish in high school, but I learned it again for you. Sometimes, I still conjugate verbs and it irritates the hell out of me. I told your mother to let you go, that it was the only way you'd ever come back, every single time you had to travel abroad. You do not have my blood. But you do have my name, my love, and my heart. You tell me if that's enough. Tell me if that makes me your dad."

He was breathing heavily when he finished, and Lucy's control shattered when a single tear rolled down his cheek. She launched herself at him, so utterly overwhelmed that she couldn't speak. His arms came around her immediately, as they always had. Steady, sure, safe.

"You are *my* little girl. Nothing can change that," he whispered in her ear. She nodded against him, her own tears streaming down her face. He hugged her harder.

They took a break. Her mother made all of them tea, and they took it into the living room. They sipped their tea and didn't rush. Lucy dried her tears and excused herself to wash up. When she returned, her parents were sitting side by side on the couch. Lucy sat across from them on the loveseat. She pulled her knees up and hugged them to her chest, feeling like she'd need the anchor. The silence and secrets crept back, and Lucy was afraid to learn too much. Did she have the same capacity to forgive as her dad?

"I made one mistake. One night. I jeopardized everything that I had, and I don't even have a good reason. That's the worst of it, I think. That I didn't even have a reason to throw it all away. As soon as it happened, I was sick. I told your father immediately," Julie said in one long swell of words. Mark put his hand on Julie's, covering it like a shield. She glanced at him before continuing.

"At first, I didn't want him to forgive me. I hated myself so much. I told him to take Char, to leave me. That he deserved so much better," Julie said, her voice cracking.

"I considered it. I left for a couple of weeks. I came to pick up Char, but I couldn't talk to your mom. I couldn't look at her. When Char told me that mommy cried all the time, I came back. I wasn't coming back to her, but for your sister," Mark said.

Lucy had to force herself to breathe as she watched the pain slowly etch itself over their features, pulling them back to that time.

"I thought I was truly heartsick. And I was. Your father was the only boyfriend I had ever had. He is and will always be the only man I have ever loved. But after three weeks of throwing up constantly, I went to the doctor."

"You were pregnant with me," Lucy whispered, not even meaning to. Her mom nodded. Lucy's stomach tilted, causing a wave of dizziness even though she was sitting.

"Everything we do is a choice. Sometimes one choice defines us—shows us who we are or who we aren't. Your mother is not a cheater, Lucy. She made a mistake. I had to make a choice, too. Move on without her or punish both of us for good. Every good thing in my life has come from being with your mom. Even the pain she caused me brought you," Mark said.

"It's not as cut and dried as that, honey. We went to therapy. I went to therapy. We fought. We cried and we healed," Julie added.

"But how did you get past the fact that she was pregnant with another man's child?" Lucy asked. She unfolded her legs and stretched them out, feeling pins and needles skitter along her skin.

"We didn't know who the father was. Until that fight. We had no idea you heard us," Julie told her. She picked up her tea, sipped at it, and placed it back down. Lucy wished she had something stronger than tea. Lucy remembered her parents worrying about Kate, taking her to the doctor, and Kate's frequent fevers. Had any of the three of them realized the stress her parents had been under at the time? Probably not.

"Kate was really sick. They thought, briefly, while running tests, that she might need a liver transplant. It was suggested that we have you and Char tested to see if you were a match. Just in case. It turned out not to be her liver, but it also gave us results we hadn't anticipated. We were so caught up in her being sick that we weren't thinking what else would come from the blood tests and screening," Mark said, his eyes cloudy like he was looking at that time in his life.

Lucy stood and stretched her legs by pacing the living room. If she had known all of the reasons—if she had never found out at all—would she have spent the last ten years losing herself? Escaping from the sting of not belonging? If she'd never found out, would they have ever told her?

"It's never changed for one second how I feel about you, Lucy," Mark said, drawing her attention back to the two of them sitting stoically on the couch.

"I am..." Julie's voice trailed off, and Lucy stopped pacing. "I am so sorry that you thought, for even one second, that having you home would bring me, us, anything but joy. I'm so sorry."

Lucy wanted to say it wasn't her fault, but that wasn't entirely true. She felt anger toward her mother, but not as much as she'd expected.

She took a deep breath. "How did you forgive her? How do you look at her the way you do and not see what she did? How do you look at me and not see it?" Lucy whispered. Her dad stood and came to her. He tilted her chin up and brushed her hair back from her face like he had when he coached her Little League games. He'd taken her chin between his thumb and forefinger and told her to keep her eye on the ball and her heart in the game.

"When I look at you, I see your mother's eyes. I hear your mother's laugh, and see her amazing capacity to give in all of the things you do. I love her. It's too much to live without her. To me, that's harder than forgiveness. All I see when I look at you is my daughter," he said quietly. Lucy wasn't even sure if her mother could hear him. And regardless of what she knew, all she saw when she looked at him was her dad. It was the only truth she needed.

He pulled her in for a hug and whispered, "Don't be mad at her. She's punished herself enough." He kissed her forehead, lingering for a moment. Then he picked up his teacup and Julie's and took them to the kitchen, leaving her alone with her mom. Lucy felt awkward standing there, so she went to sit where her dad had been.

"I ask myself every day why he forgave me," Julie said, looking down at her hands clasped in her lap. "Then I push the thought away and focus on being grateful he did. Your father is the best person I know. He makes me better, and he is part of you, regardless of DNA."

Lucy nodded. She finally felt like this was enough.

"You need help, Mom," Lucy said quietly. Might as well herd all of the elephants at once. This time, Julie nodded and took Lucy's hand. "I know."

Alex had finally caught a break. One of the security cameras they had installed had caught the back of a kid's head. It wasn't definitive, but it told them more than they had known. Their tagger was approximately five-feet-nine, right-handed, and blond. He had been wearing a nondescript nylon jacket that Alex hoped to inspect closer when he blew up some of the photos.

He poured cat food into a bowl like a zombie, wanting nothing more than to shower and sleep for ten hours. He felt like he'd aged a decade today. As usual, the best part of his day was curled up in his bed, snoring softly. She was on her side, her face so peaceful. Watching her made him physically ache for her. *Will this intensity ever lessen?* He didn't want to think about his dad, his mother, or a punk-ass tagger. Not when he could fall into bed and into Lucy. He was grabbing some boxers to change into after his shower when her phone rang on his dresser. Casting a quick glance, not wanting the noise to wake her, he pressed accept and walked out of his bedroom into the hall.

"Hello?" he said quietly.

"Hello. This is Trina. I'm looking for Lucy," a woman's crisp voice said. Apparently, Trina didn't care what time it was. "She's sleeping. Can I take a message?"

Alex moved back into the kitchen to find a pen and a scrap of paper.

"Yes. I'm Kael Makhai's assistant. I'm in charge of making the necessary travel arrangements for Lucy's upcoming trip to New York. I have an itinerary I need to send to her, so I'll need an email address. I also have a hotel booked and the list of apartments she requested Kael look in to," Trina prattled.

Alex went perfectly still. All he heard was a heavy buzzing in his ear. He squeezed the phone so tight his fingertips almost touched his palms. He accidently pressed a button, making Trina's voice come through the speaker.

"Hello? Sir, are you there?" she asked shrilly. He quickly pressed the speakerphone button to silence her back to the earpiece.

"Shit. Sorry. What?" Alex asked, his heart hammering

and a bead of sweat weaving its way down his back. He heard a heavy, put-upon sigh from the phone.

"Lucy is scheduled to be here next week for a job she accepted with my boss. Can you just have her phone me please?" Trina snapped. She then hung up, leaving Alex with nothing more than a phone in one hand, a pair of boxers in the other, and his heart in shreds on his kitchen floor.

CHAPTER TWENTY-TWO

When Lucy woke, she had that moment of foggy sadness but couldn't remember why. When her eyes landed on Alex, sitting on his window seat, watching her, she forgot everything but him.

"Hi," she said, smiling sleepily and stretching. "Why are you way over there?"

He said nothing. Just continued to watch her, his face blank. He looked like he needed to shave, his hair was messy, and his clothes were rumpled. She felt a little spurt of unease as she sat herself up.

"Are you okay? Did you just get home?"

Still nothing. Her heart beat faster, making all of her senses come alert. She was no longer sleepy, no longer sad —just scared.

"Alex? What's wrong?" She threw the covers off and moved to the side of the bed, ignoring the wave of nausea. She urged her stomach to settle down.

Everything is fine.

"You are so fucking beautiful," he said in a voice she barely recognized. Why did it sound like more of an accusation than a compliment? She felt the urge to pull the blanket back over her.

"Alex?"

"Part of the draw has always been how gorgeous you are. The thing is, you're every bit as beautiful on the inside as you are out. So when you get pulled in, you get all the way sucked in. Or at least I did. But you've never pretended to be anything you weren't, so I don't know why I let myself fall so far."

He was talking like he wasn't actually talking to her. It was making her physically ill. She held her stomach. "You're scaring me. What's wrong?" she asked.

"You told me upfront that you weren't a forever kind of girl. It's my own fault, really," he said more casually, standing. "You told me you wouldn't stay. You also told me you loved me. I guess I wanted to believe that more than the truth."

The fog cleared from Lucy's brain. She clenched her hands and stood. "What are you talking about? I *do* love you."

"Really?" He asked in such a caustic tone that it felt like he'd knocked the wind out of her.

"Yes, really," she whispered. "I've never said that to anyone outside of my family and closest friends. I don't understand what's going on."

"What's going on is our time is done. I thought I could handle you picking up and leaving, but I can't. As your family pointed out, I am, pathetically, a forever kind of guy and you're ... for now."

Lucy's stomach twisted and heaved. She covered her mouth and ran for the washroom. Too angry to be embarrassed, she dry-heaved until her stomach ached. Splashing water on her face, she tried to cool both her skin and her temper.

Alex regarded her carefully from the doorway to his bedroom. He had a glass of water in his hand, which he passed to her. She accepted it only because her mouth felt like sandpaper.

"So to recap, I lied about loving you, we're over, and I'm leaving?"

Alex winced but said nothing. She sipped, resisting the urge to toss the water in his face.

"You'll excuse me if I ask for just one detail. Where is this coming from?" she said, hoping that the anger in her voice covered the soul-searing pain. "Trina called," Alex said. He looked at her as if he'd just summed everything up perfectly.

"Who the hell is Trina?"

She saw his face blanch slightly, but he recovered and switched back to a sarcastic sneer.

"That would be Kael's assistant. Did you forget? She has all of your travel arrangements. She just needs your email," he said, yanking at the buttons on his shirt.

He wadded the shirt into a ball and hurled it toward his laundry hamper, then whirled back to face her. "And good ol' Trina, she also got together that list of apartments you wanted." His hands were on his hips, and his chest was heaving with each breath.

Everything unraveled. Like those rolls of stickers she used to get as a kid. She would unroll it, just a little, to get to the one she wanted, but then the whole thing would come undone. She couldn't catch it and in seconds, she'd be standing with a pile of stickers at her feet, and she had to wind it all back up again.

"You're an idiot," she whispered through clenched teeth. Her feet were rooted to their spot. He stood straighter. "Excuse me?"

"You believed in me when I didn't believe in myself. When the people who knew me best didn't believe in me, you did," she said softly, her fingers tight on the half-empty glass.

"A lot of good it did me," he said, but the earlier venom he'd had in his tone was gone.

Lucy laughed without humor and the motion made her chest ache. *Not him too.* Unclenching her jaw, she shook her head. "They had their reasons not to believe in me. But I've never given *you* one. I expected more from you. A lot of good *that* did *me*. You're so wrapped up in being right, you can't see how wrong you are."

To his credit, he looked stricken by her words. His voice was hoarse. "I was wrong to let myself fall so hard for a woman I knew, on some level, would never be satisfied with me and this nothing town."

"I'm sorry you feel that way. About yourself, the town. And mostly about us." She couldn't defend herself to anyone else right now. Especially to Alex. The one person she never thought would doubt her. She put the water down, as gently as possible for fear of revealing how badly her hands were shaking. She grabbed her T-shirt to yank over her tank top. Her yoga pants were on his window seat. She pulled them on over her boy-short underwear, her movements jerky.

"Running away?" he taunted. It surprised her how much she wanted to slap him.

She embraced the anger. It felt better than the sickening hurt spreading through her. "No. I'm going *home*. I've clearly overstayed my welcome here," she replied.

"Be sure to say good-bye before you head for New York," he said. Tears welled in her eyes. The empty sickness in her stomach was returning. She would not break down in front of him.

"That won't be necessary. I can say good-bye right now," Lucy said, standing quickly. Alex blurred in her vision, the sickness winding its way up her throat. She stepped toward him, but it was dark and she couldn't see. She didn't know why he was yelling her name or why she felt like she was falling. She didn't know why everything hurt so badly, and then, when her eyes drifted shut, when her face hit the soft carpet and she let them close, she didn't know anything at all.

ALEX PACED the corridor of the hospital. He wanted to punch something. He'd already flashed his badge unprofessionally and scared more than one nurse in his attempt to get some goddamn answers. *What is taking so long?* She'd collapsed in front of him. All that fury that she tried to keep hidden with her precise movements and clipped words had gone out like a light when she'd stood, blinked several times, and crumpled. He didn't even catch her, his shock was so great. He'd called her name when he realized what was happening. He'd grabbed his phone immediately, calling 9-1-1 and then her parents.

Mark had come raging through the door and picked up his daughter like she weighed nothing, even though Alex had advised him to leave her where she was. Mark had silenced him with a look and held her in his arms as she'd come to. Her speech was slightly slurred, but she was mumbling when the EMT arrived. Mark had ridden with her to the hospital. Alex should have been the one beside her, holding her hand, telling her everything was okay. Instead, he was the one who had made her collapse.

Char came barreling through the automatic doors.

"What's wrong? What happened?" she demanded, grabbing his arms.

"She collapsed. I don't know anything yet. Your dad and Kate are in the waiting room," Alex answered. His throat felt like he'd swallowed nails. Anger flashed in Char's eyes. "Not my mother," Char said, shaking her head.

"No."

"She just collapsed?" Char repeated.

"We were arguing. She got up and then she just ... went down."

His hands were shaking. He shoved them into his pockets. Mark cleared his throat, catching Char and Alex's attention.

"She's okay. We're going in to see her. We can only go in two at a time, and Kate's already in there," Mark said. Alex clenched his fists in his pockets. "We'll go in next," Alex said. Mark nodded and walked away.

Alex sat with Char for the next ten, agonizing minutes. Kate came out first and walked straight to Alex. She sat down in the chair next to him. Char stood, expecting him to stand as well, but Kate stopped him with her hand.

"She doesn't want to see you," Kate said, not looking at him. He closed his eyes. He hadn't cried since he was eight, but at that moment, he had to bite his tongue to refocus his emotions.

"What are you talking about?" Char asked impatiently. She looked back and forth between Kate and Alex. Alex stared at his feet.

"He broke up with her," Kate said. Rather than anger, he heard utter devastation in her voice. He didn't think he could be more broken. "You what?" Char yelled, earning looks from the nurses and others waiting on the cold, plastic chairs.

"She's leaving," he whispered pitifully.

"What?" Char said again, this time a bit more hushed but still surprised.

"Yes. She is," Kate said. She shook her head and finally looked at Alex. It took everything in him to find the strength to meet her eyes. She waited until he did before she continued.

"Lucy agreed to take a one-week photo shoot in New York. Kind of a trade-off for her friend taking me on as an intern. It works out perfectly. She'll come with me. Do the shoot. Help me get settled. Turns out that Kael even found some apartments for me to take a look at."

Kate stood, took Char's hand, and leaned her head on her sister's shoulder. Alex looked back and forth between them. Char's face registered understanding. "You thought she was leaving for good. You thought she was running."

Alex didn't move. He couldn't.

"You should go," Kate said. He started to protest, but she stopped him. "The doctor said she's going to be fine. Just a dizzy spell. They'll run some tests to rule things out. You have to let her go. If she wants to contact you, she will."

With that, both women turned and walked past the nurses' station. The doors slid open when they approached and then shut behind them. Alex sat, staring through the glass at their disappearing backs, wondering how—when Lucy was all that he had wanted for as long as he could remember—he had managed to chase her away when she'd been willing to stay.

Lucy was curled on her side, Kate holding one hand, Char tucked in behind her. Char had crawled right into the bed, bossy as ever, and wrapped herself around Lucy and cried. All three of them had cried. They'd washed their dad out of the small, curtained room with their tears. He'd left to get Charlotte's car and bring it around to the emergency room exit.

"Lucy?" Kate said. Lucy stared at a tiny fleck on the washed-out wall. Her body felt numb, and her mind refused to focus. Her heart was still beating, but she was certain that it was an entirely useless organ now. What would she do with it? She thought of all of the photographs she had taken that hadn't turned out just as she'd wanted. She'd shredded them. It's not like she could travel with boxes of unusable photographs. *How do you do that with a heart? Especially one that's already shredded.* She wished she could box it up. Drop it off on Alex's doorstep. *Here. You broke it, you keep it.*

"I want to go home," Lucy whispered.

"Dad's getting the car. Damn. We haven't even talked about *that* yet," Char said, rubbing her hand up and down Lucy's chilled arm. "Can you sit up? What did the doc say about your dizzy spells?" Kate asked.

Lucy closed her eyes. *Too much.* She opened them as Char eased herself carefully off of the bed.

"Just a combination of heat, running around too much, and emotional stress," Lucy said, looking away from Kate's assessing gaze. It was partially the truth. He *had* said those things.

"You're used to temperatures in South America, and *this* heat bothered you?" Char asked. Lucy sat carefully. Kate put her hand on Lucy's gown-covered thigh. Lucy pushed it away.

"I'm fine," Lucy snapped. There was a razor edge to her voice that she knew didn't hide the tears, but at least it shut her sisters up, for now. Mark pushed the pale blue curtain aside, making the little chain links on the top bar rattle. Lucy picked up the tepid water they had brought earlier and sipped.

"Car is out front. I didn't see Alex," Mark said. He looked at all three girls. No one said a word. Lucy stood, waving both of her sisters away. "I'll wait in the car," Mark said.

Once the dizzy spell had passed and the nausea had abated, she felt fine. The hospital had been more of a precaution, and it made her feel stupid. She sat in the front seat of Char's car, staring out the window, wrecked. Char pulled up to the house and Lucy noted that Alex's car was nowhere to be seen. Kate's gasp of surprise redirected her attention. Luke stood on the porch with Mia in his arms and Carmen by his side. Carmen was holding her grandmother's hand. Lucy got out of the car, oblivious to everything else, and walked to her mom. She stood in front of her and looked down at Carmen.

"I brought Grandma outside because she was worried. But she needs to hold my hand," Carmen said in her no-nonsense tone.

"That makes sense," Lucy said quietly, her throat raw but not nearly so much as her heart. She looked at her mom, who tilted her head slightly before reaching out and touching Lucy's cheek. Lucy's tears fell without warning, and she stepped into her mom, who pulled her tightly into a one-armed hug. Carmen kept a hold on her grandmother's hand, but Lucy felt the other touch Lucy's back, making them a circle. The hug, the moment, made Lucy think that maybe, one day, she might be okay. But it wouldn't be today.

CHAPTER TWENTY-THREE

*A*lex lived off of coffee, anger, and self-pity for the next forty-eight hours. He didn't go home after the hospital. He'd driven to the station, poured through the vandalism pictures, growled at anyone who spoke to him, and did everything humanly possible to avoid thinking about Lucy. Nothing worked. He kept seeing her face in the moment she'd realized what he'd been saying. He saw her falling to the floor. He saw her lying lifeless on his bedroom floor. Laying full of life in his bed. Laying underneath him ... over him. He saw her lips moving, telling him she loved him. He saw her tears. Tears he caused. He saw her on the gurney as they put her in the ambulance, and he saw Kate's profile when she told him that Lucy didn't want to see him. What he couldn't see, was how he would get over this. Over her. Past this. He couldn't fucking breathe without her.

"Hey," Sam said, startling Alex from his brooding at his office window. Sam looked normal. Happy. How were people still functioning when he couldn't breathe, and how the hell could this hurt so bad?

"Hey. Thanks for coming by," Alex said.

"You look like shit," Sam said, opening Alex's mini fridge and pulling out a coke. He cracked it open and took a long drink. Alex didn't know where to start. So he told him about the phone call, the fight, and the hospital. Sam whistled, shook his head, and sat down in Alex's chair while Alex stayed where he was at the window.

"No wonder you look like hell. Is she okay?" Sam asked, feet up on Alex's desk.

"Yes, as far as I know. She was released from the hospital. Doc wouldn't tell me much; he said she was released because I used my badge." Alex sighed and scraped his fingers along his scalp. He went to the fridge and got his own drink.

"You want her back?" Sam asked. Alex gave him a nasty look that revealed the stupidity of the question. Sam laughed it off with the ease of a long-time friend and lowered his feet. "Okay. Just checking. Want my advice?"

"Will it be any good?" Alex asked, taking a drink and wishing he had a bottle of scotch in his drawer. "Which one of us is getting married?"

"Right," Alex scoffed, "that makes you an expert." But he waited and listened when Sam spoke. "Get some knee pads," Sam said gravely.

"What?"

"You're going to be on your knees groveling for a while,

so it's best to be comfortable," Sam said. At the huge grin on his face, Alex slammed his drink down, making bits of it splash and fizz out of the opening.

"Fuck you. You don't have to enjoy this," Alex replied. His shoulders sagged.

"Come on. Don't be like that. Seriously, man. You are going to have to beg for forgiveness. You need to pull out all the stops. You want Lucy back, you need to turn yourself inside out and prove it. Show her that you know her, that you *get* her. Prove to her that you've changed—whatever you have to do. I can tell you from having things almost go south with Anna, laying yourself bare is scary as hell, but worth it if it works."

Alex mulled over what Sam had said. He had already come to those conclusions, which was why he had asked Sam to stop by in the first place. "I need your help," Alex admitted.

"You got it," Sam replied.

Lucy didn't expect miracles, but she had thought by the third day home from the hospital, something would stop hurting. People fell in and out of love all of the time. She'd been to Hollywood and she read the magazines. How did they *do* this? How could anyone survive this churning and devastation that swirled inside of her heart and her head? How did she move beyond Alex seeing her just as everyone else did?

The sun was shining through her bedroom window, reminding her that the world still rotated and everyone in it was still functioning. Knowing that didn't entice her to participate. The spot on her bed was too cozy. It needed the weight of her, and she thought that getting up would take too much effort. Kate walked in without knocking. Lucy moved only her eyes. Kate tilted her head, and Lucy would have punched her for the look of pity, but again, the effort. Kate wore a white, oversized, collared-shirt-dress that hung to her knees. She'd paired it with a wide brown belt and boots. Lucy wondered how she'd missed her sister's real passion all this time. Kate carried a brown cardboard box from Kinko's. Lucy closed her eyes. She knew what that was.

"Get up. Looking at hot men always helps," Kate said. She came to the bed and pushed Lucy's curled-up legs so that her feet fell off the edge of the bed.

"When did you become so bossy? You're acting like Char," Lucy grumbled. But she also sat up and ran a finger part way through her hair, getting it caught on the tangles. She sighed and leaned her head on Kate's shoulder.

"You adore Char, so I'll take that as a compliment. Have you talked to him?" Kate asked. Lucy took the box and ignored the question. "Let me see my handy work."

The calendars were beautiful. The front had a great shot of all the guys playing basketball on the court behind the almost-finished rec center. They were laughing and smiling. Sam was up in the air, making a shot, and Alex was guarding him at the net. Lucy inhaled slowly, painfully, certain she could hear the crumbling inside of her chest.

"You sure you want to look?" Kate asked with more gentleness than Lucy could stomach. She stood up and put the box on the bed.

She couldn't look at them with an audience. "I need a

shower. You check them and make sure everything is alright. We'll go over to the rec center when I'm done, okay?" Lucy said, pulling fresh clothes out of her dresser. Kate came over and wrapped her in her arms. Lucy let herself be hugged for a few seconds before she firmed her shoulders and her resolve.

"I'll meet you downstairs," Kate said. Lucy nodded and headed for the shower.

Under the hot spray, the scent of vanilla shampoo surrounding her, Lucy sobbed, hoping that the water would wash away the pain and the empty ache. The hardest part, other than him not believing in her—in them—was knowing that even if—when—she got through this, she would never fully be over him. He would always be part of her.

Sitting in his car outside his dad's house, far enough away that he wasn't immediately visible, Alex barely recognized himself. Here he was, spying on his own father because he couldn't shake the feeling that somehow, all of the trouble was connected to him. Sometimes, people weren't who you thought they were. He hadn't turned out to be who'd Lucy thought he was—hell, who *he* had thought he was. His phone buzzed. His hope was squashed immediately when he saw Sam's text: *Just checked it out. Should be easy enough. Won't take more than a couple of days. You owe me.*

Yeah, he owed him, even if his plan didn't work. Alex slouched down a bit, pushed his seat back, and felt the last few days catching up with him. His eyelids were heavy, and even with the windows open, so was the heat. Without warning, his dad came out of his house, springing down the front stairs, headed to his aging Durango. Hopping in, he backed out of his driveway, forcing Alex to sit up and shake off the heat. Though he didn't feel good about it, he started his car and tailed Chuck from a safe distance.

"Where the hell are you going?" Alex mumbled after he had followed behind for about ten minutes. Older homes lined the street, along with the cars people parked in front of those homes. Alex knew a few people who lived in the decent neighborhood that was just south of the main area of town. In his gut, he knew, but he didn't want to admit it or face it without proof.

Sure enough, Chuck pulled up to the curb outside of a little bungalow that was older, but well cared for. Painted a bright, cheerful yellow, it had

multicolored window boxes brimming with a rainbow of flowers. It suited its owner perfectly. Said owner must have been watching for his dad because she came bouncing out of the house, her hair not moving with her exaggerated, high-heeled steps. She had a leopard skin purse the size of a suitcase slung over her shoulder and even from where he sat, parked down the street, Alex could see she was wearing fishnet stockings. He didn't know they still made those for anything other than Halloween costumes. As they moved closer to each other, Alex groaned out loud.

"Don't do it. Stop. Please don't. Arrrg," he groused, slapping his hand hard on the steering wheel. Through squinted eyes, he watched as his dad embraced Dolores in a so-much-more-than-friends hug and then kissed her like he was going on leave for a month. Alex was suddenly grateful that he hadn't eaten much in the last few days because with what he was watching, he had a feeling it would have come back to bite him.

The rec center was ready. It needed a good cleaning—construction crews weren't known for their tidy cleanups. Still, they had gotten most of the work done at cost, so Lucy wasn't complaining and neither was Kate. Her sister had an exam that evening, and Lucy had told her she would walk home. Kate had protested, but Lucy insisted, saying the fresh air would make her feel better. It did, particularly in that moment, when day was turning to evening. When the air cooled but wasn't cold. When the heat lifted slightly and the slight breeze moved in from the lake, funneling around her, thanks to the mountains.

It surprised her that, even with the sadness that had taken up residence inside of her heart and her mind, she had no urge to leave. In fact, she was thinking about getting a place of her own. She would need one. She certainly didn't want to live with her parents forever, and she needed to start making some plans. As she walked past the Sheriff's station, she kept her eyes down, watching her footsteps. She couldn't avoid him forever, but she didn't have to see him now. She would have to talk to him again, but it didn't have to be today. She kicked a stone in her path and decided to pick up some dessert from Bean's Bakery.

OPENING THE DOOR, she held it for the high-haired woman that was coming out with a delicious smelling pie. Dolores might be stuck in the eighties, but she seemed like a sweet woman, and just the sight of her made her think of Alex and his funny stories about Dolores and the station.

"Well, hey there. Heard you weren't feeling too well," Dolores said, a wide smile on her pink lips. Lucy continued to hold the door.

"Oh, I'm okay. Just a dizzy spell and everyone overreacted," Lucy said, shrugging and feeling the need to escape before his name was said. "I've never seen Alex so beside himself. He was positively sick with worry," Dolores crooned. Lucy's heart cracked at the sound of his name. "I'm fine. Really."

Dolores smiled at her like they had some sort of secret understanding. Then her eyes widened. "Are you still looking for donations for the auction?" Dolores asked.

Lucy felt silly standing there with the door open. She caught Bean's eye from behind Dolores's back and stifled a small giggle at the baker's talks-too-much gesture.

"Of course. Do you have something? I'm trying to get everything together by Friday morning," Lucy said.

"My son is an artist and, I know I'm his mama, but my boy has talent. Serious talent. I would be thrilled to donate a few of his pieces. He's shy about offering his work, but I just keep telling him he needs to get it out there," Dolores gushed.

Lucy wasn't sure what kind of cash value a painting from Dolores's son would bring, but every artist started somewhere, so she was happy to agree.

Dolores moved out of the doorway finally, and Lucy gave up, letting the door close and ignoring Bean's wide smirk from behind the counter. She was middle-aged, blunt, and very funny. Lucy always wondered if 'Bean' was a nickname. Dolores pushed her pie at Lucy, who had no choice but to accept, then dug in her large, animal print bag.

"You come choose one or two pieces, okay? What am I saying? I can just give them to Alex, and he can give them to you," she said, laughing too hard and starting to put her pen away.

"No!" Lucy said forcefully then took a deep breath and tried to smile. "Just write your address. I'll come pick them up tomorrow night." Dolores gave her an odd look but didn't question Lucy further. She wrote her address down on the back of a receipt and traded it for the pie. "Thanks for doing this," Dolores said.

"Thank *you*. Are you coming to the gala?"

"I absolutely am. I have this gorgeous sequined dress that has just been begging for a night out," the enthusiastic blonde told her. Lucy smiled and bit her tongue.

By the time Dolores finally walked away, pie in hand, Lucy had lost her appetite for dessert. The only thing she had an appetite for was Alex. But, like dessert, she was probably better off without.

CHAPTER TWENTY-FOUR

*L*ucy sat on the porch step in the moonlight and thought about the night she'd come home. She'd been so tired and ready for a break. Africa had been wonderful, and she had especially enjoyed the last village, but it had made her crave her own village. Her own family. The night air was cool, a welcome reprieve from the heat she had felt in her bedroom, even with the window open. So she'd crept down the stairs like she had throughout her teenage years, past her parents' bedroom, and eased the door open to sit on the steps. She looked at Alex's house. She couldn't remember the last time she had seen his truck in the driveway. She wondered if Furball was lonely. Nowhere near as lonely as she was.

Even as she heard the crunch of the gravel under his tires, as her heart picked up its pace and her stomach twisted, she didn't move. She should have. She should have spared herself the agony of looking at his face, even in profile. But she missed his face so much. And his arms. The way he laughed, how he smelled and how he was always touching her. In the dark, with only a pale strip of the moon, if she were silent, if she held her breath, he would walk right by her and she could just look at him.

She heard his footsteps, heavy and slow, like the days without him. He stopped and she heard him change directions, coming toward her. Her heart hammered. It was dark. He couldn't see her. *Don't breathe. Close your eyes.* She could feel him in front of her. She could taste him, smell the sweetness of his soap and his aftershave. She squeezed her eyes tighter, trying not to inhale.

"You're going to pass out again," he whispered. How could his voice bring her so much relief when it was his words that had caused her such misery? She opened her eyes and a powerful fist squeezed her heart. He sat down on the step in front of her. The squeezing in her chest became nearly unbearable, like the fist had talons.

"I'm sorry doesn't seem like enough," he said. She couldn't talk, so he did. "You are all I've *ever* wanted, and I will spend the rest of my life regretting my own stupidity if I can't make this right. If I can't find a way to get you to come back to me. I love you, Lucy. I have loved you every single day for sixteen years. I will love you for the rest of my life, even if you can't find a way to forgive me for doubting you."

Before she could absorb his words or anything she felt because of them, he stood and walked to his own house. Once he shut the door, the windows went dark. She knew the feeling, the sudden absence of light. She folded her body and rested her head on her knees, weeping without sound. When she heard footsteps beside her, she sat up, startled.

"Mom?" she said into the darkness. Her mother stood on the porch in her nightgown. She heard the large breath her mother took, like she was preparing to take a deep dive. Then the screen door opened, and her mother placed one foot on the wooden step. Lucy sat up straight, angled toward her mom, and held her breath. Julie hesitated. Lucy could see in the moonlight that she had her eyes closed. Then she opened them and took another step. When she sat beside Lucy, all of the air she'd been holding released like she was resurfacing. Lucy's tears fell onto her lap and her chin shook. Julie trembled as well.

Lucy reached out her hand to steady her mother's, but instead, Julie's arms came around her and pulled Lucy into her side. "Come here," she said, her voice shaky. "I'm here."

Julie's tears mingled with Lucy's as they kept each other anchored and safe, treading water under the moon, both of them just trying to stay above the surface.

Alex reached for her before he remembered Lucy didn't share his bed anymore. His phone was vibrating and his head was pounding. Knocking back a few shots of whiskey when he came into the house hours ago had not erased the image of her sitting there in the glow of the moon. His phone buzzed again.

"Whitman," he answered. He slapped his hand over his eyes to block the sunlight that was streaming through.

"Hey, boss. Cal called. Seems someone not only tagged him, but also set his dumpster on fire. Figured you'd want to head over there," Mick said. Alex cursed and sat up, then swore again at the pounding in his head.

"I'm on my way. Fire department put it out?"

"They're doing it now. It's under control."

Alex clicked end without saying good-bye. Advil, coffee, car keys. He repeated the three things, almost forgot to include pants and a shirt, and was in his truck within ten minutes of the call. When he pulled up, the fire truck was loading back up. Smoke filled the air as anger filled Alex's belly. He was going to pin this punk's ass to the wall. Out of his truck, he clipped his badge onto his belt and met the fire chief halfway.

"Morning, Sheriff. Hell of a way to wake up," Quinn said. He pulled his helmet off and swiped at his dirt-covered forehead with the sleeve of his even dirtier arm.

"I can think of far better ways," Alex said, his voice clipped. Quinn, who was about his height, nodded in agreement, his sweat-slicked brown hair sticking to his forehead.

"Fire is out. Looks like the same MO as the other ones. Accelerant-soaked rag. Inspector is on his way in from Minnesota. I think we're pissing him off with our suddenly frequent needs," Quinn said, smirking and clapping Alex on the shoulder.

"Yeah, well, he can get in line. I'm pretty pissed myself. Is everyone okay?"

"Yes. Waitress hurt her wrist. She was coming out to toss the garbage into the bin, and when she saw the fire, she ran back in. A customer was coming out, and the door smashed her arm. Medics are looking at her."

Alex thanked him and went to find Cal and his staff. Danielle was sitting in the back of the ambulance, a female medic wrapping her wrist. The woman, her ponytail so tight it was making Alex's eyes hurt, glanced at him and nodded.

"You okay, Danielle?" Alex said, squeezing her other shoulder lightly.

"Sprained wrist and trampled pride," she said, smiling up at him. Her ponytail was looser, strands falling into her eyes. "No need for that. You up to answering some questions?" Alex asked.

"You're all done here. You need to go to the doctor if it's still hurting in a week, but a bit of ice, ibuprofen, and rest should do the trick," the medic told her, moving so Danielle could stand. Alex took her arm, and she smiled at him warmly before thanking the woman for her help.

Cal was answering questions with Elliot, but Alex figured his answers were the same as Danielle's. No one saw anything. When they'd shown up for the morning shift, the front of the restaurant had been tagged. The fire couldn't have been set too long before they arrived, which meant that whoever set it had an easy getaway or didn't live too far away.

"Damn jerks. Now my place is wrecked," Cal said, spitting into the gravel. Elliot walked over to where the firemen were loading up and heading out.

"It sucks, Cal, but it's not like you couldn't use a coat of paint all the way through," Alex said, unaccountably irritated. He shouldn't take his frustration out on Cal.

"You have insurance, Cal," Danielle said, rubbing Cal's burly arm.

"Yeah, I do. At least no one got badly hurt. You going to be okay?" Cal asked, frowning at Danielle's wrapped wrist. "Sure. I'm fine."

"You take whatever time off you need, honey," Cal told her. Danielle's face colored, and Alex wondered if there was something between them.

"I can't afford to take time off. I'm fine," Danielle said. Alex was about to comment when Cal's chest puffed out and his cheeks darkened to a ruddy red color.

"You think I'm going to dock you pay? Jesus, woman. Go home."

Alex watched the exchange, feeling like he was peeking through someone's window. Danielle looked at her feet, and Cal stared at Danielle. *Definitely something going on.* Elliot joined them again just as Danielle spoke in an almost-whisper.

"I didn't bring my car," she said to Cal. Elliot's eyebrows raised and waggled at Alex, who cut him off with a stern look. "I'll take you home, Danielle," Alex said.

"I don't want to be any trouble," she replied. Alex sighed. Elliot grinned. Cal put his hands on his hips and nodded at Alex. "Let's go," Alex said. He turned to Elliot. "You got the pictures and the rest of this?"

"Sure thing, Sheriff," Elliot replied in his laid-back tone while giving a mock salute.

Lucy walked up the corridor of the university. It was

about a half-hour drive from her house, but not far from the address Dolores gave her. Things were falling into place. They would spend tomorrow decorating for the gala and getting ready for the auction. Her friends had come through for her, and so had the town. She was more excited than Kate to unveil the new rec center. Kate's mind was occupied with her last final exam and packing for New York. She was trying to downplay her excitement because of the recent chaos, but Lucy was happy she was so thrilled. Everyone else would come around. Char and Luke were planning a Sunday brunch as a send-off.

It smelled like Axe in the hallways, and Lucy half expected the elevators to open and reveal twenty-somethings with disheveled clothing, just like in the commercials. *Too much T.V.* Her dad's office was on the second floor. His door was closed, but Lucy could see through the top half of the door that he was alone. He was talking on the phone, so she knocked softly. When his face brightened at the sight of her, it stitched up one of the torn pieces inside of her. He waved her in, and she closed the door quietly behind her.

"Okay...Yes...Take a look at the syllabus online and just email me...You're welcome."

Lucy stayed by the door until he hung up. When he did, he came over and embraced her. His hugs were all encompassing. There was no room for doubt inside the circle of her dad's arms.

"How are you, honey?" he asked, kissing her forehead and pulling her into the room. They sat side by side on his pale blue leather couch. It was a strange focal feature in an otherwise studious office.

"I'm good. I came to pick up some logo wear for the auction. The bookstore agreed to donate hoodies, shirts, and hats."

"Right. And to see me," he said. He leaned forward, hung his arms between his legs, and considered her. He didn't ask anything, but he had that look that demanded, gently, that she tell him. And that he'd wait until she did.

"We broke up." Getting the words past her throat caused more pain than she'd thought possible. They were just words. Words shouldn't hurt, but those ones had daggers.

His lips firmed and he nodded. He put his hand over both of hers, which were clasped on her knees. "I know. Do I need to kick his ass?"

Lucy laughed, and the feeling felt foreign to her. She hadn't had any happiness inside of her for days.

"He thought I was leaving. He assumed I was leaving. Kate is leaving, but he thought it was me," she said, her words feeling as jumbled as her heart. Her dad sighed heavily but said nothing, which made Lucy babble. "He was the only one who didn't doubt me. Until it mattered. I've never told anyone I love them—other than you guys, and obviously, *that's* a little different—but I told him. And I meant it. I mean it. I do love him. I let myself need him, and he didn't trust me when it really counted. I know he's sorry. I know that he misunderstood, but he..." Her voice broke, but she didn't cry. Her dad pulled her into his side and kissed the top of her head.

"He was supposed to be the one who never doubted you, the one who never pushed you away. He was supposed to *know* that you wouldn't leave him," her dad finished. Lucy nodded. She pulled away and rose from the couch to grab a tissue from her dad's desk.

"It's like he was just waiting for me to let him down." She wiped the corner of her eyes before the tears could fall.

"We've done that to you as well. We've doubted you and teased you about your tendency to roam. But that's not all that you are. You're so much more, Lucy. I'm sorry that it took us so long to see that."

She rested against the edge of his desk and looked at him, grateful for his words. "Thank you."

He nodded and leaned back comfortably on his blue couch. His perfectly pressed dress pants and button-up shirt looked at odds with the retro style furniture.

"Sometimes, in moments of panic, our worst fears fly out of our mouths before we have a chance to process them in our brains," he said thoughtfully. "He gave me his house key. I accepted it. How could he think I would leave?"

"Wow. Well. I think I should kick his ass, but we'll come back to that," Mark said, his eyebrows pinching together. "The thing is, Lucy, even if you weren't a traveler, a wandering spirit, anyone who loves with all of their heart secretly fears losing the person they've given their heart to. It's human nature to fear losing what you love the most."

Lucy thought about that. Alex didn't even like to travel, but there were moments that she felt so overwhelmed with loving him that she *had* feared she would mess it up, wreck things between them.

"So now the worst has happened. You've lost each other. What now?" Mark asked, coming to his daughter and standing in front of her. "I don't know."

"I guess you need to figure it out. And make a choice that you can truly live with."

Lucy didn't feel like she had a choice. Her heart had already given itself over to Alex like a traitor.

"How's Lucy?" Danielle asked as Alex pulled his truck up to the curb outside of her apartment.

"She's okay. We broke up," Alex said. The words tasted foul in his mouth. He shut the truck off and came around for Danielle. He took her arm as she got out of the truck.

"I'm sorry. She's a really good person. So are you. You guys ... fit. That's too bad."

They walked up the narrow path to the three-story building, and Alex thought that was such a simplistic way of summing it up. "It sucks. I hurt her and there's no excuse for that."

Danielle struggled with keeping her purse open and digging in it without jarring her wrist. Alex took the purse and held it open for her, not even daring to navigate its depths.

"Lucy makes you want to be a better person," Danielle said softly, pulling her keys up and out. Alex locked eyes with Danielle's; it was the perfect way to describe Lucy.

"She's the best person I know. When she needed me to believe that, I doubted her," Alex said, unable to cover the regret in his voice. Danielle put the key in the lock, but Alex turned it for her. She paused once he had opened the door.

"She forgave me when she didn't have to ... because I asked," she said, encouragingly. Lucy didn't talk about the tension between her and Danielle, so Alex had never pushed.

"What happened?" he asked now. Her lips firmed and her eyelids lowered. She brought her gaze back up to his before she spoke. "I slept with her prom date," Danielle told him, contrition in every word. "On the day of prom."

Alex sucked in a breath and Danielle's cheeks turned red. "How did she find out?"

Her blush spread, making her whole face pink and she cast her eyes down.

"He and I lived a few doors down from each other, and he'd asked if I could come in and show him how to tie a tie. Lucy stopped by. He thought she'd just let it go. No big deal. That's what he said to both of us."

All these years, all the rumors—which had been fast and furious immediately after graduation—and Lucy had never defended herself. She had never spoken badly of Danielle, and she had let others think what they wanted. Even if what they wanted to think was that Lucy was just unreliable, the Aarons sister that couldn't even sit still long enough to make it to prom. She had taken off shortly after.

Alex thought of how humiliated she must have been. But she hadn't let it define her. Because Lucy was so much more than what people saw in a passing glance. As he had told her, she was everything. Alex realized he was still gripping the door, holding it open for Danielle when she stepped into the small but clean lobby of her building.

"Thanks for the ride, Sheriff."

"No problem. Get some rest."

He turned to go, but she called his name, so he turned back. "Don't wait as long as I did to tell her how sorry you are."

With a shy smile, she let the door close. For the first time in too many days, he found the energy to smile back.

CHAPTER TWENTY-FIVE

*L*ucy parked her car in the driveway of Dolores's exceptionally bright home. It was a nice street in a quiet neighborhood with slightly outdated homes. She could probably afford a home in this area. It didn't have the same quaint charm as her parents', but it also didn't have Alex across the yard. She knocked on the front door, unexpectedly charmed by the cheerfulness of her window planters. She couldn't name any of the flowers, but they made her smile.

"Oh, you made it! Come on in. Andrew isn't home. He's out with some friends, which is just great. He doesn't get out enough. Anyway, between running errands and working, I haven't even had a chance to talk to him, but I just know he's going to be so excited that one of his paintings is going to be part of something so special," Dolores said in one long-winded breath.

Much like Dolores, the home was colorful. It was less cluttered than Lucy would have expected, but every color imaginable existed between the front door and what she could see of the living room. There were two steps down into the sitting area where a red velvet couch sat across from a white leather one. They looked like the angel and devil version of couches. Lucy wondered if Dolores chose where to sit based on her mood. On the walls, there were photographs of Dolores and her son. He was a good-looking kid despite the sullen frown that graced most of the pictures. Dolores's smile in each photo made up for his obvious lack of enthusiasm.

"I just have to grab a couple from his room, okay?" Dolores said excitedly.

"Sure," Lucy replied, hoping that the art would sell. Dolores would be so disappointed if they didn't. Lucy took the steps down into the sunken living room and moved toward the fireplace, drawn to the abstract painting that hung above it. The colors were beautiful, dark swirling with light. If this was the quality of Andrew's work, there was a good chance that his art would bring in some money. Lucy's eyes were caught in the movement of the lines, the way they merged together, not quite circles, not quite meeting in the middle before they burst away from each other in new colors. She tilted her head a bit, stepped closer, and when the lines in one corner merged into a heart-like shape with a curved tail, she sucked in a breath.

"TOLD YOU HE WAS TALENTED," Dolores bragged, her heels click-clacking over her laminate floors. Lucy turned, wide-eyed. Dolores had two small canvases. She placed them on the couch so Lucy could see both. One was abstract like the one over the fireplace, but now that Lucy knew what she was looking for, she spotted the heart symbol immediately. It was harder to spot in the second print of a woman's back, the delicate curves of her hair flowing over her shoulders. A blanket was pooled at her hips. In the cascading movement of the blanket, the symbol, was nestled quietly. Lucy bit her lip, struck by the beauty of the paintings and the reality of them. She needed to talk to Alex. *Breathe. Stay calm.*

"They're amazing. You're sure he won't mind parting with these?" Lucy asked, hoping her voice sounded normal. To her own ears, it was tinny and far away.

"You know what? If I wait for him to believe in himself, I'll be waiting forever. Sometimes, you have to give the people you love a nudge in the right direction."

Lucy nodded and forced herself to meet Dolores's proud eyes. She was so happy for her son. She truly had no idea. Lucy thanked her several times, desperate to get out of this woman's house, desperate to see Alex, and desperate to avoid running into the town's vandal and arsonist.

Alex knocked harder than he'd meant to on his father's door. He could hear Chuck inside, music blasting. Jesus, it was like they'd reversed roles and his dad was now the teenager. Loud music, sneaking around, making out with women... Alex shuddered as the image flashed in his head. Chuck yanked the door open, scowling at his son.

"Why the hell are you mad at my door?" he barked, looking back and forth between Alex and the door.

"I'm not. I'm mad at you," Alex returned. He was ready

for this, braced for the fight. His dad was strong enough to take it, and Alex could really use a punching bag to unload everything that had happened in the last week.

"What else is new?" Chuck asked, walking away, leaving Alex to follow. Alex closed the door quietly to compensate for the desire to slam it. The television was blaring and the sounds of the game show pressed on Alex's already-stretched nerves.

"You're fucking Dolores."

Chuck whirled, and Alex wondered if he had ever seen his dad that angry. He clenched his hand around the remote, the knuckles turning both red and white. He clicked mute, and the silence was louder than the show had been.

"You watch your mouth," Chuck said, his voice barely controlled.

"That's not much of a denial," Alex said, ignoring the obvious signs of rage boiling beneath his dad's surface.

"I don't have to confirm or deny anything. This is my goddamn house, and you'll speak respectfully of her or you'll get the fuck out of it," Chuck boomed. He threw the remote onto the couch but kept his fists clenched. His anger doused some of Alex's. This kind of anger didn't come from a fling or a backroom tryst. His dad cared about Dolores.

"Do you love her?" Alex asked, shocked at the possibility.

"Of course I love her, you idiot. You think I'd be running around with her if I didn't? Protecting her and hiding things from you until I figure out what the hell is going on?"

"Why didn't you just tell me that?"

"Firstly, it's none of your business. We didn't expect it, but you with your stick-up-your-ass ways... We didn't want to say anything until we were sure there was something to say. Now we're sure. I'm going to ask her to marry me," Chuck said, defensiveness clinging to every syllable.

Alex took a step back, pushed his hands through his hair, and stared at his father. "Holy hell. Marry? How long have you guys been together?"

"Not that it matters, but about six months. When you know, you know," Chuck said, unclenching his hands.

"Like you knew with mom? That worked out real well," Alex snapped. His phone buzzed, but he ignored it.

Chuck's shoulders slumped. He shook his head at his son and sat on the couch. Alex took the chair across from him.

"Your mother and I didn't handle our divorce well. I shouldn't have left. She shouldn't have left you. We screwed up. I've tried to make up for it. I've tried to be a good father to you since the minute she dropped you here. Obviously, I didn't do so great, even when I was given a second chance," Chuck said. He was looking at Alex like he was just coming to this realization.

"I never said you weren't a good dad," Alex said grudgingly.

"I was angry at her, too. I didn't think about how that would affect you. Over the years, you let it go. You forgave without even meaning to. I should have told you that I wasn't angry anymore. That it wasn't just her fault. I should have talked to you about how she left."

331

"What difference would that have made?"

"Maybe you would have felt less abandoned. I don't know. Hindsight is a kick in the ass. She loves you, Alex. She always has."

"Not enough to stay. And that's not what this is about," Alex said, jumping to his feet, sick of the pressure in his chest.

"It damn well is. Your suspicious nature makes you a good cop, but it makes you wary of anything good. Like it can't last. Like somehow, the good will slip away no matter what you do. That's bullshit. You don't want the good to slip away, then you hang on tighter. You hang on to it harder than you hold on to the anger and the bitterness, or you'll end up empty and alone. I don't want to be empty and alone anymore, so even if it pisses you off, I'm hanging on to

Dolores."

Chuck stood as well, to punctuate his words. They stared at each other, stuck between the past and the present. Move forward. Let go of the past. If he were honest, Alex knew that he wasn't angry at his mother anymore. She'd been trying to get in touch with him for a good five years now, but he hadn't been strong enough to forgive her. *A man who needs forgiveness ought to be able to give it.* Especially after all this time.

Lucy's fingers were shaking as she texted Alex that she needed to see him. She met Kate and Char at the rec center. They were hanging tulle elegantly along the sparkling white walls. Music was coming from one of their iPods. Tables were set up but not dressed and packages lined the walls, all items to be auctioned.

"Look who decided to show up," Char joked, then looked stricken. "I'm just joking."

"I know. You guys, I know who the arsonist is," Lucy blurted. Char dropped the tulle she was holding, and Kate gaped at her from where she was standing on a stepping stool.

"What are you talking about?" Char asked.

Lucy told them everything, barely pausing when she spoke. By the time she finished, she was out of breath like she'd run a marathon without water. Her hands were still shaking.

When his dad went to grab them both a drink, after some of the tension had ebbed, Alex grabbed his phone to check his messages. His heart thundered when he saw there were several texts from Lucy. He scrolled through them, and his heart marched its way up to his throat, pulsing painfully when he got to the last one. *It's Andrew. Dolores's son. He's the tagger. Alex. Phone me. PHONE ME. PLEASE.* Chuck walked back into the living room, two Coronas in one hand and a bag of Doritos in the other. Alex stood.

"Dolores's son. His name is Andrew?"

"Yeah. Moody kid. Not thrilled his mom is going out with me. His dad took off a few years back, and the kid blames Dolores. You two will have something in common," Chuck said, holding the beer out. A smile spread over his face, "You're not going to be all needy having to share my attention, are you?"

Alex didn't take the beer. He put his phone in his pocket. "Is he at home?"

"Who?" Chuck was looking at him like he'd lost his recently found mind. He put the beer and the chips on the coffee table. "Andrew! Dolores's son. Where do I find him? At her house?"

"How the hell would I know?" Chuck looked at his watch. "He's out of school by now. Why? You want to meet your soon-to-be stepbrother that badly?"

"Yeah. I really do. The sooner I meet him, the sooner I can arrest him," Alex replied.

The three sisters were sitting on the floor of the main gymnasium. The smell of paint and new wood surrounded them as her sisters processed what Lucy had told them. Her phone rang.

"Alex?" she answered, pulling herself up off of the floor. "Where are you?"

"At the center," Lucy replied, looking at her sisters.

"Stay there. I'm on my way," Alex said. Lucy felt like things inside of her shifted back into place with his words.

She put her phone down and told her sisters he was coming. As she walked back toward them, she smelled it. Smoke. She looked around to see where it was coming from.

"What is that?" Kate asked, standing. Char stood as well and walked to the double doors at the front of the open room. She pushed on them repeatedly.

"What the hell? Something is blocking the doors," Char

said. Lucy's neck heated—she felt too warm. She forced herself to breathe. The doctor had told her to avoid stress. *Cause that's possible.* The rec center consisted of a huge gymnasium, a smaller gymnasium, and a few rooms between them that would serve as classrooms for the various kids' programs that would be offered. And, Lucy hoped, where she could offer photography classes.

"Check the other door," Lucy said, heading out of the main gym and down the small hallway. She passed the boys' bathroom, the girls' bathroom, and turned into one of the classrooms. There were windows, but they pulled open in a V-shape from the top. She walked to the classroom door. It didn't budge when she tried to open it. What was blocking the doors? *Do not panic. For now.*

Alex explained to his dad on the drive to the rec center. Chuck argued and refused to believe him, calling Alex petty and childish. But he also called Dolores and asked her where Andrew was. Alex called the station and sent Elliot and Cam over to the center, just to be sure. He had a bad feeling and good instincts.

When they pulled up, his heart slammed into his ribs. He saw smoke. Elliot and Cam were out of the patrol car, guns drawn. They saw Alex and Chuck. Elliot motioned to the side of the center with his hand. Alex pulled his gun. He heard the fire engine in the distance, amazed he could hear anything over his own heart. He saw the two-by-four that was shoved through the front doors of the building. Alex signaled for them to cover him while Chuck moved to release the two-by-four. Around the side, Alex saw the blond-haired kid that had eluded him for months, crouched low and holding a long twist of newspaper, lit at the end, against the wood of the building. Sam had purposely used an anti-accelerant paint. Alex hadn't known that such a thing existed. It could still flare up, but a chemical formula kept it from happening quickly.

"Put your hands up, Andrew. Put the fire down and stomp on it," Alex said, firm and low. Andrew flinched, his shoulders hunched. He stayed where he was, crouched in the same position, but he put the fire down.

"Stand up," Alex demanded. Andrew stood. Turned around. The extent of the anger that Alex saw on his face surprised him. And sadly, reminded him of the kid that he, himself, had once been. Andrew said nothing, just stood facing Alex with a sneer on his face, his hands by his sides.

"Someone is at the front," Char yelled. "Lucy!"

She could hear her sisters yelling her name as she came back into the main gym. Chuck came through the doors, followed by Cam.

"You girls okay? Let's get you out of here," Chuck said, grabbing Char and Kate's arms, pulling them forward as Lucy joined them. Cam stowed his weapon and took Lucy's arm.

"Are you alright?" he asked.

"Yes. We're fine. What's going on?" Lucy replied.

"Can't say just yet," Cam said as they exited the building. The fire department pulled in, sirens blaring. Dolores's car pulled up at the same time. She was out of the car before the fire engine had parked.

"Where's Andrew?" she screamed. The firemen yelled as they set up to put out the small fire that was spreading along all of the greenery that had been planted.

"Calm down, Dolores," Chuck said, releasing Lucy's sisters. The firemen went to work on the bushes that lined the wall of the rec center.

"Don't tell me to calm down! He's my son! He's just a kid," she yelled, pounding on Chuck's chest. He took both of her arms and pulled her to him, fighting

her struggling.

"He's with my son. Just calm down. Everything will be okay," Chuck said.

Cam pulled Lucy over to the squad car, and her sisters stayed by her side. Alex came around the corner of the building a moment later, nodding to the firemen. He had a sulky looking teen by the arm and was dragging him along. Elliot followed behind, gun still drawn.

"Seeing as we're going to be related, I didn't slap the cuffs on him," Alex snarled to his dad. His eyes found Lucy's.

"Of course you didn't! What is the matter with you? What's going on?" Dolores continued to screech, rushing Andrew and throwing her arms around him, tears streaming. Alex let him go and came to stand in front of Lucy.

"Are you okay?" he asked quietly. She nodded. He reached out to touch her, but pulled his hand back and looked at Eliot.

"Get these girls home. We'll deliver their cars later," Alex instructed, his tone hard and cold. Lucy wanted to protest but changed her mind.

"Ladies, if you'll allow me to escort you," Elliot said, smiling at them. Recovering from their scare with more ease than her, Kate smiled back at him, a little too brightly for Lucy's taste. Char took her hand and squeezed it. Kate called shotgun while they climbed into the back.

"You get to explain to Dad why the cops are bringing us home," Char said to Lucy.

CHAPTER TWENTY-SIX

*A*lex stood outside the interrogation room and rolled his eyes at Dolores's dramatics. "Dolores, your kid has been setting fires and defacing buildings for months. We have proof."

"He's sixteen, Alex. He's been through a lot."

"Dolores, let Alex do his job. He's good at it," Chuck said, surprising Alex. If they did marry, this was going to make for some interesting Christmases. Chuck pulled Dolores into his arms. He murmured something softly, showing a side of himself that Alex had never seen.

"You can sit in," Alex said to Dolores, opening the door, "but don't interrupt."

Dolores sniffled and looked at Chuck. Her black mascara was holding strong through the waves of her tears. She followed Alex and took a seat beside Andrew, who stared straight ahead, not acknowledging either of them.

"You've caused a lot of trouble, Andrew," Alex said, taking a seat in one of the two chairs opposite Dolores and her son. Andrew shrugged. Dolores started to speak but stopped when Alex looked at her.

"We have you on numerous acts of vandalism, four acts of arson, and attempted murder," Alex said, trumping up the last charge. Dolores gasped loudly. Andrew, finally, made eye contact with Alex. He kept his face passive, but Alex saw the fear and anger in his eyes.

"I didn't try to murder anyone," he spat, sitting up a bit straighter. His T-shirt was the kind of worn material that kids bought that way, even paid extra for. His hair was a little long around the sides, but he was a good-looking kid, despite the scowl.

"There were three women inside the rec center," Alex stated. "I just wanted to scare them. Scare you."

It wasn't often a suspect or a criminal surprised Alex, but Andrew managed to do that, repeatedly. "Me? Why the hell would you want to scare me, kid?"

"You mess with my life, I mess with yours," Andrew said. Dolores fidgeted, all but bursting with the need to say something.

"You're going to have to clear things up for me here. How on earth did I mess with your life? I don't even know you," Alex said, reaching for patience. Andrew looked at his mother.

"Your dad is screwing my mom. It's fucking up my life. Your family messes with my life, I mess with yours," Andrew said, some bravado puffing his chest out.

"What are you talking about? And watch your language," Dolores said shrilly.

"When Dad comes back, you think he's going to be

okay with you screwing some retired, has-been cop?" Dolores's face paled and she looked at Alex, her eyes pleading.

"Could we have a couple of minutes?" she asked. Alex pushed back from the table and left them alone.

Lucy lowered herself into the bath and tried to soak away the last week. She closed her eyes and breathed in the mini bubbles that popped here and there. The gala was tomorrow. New York was Sunday night. She would be there for one week. Then she would come home. And start again. With Alex or without. She tried to imagine both. He'd made a mistake. She'd taken it hard because she wanted so badly for someone to see her better than she saw herself. She tried to reverse the situation. If she'd jumped to conclusions, hurt him and doubted his feelings, would he have forgiven her? She knew, without a doubt, that he would have. It's what you did when you loved someone. When your life was better with them than without. When they were more than the mistake they had made.

Unable to shut her mind down, she got out, dried off, and went to her room. She would put on some cozy clothes, go over her list for the gala tomorrow, and then grab something to eat. In her room, she yanked a T shirt she had stolen from Alex over her head and pulled on a pair of loose cotton pajamas. She sat down on her bed, her back against her pillows, and picked up her list. Her eyes fell on the black photo album that Alex had given her. She picked it up, opened it, and stared at the first pocket. She shook her head and closed it, put it aside, and looked at her list. Her eyes drifted shut and she let them. Just for a minute.

Alex and Chuck watched from the two-way glass as Dolores and Andrew fought, cried, and fought some more. Alex was drained just from observing. Andrew's dad had left them a few years ago, but Andrew was sure he'd be coming back. In fact, he'd contacted his dad, and his dad had said he wanted to see him. Soon. Then Dolores took up with Chuck and started spending her time with him. Andrew got kicked out of art school and came home to find that his mother was fine without him. He'd originally thought the vandalisms would keep Chuck busy. The kid hadn't even paid attention to the fact that Chuck wasn't the sheriff anymore. When he'd realized it, he just kept going, seeing as Chuck's son was in charge. Andrew rationalized his actions like a man and pouted like a child. Back and forth until Alex's head hurt from watching.

"Bottom line, the kid needs help. He's done some stupid shit just to get mommy's attention," Alex said, arms folded across his chest. Chuck stood beside him with the same stance.

"Kind of like taking up with the wrong crowd?" Chuck asked. Alex didn't know his dad knew about the last few months he and his mother had spent in Chicago. He didn't reply, just shrugged.

"He could have really hurt someone," Alex said. "You're right."

When Chuck left it at that, Alex wasn't sure what to do

with it. Being right didn't make things easier, especially with so many intersecting variables. He didn't feel at all vindicated, like he usually did after closing a case. Where they went from here—all of them—was what mattered now.

After all of the highs and lows, the drama and the tears, Lucy found the gala to be a bit blah. In truth, she found everything to be a bit blah. She had fallen asleep and woken the next morning with a list of things that hadn't been done. She hadn't heard from Alex, and even though she had enough things to keep her busy, the fact that he hadn't called weighed heavily on her.

She spent the day running errands, making herself stop to rest, to eat, to breathe. When she started thinking about Alex, she went back to being busy. As the town came together, dressed in their fanciest clothes, Lucy stayed on the edges, capturing the moments without wanting to be part of them. It was the only way she could function right now.

She would go to New York on Sunday, and when she got back, she'd put the pieces back together. The one thing about not rushing off to a new continent was that she had time to sort things through, rebuild, and heal. It didn't have to be tonight. The music swirled around her like a warm blanket, slow and sultry. Glasses clinked and people laughed. Lucy listened to the soothing sound of her camera, blocking it all out and taking it all in at the same time. Until a hand touched her shoulder. Without moving, without looking, she knew the weight of that hand, the feel of that touch.

"You look stunning," Alex whispered, his breath

fanning her ear. She would not let herself lean back into him. Swallowing the knot in her throat, she turned to face him, lowering her camera. His eyes, even in dim, twinkling light, showed his fatigue.

"You should talk," she replied, taking in his suit and tie. With her heels on, she was closer to his height and could meet his gaze evenly.

"*We* should talk," Alex said, moving into her, reaching out his hand to touch her. He pulled it back instead. Her breathing slowed while her heartbeat sped. She closed her eyes, trying not to inhale the scent of him. Taking a small step back, she opened her eyes.

"Not now. I have to take pictures. I have to help Kate."

She hated the sadness in his eyes almost more than she hated the emptiness in her chest. "When?"

"When I get back from New York," she said, knowing she needed him to be sure, of both of them. Knowing that she needed the time to pull herself back together and prepare herself for whatever happened. His face fell, but he nodded.

"We're cutting a deal with Andrew," he said, changing the subject. They walked the side of the room, through the crowd. "Oh."

Alex's hand grazed hers, and she fought the ache it caused, remembering how perfectly their hands and bodies fit together. They walked to the buffet table, and Alex poured them both some punch.

"He'll be going to counseling. He'll also be doing community service until he's eighteen. He's seeking treatment for depression and anger. Dolores will also be doing family counseling with him. He'll have an imposed curfew until he's eighteen, and if he violates any of the conditions, he'll have to do time at a facility for troubled youth."

"Wow," Lucy said, taking a sip of the sweet punch.

"Yeah. That's the family deal," Alex said with an unhappy smile. "I'm sorry, what?"

He told her about Dolores and his dad. She didn't know what to say. He told her about his mom. "I'm so sorry. Will you phone her?" she asked, putting her glass down.

"In time. I don't want to look back and realize I should have tried harder, that I should have done more," Alex said. Lucy nodded in understanding, her throat too tight to speak. Alex reached out then, tracing his finger softly down her face.

"Alex."

He leaned in to kiss her gently, but she turned so his lips only brushed her cheek. His face lingered near hers, his eyes closed like he needed this moment of nearness.

"I love you. I'll see you when you get *home*."

Lucy watched as he weaved his way through the crowd and more firmly inside of her heart.

CHAPTER TWENTY-SEVEN

*L*ucy didn't see him at first. She felt like she was on a conveyer belt of people, being shuffled out of the terminal. She walked to the baggage claim, her mind cloudy and tired. She waited for her bag, irritated when it seemed to come last. Lifting it, she turned and almost ran into him.

"Let me carry that for you," Alex said. His face was smooth, and his eyes looked her over like he was hungry just for the sight of her. Seeing him was doing strange things to her heart, her stomach, and her ability to talk. The loudspeaker crackled, telling passengers it was the last boarding call. Not for her. She was happy to stay off of planes for a while. There had been enough turbulence to unsettle even the most seasoned traveler. Alex pulled the large bag from her, leaving the camera bag on her arm.

"What are you doing here? You shouldn't be here," she said, her voice tired and squeaky. "Why not?"

"This isn't... I've been on a plane. I'm all ... plane-y.

This isn't what I planned," she stammered. He hooked the bag on his own shoulder and took her elbow to lead her away from the baggage claim.

"What did you plan?" he asked.

"I was going to go home. Rest, clean up, and then come to you. To talk."

"Hmm. That's a good plan," he conceded, looking at her with that smile that undid everything inside of her. "I had a plan, too." She stopped and looked at him.

"What's your plan?"

He stepped closer, stealing her space, and leaned his face close to hers.

"My plan is to *always* pick you up at the airport. Unless I'm already with you. Then my plan is to drive us home."

He took her hand and continued walking through the airport. She didn't know what to say, so she let him lead. He held her hand for the whole ride home. She watched his profile, drinking in every angle of his face. It was such a good face. When he pulled up outside of his house, he turned the truck off but gripped the steering wheel. She waited in the silence. He looked over at her. Both of them undid their seatbelts.

"I was a jerk. I jumped to conclusions, and you deserved more than that. I told you that I believed in us enough for both of us, but when the chance came to prove it—to prove I believed in *you*—I didn't. I was scared. Scared that I wasn't enough reason for you to stay."

She squeezed his hand, trying to find the words that were swirling inside of her, free-floating like dust particles. Almost impossible to catch.

"I wasn't sure, either. The whole time, I wondered if the feeling of needing to pick up and go would wash over me again. I didn't know how I would do it. It's never been hard for me to leave. I overreacted because I didn't believe in myself. I expected you to believe in me enough for both of us."

"I should have. I do," he said, his voice quivering slightly.

He got out of the car and came around to her side. He led her across his grass, confusing her by going around the side of his house. He stopped outside of his shed and stared at it, then turned to face her, letting go of her hand. He pulled a thin, rectangular packet out of his inside pocket and a key out of his jeans pocket. He held both in his palms.

"What is this?" she asked, looking back and forth. The white packet had a travel agency logo on it. The key was just a run-of-the-mill key. "You choose. It doesn't matter to me which life we have, but it has to be together," he said.

"What?"

She looked up at him and down at the items in his hands, not understanding.

"If you want to pick up and go every month, we will. If you want to stay here, live in this town, and just travel on holidays, we can do that."

"You don't like traveling. You love this town. Your house," she said, baffled.

"I love *you*. You're my home, Lucy."

Her lips trembled. She still didn't fully understand, but she liked the parts she did. "What's the key?"

He handed it to her and gestured to the shed. Narrowing her eyes, a smile fighting its way to her lips, she unlocked the door and opened it. Inside had obviously been renovated recently. There was still traces of sawdust on the tiled floor. The walls had built-in shelving, and a long, high table stood in the center of the room. The sunlight was coming through the windows, but she could see the blackout blinds hovering above them. There was a door just to the right of the entrance.

"Alex, what is this?"

"It's yours. You were talking about a place of your own. Sam researched photography spaces and did the best he could, but if the darkroom, through there, isn't right or you want something different, he'll come back and change it."

She turned to face him. He still held the packet in his hand. She took it and opened it. It was a travel voucher. Enough for them to go anywhere they wanted. He put his hand in his coat pocket and pulled out a small, square, black box. Lucy gave a strangled gasp when he went down on one knee and looked up at her.

"Lucy, I love you. I believe in you, and I believe in us. I will spend every day, for the rest of my life, proving that to you. Loving you. I want to marry you. I want to spend my life with you. More than that, I don't want to spend another day without you. Will you marry me?"

She bit her lip and covered her mouth with her hand. He stared up at her. "I'll be right back," she blurted and dashed out of the shed toward his truck.

ALEX GOT up off of the floor, trying not to freak out. She hadn't said no and run off. She said she would be back. And she was, moments later. She had the photo album he had given her, and she handed it to him. His heart sank to the floor as he took it. He looked at her and wondered if she could feel the pain emanating from inside of him. Her hands were shaky as she brought them to her mouth then lowered them.

"I didn't think I had a place here—in my family, in this town. I spent all my time traveling because I thought that I would be able to find myself—figure out who I was and what I wanted. It wasn't until I stood still that I realized what I wanted is right here. My place, the only place that truly matters, that I truly belong, is with you. So when you open up that photo album, if you still want me to marry you, if you're sure, then my answer is yes."

He looked at her and down at the album in his hand, wondering what the hell she was talking about. Of course he was sure. He opened the album, certain he would find the key he had given her sitting in the top pocket. But instead, he saw a small, somewhat grainy photo. He pulled it out of the pocket and brought it closer. The thin film of the ultrasound tape felt smooth in his fingers. He looked at Lucy, who was all but vibrating.

"You're pregnant," he said, in awe. Disbelief washed over him. He looked at the tiny outline, a speck, really. He wondered how he could love something already that was barely the size of his thumbnail. He put the photo back in the pocket, closed the book, and placed it on the table behind him. He pulled her into him, staring in awe down at her stomach and placed his hand there. When he looked up, she was crying and biting her lip. "You haven't answered my

question," he said, his voice rough with emotion.

"Are you sure?" she whispered. He pulled the ring out of his pocket, slipped it onto her finger, and without giving her time to even look at it, yanked her close, covering her mouth with his, desperate to show her how sure he was.

"You're everything. You. Both of you. I'm sure. Say yes," he said between kisses, running his hands over her. Her hands moved over him, anchored themselves around his neck.

"Yes."

She kissed him as frantically as he kissed her until she finally pulled back, breathing heavy, and looked at her ring. "We're going to get married," she whispered.

"And have a baby," he replied, still awestruck. She smiled so brightly it made his pulse race. She put her arms around him, snuggling into him. He kissed her again, whispering that he loved her, elated when she whispered that she loved him, too. Leaning back slightly, she framed his face and looked at him. He rested his forehead against hers as her eyes twinkled.

"What?" he asked, grinning.

"Nothing. I'm just really glad to be home."

ACKNOWLEDGMENTS

Thank you to everyone who has supported my writing. My mom and brother from the time I was a little kid. My best friend from the age of 13. My husband, who still thinks my worst book is my best book because he always sees the best in me. My kids, who not only make me so proud but are incredible writers themselves. My go-to readers: Bren, Tiff, & Tara.

This was a tough one...this book. It got a lot of requests from agents but something was missing. That's hard as a writer, to step outside your own work and try to figure out WHAT is missing. I was incredibly lucky to have a supportive group of writers that I could reach out to, that helped me keep going. Taylor Jenkins Reid may not know it, but a lot of her kind words have kept me going despite how hard this journey sometimes seems. And with Falling For Home specifically, Rosie, Ami, and Louise were incredibly supportive and helpful with their time and their encouragement.

To the incredible authors who agreed to help me host a Facebook party; who offered their time and some great giveaways. Thank you to Shannyn Schroeder for reading the book before all the edits were done and still saying something nice about it.

I'm thankful for the great people I've connected with on Twitter and Facebook. It's not just raising a child that takes a village, so truly, thank you. And thank you to Penner Publishing, the authors there, and to Jessica and my editors for believing in my work, even in the moments I didn't.

Finally, thank you, readers, for reading. I feel incredibly lucky to have anyone read my books, so thank you for that. I hope you enjoy Lucy and Alex. I'm particularly fond of them.

ABOUT THE AUTHOR

Jody Holford lives in British Columbia with her husband and two daughters. She's unintentionally funny and rarely on time for anything. She loves books, Converse shoes, and diet Pepsi, in no particular order.. Whether she's writing contemporary romance or cozy mysteries, she's a big fan of love and finding happily ever after. Probably because she's lucky enough to have both. Learn more and signup for her newsletter on her website: http://www.jodyholfordauthor.com/

- facebook.com/Authorjodyholford
- twitter.com/1prncs
- instagram.com/36jody
- bookbub.com/authors/jody-holford
- amazon.com/Jody-Holford
- pinterest.com/jholford

ALSO BY JODY HOLFORD

Britton Bay Cozy Mysteries
Deadly News

The Love Unexpected Series
Let It Be Me
Never Expected You
Story of Us

The Kendrick Place Series
More Than Friends
The Bad Boy Next Door
Hate to Love Him

The Angel's Lake Series
Falling for Home
Falling for Kate
Forever Christmas

The Some Kind of Series
Some Kind of Christmas
Some Kind of Love

Some Kind of Forever

Some Kind of Always

Standalones

With These Shadows

Caught Looking

Damaged

Always Time for Christmas

Made in the USA
Middletown, DE
06 October 2022